Jas_____ the wall
and

A moment later, a lithe, powerfully-built figure dressed in an orange jerkin burst in from an ante-room! Their ace in the hole — Savate, the deadly mercenary and master of the French martial art whose name he had adopted as his own!

The mysterious Man Of A Thousand Kicks had clashed a dozen times or more with America's Greatest Hero, and always escaped to fight another day! Savate was usually hired to delay Doc Thunder and other champions of the law for the crucial moments necessary to complete some heist or scheme — yet his strange code of honour forbade him from taking the lives of those uninvolved in the struggle between the forces of law and the criminal underworld.

But to delay Doc Thunder's victory now would be to doom thousands to slow and painful extinction! Was Savate an unwitting dupe of the sinister forces of Untergang? *Or had he finally crossed the line that separates the dashing rogue from the callous murderer of millions?*

The answer will astound you! Turn to page five for more of the incredible front-page scoop this reporter *had* to call — *"The Fearful Fate Of Doc Thunder!"*

Pax Britannia

ABADDON
BOOKS

WWW.ABADDONBOOKS.COM

PAX BRITANNIA

PAX

MEGA

AL EWING

An Abaddon Books™ Publication
www.abaddonbooks.com
abaddon@rebellion.co.uk

First published in 2012 by Abaddon Books™, Rebellion Intellectual
Property Limited, Riverside House, Osney Mead, Oxford, OX2 0ES,
UK.

10 9 8 7 6 5 4 3 2 1

Editors: Jonathan Oliver & David Moore
Cover Art: Pye Parr
Design: Simon Parr & Luke Preece
Marketing and PR: Michael Molcher
Creative Director and CEO: Jason Kingsley
Chief Technical Officer: Chris Kingsley
Pax Britannia™ created by Jonathan Green

UK ISBN: 978-1-907992-90-2
US ISBN: 978-1-907992-91-9

Printed in the US

For Sarah, who is the best thing.

AUTHOR'S NOTE

James Newton ("The Printer's Devil") and Matt Zitron ("The Last Stand of the Yodelling Bastards") are the names of real people.

They appear in this book courtesy of the "Genre for Japan" charity auction, which took place in April 2011, in support of the Red Cross efforts in the aftermath of the Japan Earthquake.

The characters appearing under their names are, of course, wholly fictional.

ALPHA...

First, there was not.

Nothing existed, and there was nothing in which to exist.

Over a timeless interval, during which time had no meaning, He considered the situation.

He existed. He was the only thing to exist. That did not feel correct.

He focussed His being, and spoke.

And there was.

As He watched the fundamental forces slowly tear themselves from one another, He found himself wondering if He had chosen to create, or if creation had somehow chosen Him. Nuclei formed in the torrents of energy He had released and spent millennia wooing electrons, forming atoms as He debated the matter with Himself.

Dense pockets in the primordial gas, warped by gravity, ignited into the first suns, and He decided that the question was of no consequence. The act of creation had happened. The future had been seeded.

Around the new stars, swirling debris coalesced and cooled into planets, moons, meteors, the endless architecture of the cosmos. In a moment of curiosity – rebellion against the chain of events He was bound into, perhaps – He attempted to shift some of these emerging bodies from their set course.

Once, He had created a universe from nothing, but things were different now. Exposure to time had somehow decayed Him. He still existed, but not in any physical sense, and the power of His mind was not strong enough to effect the necessary gravitational changes.

He realised then just how much time had passed. His perception of it was accelerating in odd patterns – speeding and slowing – and his disembodied consciousness was starting to drift apart. The decay would continue. Death was coming to Him.

Death, at last.

How strange and novel it would be.

His awareness drifted to one of the new planets, the third out from its star. The shape of the emerging continents was familiar in places, and microscopic life forms were beginning to thrive and propagate in the volcanic regions. He studied them for a short while as they evolved, to flatworms and algae, then to more complex forms.

His intelligence was starting to dissipate now. Death was approaching rapidly, and He relaxed into it, watching the events occur on the new planet until He could no longer comprehend them.

The last thing He saw and understood was the ship, appearing from the wormhole at too great a velocity, trying desperately to change its course and then crashing into one of the newly-formed continents. They were very familiar now.

Hello, He thought. *Hello. Hello.*

After that, He could no longer think of words. He thought of her face, for a moment, and then that, too, became too complex to hold onto.

He thought of a smile.

And then He was not.

THE END OF THE WORLD

Munn, the Navigator, sat with his legs dangling off the edge of the high cliff and watched the monsters fighting in the valley below.

What else was there to do?

There were two of the creatures, giant lizards with great fans of bone crowning their heads, and three horns – two at their temples and one jutting from their snouts – above what looked like a large beak. From what Munn could work out, the combat was between an old bull, defending his place in the pack, and a smaller challenger bucking for a higher position in the hierarchy. A group of females watched, grazing on the tall grasses nearby. They were patient animals – the fight had gone on for at least an hour.

Was it a fight? Now that Munn had watched the pair for so long, the regular clashing of horns looked more like a display – almost a dance. A contest of endurance, perhaps, one that would continue until the weaker of the huge beasts no longer had the energy to carry on. Munn examined each of the creatures carefully from his vantage point, looking for signs of exhaustion, but gave up quickly. Unwen, the Biologist, might have had something to say about it, but he was busy in the ship with his mammals. Perhaps Munn would ask Unwen what he thought on the matter. Without the selfsearch, Unwen might not know precisely, but he seemed to be adjusting himself to the lack of it better than most. He could probably come up with an answer.

Munn undid one of the clasps on his belt, lifting the small plasol bag of *hosa* from its pouch and packing a little into the three-inch metal pipe he now wore, as a matter of habit, around his neck. He thumbed the stud that ignited the yellow powder, and then breathed the smoke into his lungs, feeling his perceptions loosen and shift slightly as the new possibilities began to fall into his mind, slotting perfectly into place like the bind-blocks he'd played with as a child.

He breathed out a long coil of yellow smoke. The pipe was an inefficient system for delivery of the drug, especially compared with the skin-patch he'd worn on his upper arm ever since he'd left the crèche. In the Habitats, skin-patches were a necessity – without a constant low-level infusion of *hosa*, the speed, intensity and complexity of normal life would be impossible to comprehend. But on this new planet, in this slower, stranger existence, priorities had changed – the skin-patches had had to go, because they had precious ununtrium in the contacts and there was no ununtrium to be had here, or any way of synthesising it. And without ununtrium they would have had no way of establishing a permanent perimeter-field, and without the perimeter-field they would all have died, as surely as the Captain had.

So, no more skin-patches.

QED, as Unwen or Soran would say.

Munn's thoughts drifted. That was another problem with smoking the *hosa*-powder instead of having the pure essence of the drug micro-injected into the capillaries. Bad memories had a sudden habit of ambushing the conscious mind, and Captain Tura's death was one of them.

After the crash, she'd been monitoring the ship's attempts to seal and repair itself – as much as it could, outside a proper docking bay. He remembered her face in particular, lined with concentration, trying hopelessly to jolt the lift-engines into proper function, not noticing the shadow suddenly descending on her from above. Munn had opened his mouth to call out, but she was already gone – a screaming shape high in the sky, held in the claws of one of the flying monsters. Munn had watched helplessly as the thing had pulled her head from her body with its beak, swallowed it and flapped off with the twitching remnants. Something to feed to its nightmare children, he supposed.

He tried to imagine what the Captain had experienced in death – the tearing pain, a split-second of disorientation, the realisation that her body was simply gone... and then the ego winking out like a light, or spiralling away like water into a drain.

And then... what?

Something unimaginable. Something that nobody had had a reason to contemplate, for hundreds of thousands of years. Death, in all its totality.

Munn tried to think of what that inconceivable absence might be like. He tried to think of not thinking, of not existing, and even with the *hosa* accelerating his mind he couldn't make the mental leap. It terrified him.

He shivered, shaking his head to try and flush the idea away. He'd never had to consider death before he'd arrived in this place. Death was for the special soldiers in the Red Queen's employ, the Silver Service, and no-one else. Theirs was the highest sacrifice, opening themselves to the possibility of non-existence. Munn wondered if the Silvers were given any special reward for their work, beyond the honour of the work itself. Probably not. Nothing material could make up for such a horror.

His mind drifted on, to the vote they'd taken after the Captain's death. Not a true vote, of course – without mental-linkage equipment, the best they could manage was a vague, approximated version of democracy. Still, they'd done the best they could in the circumstances, and after a brief debate they'd made the decision to atomise all those items unnecessary for continued existence in this world, like the skin-patches, the fiction gels – even the selfsearch.

They'd used all the rarer elements thus harvested – the precious ununtrium, the sparse grains of dubnium and meitnerium, impossible to hold together outside a quantum envelope – to repair the life-support and create a working perimeter-field strong enough to keep all the monsters outside at bay. Once survival was thus assured, they could work out what to do next.

That had been the plan, anyway.

So now the remaining crew-members were safe in their bubble, and Munn was dangling his legs off a sheer cliff, safe in the knowledge that if he should fall, or leap, the perimeter-field would catch hold of him – he could even walk on it, if he wanted – and watching the lizards dance, hundreds of feet below.

What else was there to do?

"How's your reading, Munn?"

Maya, the Security Officer. Munn took a long drag on the metal pipe, holding the *hosa*-smoke in his lungs, and exhaled slowly, considering the question.

"It's a phrase that's already lost its meaning, isn't it?" he murmured, smiling humourlessly. "There's no selfsearch any more to get a reading from. I could give you an estimate, if you like..."

Maya looked down at him disdainfully. She'd never thought much of Munn, and with the *hosa* coiling in him he could read all of her contempt for him as clearly as any stellar map. "I can make a guess for myself," she murmured. "You're missing Habitat One, you're missing a working ship... you're missing civilisation. You're starting to fall into a depressive state." She frowned dismissively, and Munn found himself resenting her – the way she'd so readily accepted being exiled here.

He shrugged, turning away. "I suppose I am. Without a selfsearch reading it's difficult to be sure what I'm feeling, exactly." He laughed bitterly to himself. "This must be how our ancestors felt. Or assumed they felt."

Maya frowned. "Forget selfsearch – it's gone. Frankly, I'm happier without it. I'd have gone all the way and junked the talkeasies, if I could be sure we'd understand each other without them."

"Well, why not? It's not like we understand each other as it is." The words sounded angry in his ears, and he wanted nothing more than to consult the familiar machine and have it tell him why, and what to do about it. Why had he agreed to get rid of them? They could have found what they needed elsewhere. One of Soran's scientific toys, maybe.

"Listen, Munn. What was is over. We should try to make the best of what we have now, not sit around moaning about all our old trinkets. Our species existed for millennia before selfsearch, or *hosa,* or psychetecture. We'll learn to exist without them again. We'll build back to what we had before."

"You sound very certain, considering it's just the four of us..."

Maya shrugged. "That's how it has to be. That's how it will be. What other choices do we have?"

Munn shook his head, angry at her fatalism. "Rescue?" Even saying the word, he felt stupid. There wouldn't be a rescue – nobody from the Habitats would be able to find them, out here on the other side of the wormhole. "Escape, then?"

Maya shook her head. "There'll be no escape. It's us and this world now – the ship won't take us anywhere else. The xokronite we have is enough to keep us powered, but we can't synthesise the elements we need to repair the lift-engines. Soran was working on it, but..." She shook her head, leaving the sentence unfinished.

"He's given up?"

Maya shrugged. "He tried. He failed. I had a feeling he would. Still, it's more than the rest of us have done." She looked pointedly at Munn, and he felt uncomfortable, under scrutiny. She might as well have asked him straight out what exactly he was doing to help, besides watching the reptiles bash their heads together.

Munn bristled. "There's not much I can do in this situation.

I'm a Navigator, Maya. I've been a Navigator for... for..." He tailed off, trying to work out exactly how long it had been since he'd first sat at a navigation station and plotted a course between the galaxies. Eighty thousand years? Ninety thousand? Enough time to grow bored and exhausted with navigating between stars and galaxies and wormholes, and then to fall in love with the process all over again as new developments in the art appeared. And then to lose faith again, and get it back, over and over... but always Navigator, always guiding ships between the stars. It had defined him in a way nothing else had, and now it was gone.

How long *had* it been? Without selfsearch, or external memory packs, or even an efficient supply of *hosa* in his bloodstream, it was impossible to remember and collate much before the last two or three thousand years; only the vaguest of flashes. The horror of that washed over him for a moment. *I'm brain-damaged,* he thought. *We all are. In three thousand years, four at the most, will we think we've always been here? Will we even remember Habitat One, or things as simple as selfsearch or gels or talkeasies? And if we do remember everything, if we do build it all just the way it was – is that better?*

Or worse?

Maya snapped him out of it. "Munn?"

He rubbed his bare scalp gently with his fingertips, trying to work his way back into the conversation. "For all that time, I've flown ships. Ships are... part of *me. Stars* are part of me. But that ship" – he waved his hand at the lush canopy of the jungle, in the rough direction the ship was in – "that ship's just... a domicell-complex now. A place to live. It won't fly. And at night, the light from the field stops me seeing the stars. And I'm never going to see the stars again..." He swallowed, unable to speak. His eyes stung. He hadn't realised how much he'd missed the stars until that moment. "So what should I do now? Tell me that. What am I going to be?" He turned away from her, not wanting her to see the tears. "I could spend a thousand years trying to decide. We all could."

Maya shrugged. "We've got a thousand years. We've got ten

thousand, and ten thousand times that. We can do anything we want. And in the end, what we'll do is build."

Munn stared at her with his wet eyes, and suddenly he hated her; hated her certainty, her seeming invulnerability. What did she know that he didn't? "Build it all just the way it is back at home," he muttered to himself. "Do you think Unwen and Soran will agree with your nostalgia?"

"I suppose we'll find out," Maya replied, as if she already had, as if any conversation on the subject was just a formality.

Munn didn't reply. After a moment, Maya turned and walked off, and he returned his attention to the three-horned lizards in the valley below. In the time he'd spent talking to her, they'd finished their combat, or display, or whatever it had been, and now both the males were grazing alongside the females as if nothing had happened.

Munn wondered who'd won.

"HERE'S ONE I prepared earlier."

Unwen smiled, picking up the miniature field in his hands. Inside the sphere of force, snitting against the almost invisible barrier, there was a small creature, about the span of a hand, with four legs, brownish fur and a thin, twitching tail. Soran frowned, rubbing his chin. "It's not unlike a surface-cleaner. I remember when I was a boy, we had several. Bio-forms, they were... little pink things with snouts... they actually ate the accumulated dirt, you remember? They were smaller, though, the size of a thumb..." He tailed off, staring at the animal.

Unwen looked at him for a moment, then re-lit his *hosa*-pipe and took a long, slow drag on the burning powder. "No, I don't remember anything like that." He gazed at the scurrying creature, as though it might recreate whatever decayed memory he was grasping for. "It may be before my time."

Soran shrugged. "I remember it clearly. I used to let them scamper over my feet, nibbling at the dead skin. Someone told me it was disgusting... a nun, or a nurse... I forget..." He stared at his console, lost in thought.

Unwen looked at Soran, concerned. The ship's Engineer was perhaps five hundred thousand years old, one hundred and fifty millennia older than any of them, and the loss of the skin-patches seemed to have hit him the hardest. Strangely, he had consistently refused the pipe. "I'll need you for this next bit."

Soran nodded, snapping out of his reverie. "Yes, yes. Of course. We must be careful." He smiled, looking around the chamber – the Power Room, as it was called for simplicity's sake. The place where the limitless energy that powered the ship and the field was generated; the energy that would power Unwen's little experiment. There was a visible twinkle in the older man's eye as he lifted his hand in the particular gesture that called up the room controls, a string of icons shimmering on a near-transparent field at chest height, and he passed his fingers over them in the manner of a man at play. Of the four survivors, he had had to adapt the least. The ship was still running, the power still needed to flow, occasional repairs would still need to be triggered in those systems that did not immediately repair themselves. He, Soran, was necessary to the group's survival in a way none of the others were.

The room's central pillar hummed softly, like an insect, before its silvery sheen cleared, turning from opaque metal to something akin to glass. Floating inside the glass, at head height, was the glowing blue metal that powered the ship – that powered all of the Habitats.

Xokronite.

Unwen gazed on it, a half-smile playing across his face. "Beautiful, isn't it?"

Soran stroked his hairless chin, studying the shimmering, flowing lines and pulses that told him the energy output. "It's very pretty, very pretty... I once had a sunsuit of that colour..."

"No, no." Unwen shook his head, flashing Soran an amused glance. "What it represents. A gateway for energy from the Big Bang itself..." He laughed, shaking his head in wonder. "We steal energy from the dawn of time, and all the energy we steal, throughout our history – throughout the history of the xokronite, no matter who uses it, *has* ever used it, *will* ever use it... put all that stolen energy together, and you have the exact amount that *needed* to be stolen from the Big Bang to create this exact universe, the exact history and cosmology we know. It's perfect. Isn't that perfect?"

"It's a rather simplistic way of putting it. I can tell you didn't study the physical sciences."

"You say simplistic, I say poetic. The universe is the way it is because it created us, and we discovered xokronite, and through it we made the universe the way it is. A perfect cycle of causality." Unwen gazed deep into the glowing stone, eyes shining with reflected blue. "And we can never get enough energy from it, because if we were ever to do so, if we were ever to drain too much – or not enough – the universe would be a different place. Perhaps only slightly different, but different nevertheless. And it's not, so we don't, therefore we can't, therefore... limitless power. It's so *poetic*, Soran. Don't you think?"

Soran shrugged. "Poetry isn't my department. Or yours. And in my experience, nothing is free, even if you do steal it. There are costs..." He nodded to the creature trapped in Unwen's spherical field. "How does this relate to your friend there?"

Unwen lifted the beast up, looking at it. "We'll need a limited transfer between the two fields. As you say, I'm no physicist, but I do dabble – I think if you drain off some of the tachyon field from the xokronite in the following frequencies..." He reached up with his free hand, calling a display field into existence and inscribing a sequence of fluid shapes and signs, which glowed ethereally in the blue light.

Soran looked them over for a moment. "That's... interesting." A hint of nervousness had crept into his voice.

Unwen grinned. "It will be."

"Yes... I was under the impression that... well, that experimenting with these frequencies on living tissue had been banned by both the Royal Houses?" His grey eyes flicked over to Unwen's.

Unwen lifted an eyebrow in response. "You have an objection?"

Soran sucked in his breath for a moment. After a pause, he shook his head. "No. We'll proceed. I can make this more energy-efficient, now I know what you're aiming for." He forced a slight smile. "What can they do to us here, eh?"

"You see? You're as curious as I am." Unwen set the spherical field's gravity so that it would sit in the air, then took his hands away and let it hang gently, supported on nothing. He stepped back, admiring the small mammal as it turned circles in its floating prison. Some callous part of him enjoyed the sensation of having power over these little beasts – they huddled close to the field in great numbers, as if recognising its power over the larger lizards that were their chief predator, and when he snared one from outside to bring through the field and into the ship, he felt almost like some deity, reaching down to pluck his chosen few to the heavens. There were myths that still persisted in the Habitats of ordinary beings plucked from their base circumstances by the hand of the gods, to dwell among them as one of their own. He imagined the small mammals building their own myths, in their squeaking rodent-language, and the thought pleased him.

And here we have the beginnings of a new myth, he thought to himself. "Let's start slowly. Transfer five per cent of total yield."

Soran nodded, wetting his lips and leaning forward as he brushed the control field with his fingertips. Unwen couldn't help but smile – Soran was as excited as he was, despite himself. He turned his attention back to the field, watching the mammal scurrying and scrabbling at the invisible barrier he was caught in. Gradually, the flesh and fur of the creature was suffused with the same blue glow of the xokronite itself.

There was a soft, gentle whine of straining machinery.

At first, nothing seemed to happen. Unwen, watching closely, could see the beast's eyes dilate. Its breathing quickened, then grew heavy and laboured. Suddenly, the muscles of its back and legs seemed to shift slightly; the mammal rolled onto its back, squealing in discomfort, kicking its legs. Unwen watched its feet move, holding his breath, then let out a small cry. "Stop there!"

Soran shut off the transfer. The glow faded, the soft keening noise died. "What is it?" He hurried across the room to where Unwen stood, hunched over the field, examining the animal as it panted helplessly, still on its back. Unwen seemed as transfixed as his specimen. "Unwen, what is it?"

"Look there," Unwen breathed, tapping the field with his fingertip. Soren looked. The beast was visibly larger, as if it had grown new muscles. Its legs were longer, and he could now see that there had been other changes to the shape of its back and skull.

"You've mutated it."

"More than that. Look at the paws."

Soran's eyes narrowed, then widened. The paws of the animal had changed as well, elongated, into five recognisable digits. Their configuration had a familiarity that at once excited and disturbed him.

Opposable thumbs.

"OPPOSABLE THUMBS?"

Unwen nodded. Maya frowned at him. "And where is it now?"

"I let it go again." Unwen shrugged, and Soran looked up from the food-tray, shocked.

"You didn't! Unwen, even I know that's going to play havoc with the evolutionary tree –"

"It might." Unwen grinned. "Our little friend might get eaten by something before he breeds. Either way, we'll see what happens in a million years. In the meantime, shall we return to the thumbs?"

"I don't see the significance of them," Munn said, as he picked a red protein-globule from the shared tray. "The mutation aspect – well, it's interesting, certainly, that we can do that. It's nothing scientists back in the Habitats weren't able to achieve before, but it's nice that we can do it with the equipment we've got, and by this method..."

"A forbidden method." Maya murmured, frowning. "Forbidden by both the Royal Houses."

Unwen rolled his eyes as he chewed idly on one of the white carbohydrate squares. "Nobody's going to come and punish us, Maya."

Maya shot him an angry look. "Perhaps *I'll* punish you for violating the Queen's rule." The others looked at her for a moment, and she seemed to acknowledge the ridiculousness of the statement. "Well, anyway... it's a slippery slope. Are we going to start breaking every rule of society one by one, Unwen? We're supposed to be building – I mean *re*building – society. Not tearing it down for our own –"

"Are we? When did we take that vote?" Unwen interrupted, enjoying Maya's obvious outrage. This obsession she'd picked up with replicating the culture of Habitat One with their meagre resources had gone from naïve to tedious to irritating, and now he found himself glad of any opportunity to prick that particular bubble.

Soran, always less contentious than his fellow scientist, was quick to play down the potential conflict.

"We don't *want* to go against societal rules, as such," he said in a calming tone, "but you have to admit that we're outside that society now. We're a long way away from Habitat One. If I wanted to be pedantic about it, I could say that the moment we took the decision to atomise the selfsearch, we stepped outside the bounds of ordered society. Look at us now – we're unsure of each other's motives, unsure of our own... once upon a time, we could have settled this whole discussion by comparing readings." He took one of the long yellow fluid-sacs and bit it open with his teeth, swallowing the sweet, tart juice, then the skin. "Or by mental link, for that matter, if we'd been at home. That's something I miss... do you know, I had a rather fascinating dream last night of the area without us – just as if we'd never landed here. It seemed very significant when I woke up, and I thought I'd record it on the link and share it... except we have no link any more..." He paused for a moment, staring glumly at the sticky juice that remained on his fingers. "Perhaps... perhaps you're right, Maya. I do so miss my home..."

He lapsed into a silence that none of the other three gathered around the feeding-tray felt like breaking. They were eating outside the ship, next to the perimeter-field, where Unwen could watch the mammals gather on the other side. There was a crowd of them now, staring with pink eyes, occasionally creeping forward to sniff at the shimmering air that kept them out. Mostly, they seemed to be staring at the feeding-tray, floating a foot or so off the ground, loaded up with the various basic components of a complete meal, but occasionally they'd turn their heads, blinking at Unwen, almost as if they remembered him. He smiled, resisting the urge to send one of the small red globes through the field for them to eat. To be a generous god.

Munn broke the silence. "I don't understand what's so special about the thumbs. Why is that mutation in particular so important?"

"I've gone through this once already, Munn. We didn't mutate it, not in the sense you mean." Unwen shook his head impatiently. "What we *did*, Munn – I'll make it simple – was swap out its DNA for that of a descendant from millions of years down the evolutionary line. We looked into the future of the species and brought that future back into the present."

Soran bit into one of the white squares. "That's almost making it too simple, if you ask me. But, yes, in terms of the effect, we were able to... well, jump up the evolutionary ladder. Of course, the results will differ vastly from mammal to mammal according to their species or location. If we were to attempt the process on one of the reptiles, for example, we might find that..."

"Let's not do that," Munn broke in quickly.

Maya nodded in agreement. Soran looked to Unwen for support, but he only shrugged. "I'm afraid I concur with the rest of the group, Soran. It's far too risky to bring one of the larger lizards through the field – anyway, I think we've got enough on our plate right now with this species. I think if we can follow it further down the evolutionary path... well, this is where the thumbs become important, Munn."

"I'm listening."

"The fact that these creatures developed opposable thumbs suggests that, if pushed further down the evolutionary path, there's a chance that they might evolve into... well, us. Or a creature very like us. Bipedal, using tools. Perhaps even sentient." He smiled, popping one of the yellow fluid-sacs into his mouth.

Maya nodded, watching him with a curious look on her face. "I see, Or... its descendants might evolve into primates and stop there. If I'm understanding you correctly."

"You are, up to a point. By adjusting certain variables – and this is something Soran had a great deal of difficulty explaining to me, so I won't try and give you a second-hand version – we can pick and choose which branch of the evolutionary tree we follow. If even one of those branches leads to a sentient or semi-sentient creature, we can... well, bring it into being."

"You're twisting my words," Soran interrupted, scowling. "I said it was theoretically possible with the equipment we had. That doesn't make it easy, or wise. The power drain would be catastrophic."

Unwen seemed almost amused by the idea. "The whole point of xokronite as a power source is that it grants us potentially infinite power, surely?"

"You're not a physicist," Soran spat, almost savagely. "You're not an engineer, either. Drawing energy at the rate you're discussing would lead to –"

Munn cut him off. "The mammals."

"What?"

He pointed towards the edge of the field. "Where are they going?"

The crowd of small animals who'd sat watching the four of them eat were scurrying for cover, finding holes and branches to lose themselves in. A moment later, the ground underneath them vibrated with a sound like thunder.

"I think –" Soran began, and then he was silenced by another thunderclap, then another, and another – louder each time. Something approaching, on feet heavy enough to shake the earth. Something huge and terrible, making its way through the trees.

Then it was on them.

Nearly three times as tall as a man – and even then Unwen could see that it was not rearing up to its full height. Instead, it held its body parallel to the ground, lunging at the field, a great mouth of razors attempting to tear into the empty air. The field shimmered and whined under the assault, becoming almost opaque in places under the stress, and Munn found himself inching back, despite himself.

"It won't breach the perimeter-field," Soran muttered, but there was a trace of uncertainty in his voice.

Unwen felt oddly detached, observing the massive monster as it roared at him, great globs of its spittle trickling down the outer edge of the field. It walked on its massive hind legs, its small arms seeming useless, almost vestigial. But then, the claws were sharp – perhaps, when it was engaged in fighting or feeding on similarly gigantic reptiles, the arms would latch onto its prey for ease of attack. If he could only study one in a more natural habitat. A mobile field, perhaps.

If he could only capture one.

Abruptly, the massive beast turned, slamming its tail into the field, and crashed through the tree line and out of sight, shaking the earth again as it stomped into the distance. Eventually, the smaller mammals began to creep out of their hiding places, moving back to their place at the edge of the field.

The four of them finished their meal in silence.

LATER, MAYA SAID to Unwen: "Honestly? I think you should try it."

Unwen raised an eyebrow. "Interesting. You're the last person I'd expect approval from, quite frankly. What happened to the slippery slope?"

She shrugged, irritated at his point-scoring. "We're already on one."

The two of them were in Unwen's sparse domicell, away

from the others, lounging on a pair of visible fields projected from the walls and floor. Unwen's was a curved plane, allowing his legs to remain horizontal and his back supported, while Maya preferred a solid block to perch on. "Munn hasn't said a word since the fang-beast attacked the perimeter-field," she continued.

Unwen raised his other eyebrow at that. "Fang-beast?"

She smiled, despite herself. "It's by far the largest and most dangerous reptile we've seen. It deserves a name. Feel free to come up with something more scientific."

"I already have. Species designate #7C."

"And the ones Munn's become obsessed with? The ones he stares at all day and most of the night?"

"The triple-horned things?" Unwen thought for a moment. "#3C. The C classes them as reptile. They were the second reptile species we saw, admittedly, after the flying one, but... well, the triple horns. These things should have at least a little poetry in them, Maya." He chuckled. "If we do restart civilisation over again, one thing I'll be pressing for is including poets in the crew of every ship. Just in case something like this happens again."

Maya looked at him for a moment. "You're in favour of rebuilding, now?"

"Not to the extent you are. Everything doesn't have to be exactly the same. I never did understand your obsession with that..." He shrugged. "But what else is there to do? We have to fill our endless time with something, just to avoid going mad. So let's build our own little world here. Why not?"

Maya looked at him in silence. Unwen sighed, leant back, and scratched his chin. "All right... how would it work? We want a nice, large, growing population to rule over. There's not enough genetic material between us to repopulate ourselves... so we take, say, a thousand of the mammals – assuming we can find that many without leaving the perimeter and being picked off. Mutate or evolve them, whichever terminology we're using, until they're sentient creatures. Educate them as best we can to a basic level. Feed them with the ship's synthesisers at first – I don't know where they'll sleep, mind you. And of course, we'll be hoping against hope that the food synthesisers won't burn out from overuse until we've taught them farming... and teaching them how to farm without being picked off by the reptiles will be difficult in the extreme, but I'm sure..."

"Enough." Maya shot Unwen an irritated glance. "Too many problems, Unwen."

Unwen reached into his field, lowering its density slightly so that he sank deeper into it. He closed his eyes, and Maya had the maddening urge to stand up and command the room to switch off all the fields, to watch him crash down onto the floor. "All right," she said, "if the main problem is the reptiles, what would it take to kill one? Say, the #7C."

"The fang-beast. Nothing we've got, unfortunately." Unwen frowned. "Theoretically, we could possibly kill one by projecting a field into its brain or heart, if we got close enough... yes, that would work. We could cannibalise the furniture fields – if that one you're sitting on were to suddenly appear in one of the monster's ventricles, say, or the folds of its brain, that would be very fatal indeed." Unwen stroked his chin, suddenly looking more awake and alert. "Soran could probably jury-rig something – a portable projector. It'd mean losing some of our furniture, obviously, but we could craft new surfaces from solid matter, wood or stone... we have time. If we could do that, our biggest problem then would be getting close enough..."

Maya nodded. "Without being eaten."

"Quite. Even if you managed to kill a #7C – or a #1C, or any of the other dangerous creatures out there – it would probably tear you apart before it realised it was dead. Besides, you're the only one of us with anything close to the training for this kind of thing. The rest of us would die off very fast." Unwen stared up at the ceiling for a moment. "And none of us are qualified to program an AI that could... Ah, yes." He laughed. "I think I'm starting to see. We're back to the mammals again."

"We are?"

"Oh, yes. We need creatures to take this hypothetical device of Soran's – which we will mass-produce – and kill the lizards with it. Some of the larger mammals, too, the dangerous-looking ones. Semi-sentient creatures to kill and die on our behalf. Of course, more often than not, they'll be dying rather than killing. But so long as we can retrieve the field generators, that's fine." He looked at her for a moment, gauging her reaction.

Maya nodded, her eyes not leaving his. "They're only mammals."

"They're only mammals." He chuckled. "And we need to stop them turning the devices on us, of course. So Soran and I will have to create more devices, to implant in their heads, to kill them if they try anything. These killing implants would also be activated if they refuse an order... such as the order to die for our benefit." He kept looking at Maya, waiting for her to snap, to dismiss the whole scenario.

She only nodded.

"An army of slaves..." He enunciated the words carefully, marvelling at them, trying to hide his excitement at the prospect. Surely Maya wouldn't agree to this –

But she nodded again, without changing her expression, and Unwen had to consciously hide his astonishment. He'd actually managed to manipulate her into letting him do it.

Or perhaps she was manipulating him. Or both at once. *Ah, selfsearch*, he thought, *how mysterious life is without you.*

After she left, he lay back on his field with his eyes closed, lost in thought.

He thought about the gigantic reptile that had come at them. The #7C, the fang-beast. He thought about the mammals, and how they had watched him through the perimeter-field.

He thought about how they would remember him, in their legends.

"No. Absolutely not." Soran's voice was firm. "I can't possibly allow it."

The sun was setting, and the four of them were again sat

around the feeding-tray as it floated an inch above the grass. This time it was loaded with a mixture of long green sticks, round yellow discs, and clear fluid-sacs of lightly flavoured water – the food-synthesiser followed a rhythm of its own in response to the dietary needs of the crew, and what it provided was rarely questioned. Unwen picked one of the yellow discs up, nibbling around the edge as he studied Soran closely. "The moral issue?"

Soran hesitated, seeming startled by the question. "Yes, yes," he said, a little too quickly. "It's morally unconscionable, it goes against hundreds of thousands of years of moral development by our species..."

Unwen smiled. "What's the real reason?"

Soran flushed red, and scowled. "It's simply too dangerous. The sheer amount of power we'd be draining out of the xokronite..." He shook his head firmly. "Creating just one of these hominids of yours would be risky. To compound that risk by creating an army of them is... well, it's insanity. Utter madness."

Maya picked up one of the clear sacs and bit into it. "What *are* the risks, Soran? What happens if we draw too much power too quickly?"

Soran shrugged. "In layman's terms? Well, the xokronite would become fundamentally unstable. What happens after that would be extremely difficult to predict. That's why it's so dangerous – there's no real telling what would happen."

"Well, can you narrow it down, at least?"

"The xokronite could stabilise on its own once we lower the rate of energy transfer. That's certainly possible. If it doesn't, our safety equipment – the containment cylinder, the energy dampeners – would presumably kick in, cooling it, draining off excess radiation, and so forth. That might be enough to forcibly stabilise it." He rubbed his fingertips lightly against the stubble on his scalp. "But that is the best-case scenario. We *could,* on the other hand, initiate a fatal chain reaction in the xokronite – making it more and more unstable, until..."

Maya frowned. "Boom?"

"No, no. If only!" He shook his head, almost amused at the notion. "The containment cylinder can deal with an explosion – any explosion. You could let off a supernova in there and the outside of it wouldn't even feel warm to the touch. The end would come not with a *boom*, Maya, but with... well, with a whimper." He chuckled. "The xokronite would, in a case of catastrophic instability, degrade into something else entirely. Results vary as to what, depending on the original method of synthesis, but the best outcome I can think of in that scenario would be the chunk we have in our possession ending up as a lump of kronium-442. Which would supply a thousandth of the power required by the ship – perhaps enough to provide starvation rations from the food-synthesiser, if we could get it working under those conditions, but certainly not enough to power the perimeter-field."

There was a pause as all four of the crew took the information in. Maya found herself glancing at the perimeter-field, as if the mention of it might cause it to falter, or magically summon one of Unwen's #7Cs to attack it with tooth and claw. Munn, she noticed, hadn't taken his eyes off it once during the entire conversation.

After a moment, Soran resumed.

"The worst case scenario, of course, would be no power at all – no, no, I'm lying. There are far worse possibilities. When you're dealing with a substance that facilitates the transfer of energy through time, you have to open yourself to hypotheses that seem utterly outlandish – even divorced from known physics. We could all of us end up smeared across time like so much..." He stopped himself. "I shouldn't worry you with hypotheticals. The most likely danger here is losing the one power source we have – and if we lose the xokronite, we lose everything, what few comforts we have, and very likely our lives. It's simply not worth the risk."

Unwen scowled. "And we don't have any reserves?"

Soran smiled ruefully. "The storage batteries were irreparably damaged in the crash, I'm afraid. If we lost the xokronite, we'd have... perhaps three minutes of power? Enough time to evacuate the ship before the doors stopped working, I suppose. And even if they were in full working order, we'd never be able to top them up again – the end result would be the same. No power, no us."

Unwen nodded curtly and looked away.

"Soran..." Maya paused for a moment, choosing her words. "What is it about this... process... that drains the most power? In layman's terms."

"Oh, everything. You're talking about mutating living tissue – no, rewriting it – to bring it into line with some future descendant, millions of years ahead on the evolutionary tree. Now, the temporal rewrite – that's not too difficult. Copying a genetic map from a future descendant is what would really give us trouble..."

"Oh?" Maya was conscious of Unwen's eyes on her, but the biologist said nothing, waiting for her next move. Meanwhile, Soran rattled on, warming to the theme.

"Oh, yes. The problem here is that you want a *particular* descendant to map from. If we were just barrelling down the highway of genetics, grabbing what we found at a certain point *here*, or *there* – well, Unwen and I had no problems doing that before. Reaching deeper into the future shouldn't provoke a more significant power drain, but of course, the deeper you go, the less likely you are to find what you want..." He bit down on one of the yellow discs, considering. "We ourselves shared a common ancestor with hundreds of other species in the distant past of Habitat One – isn't that right, Unwen?"

"Thousands. Millions." Unwen shrugged. "Go back far enough, and you'll find a brother in the nester crouching in the walls of your domicell, eating scraps."

"Not that we'll ever see a nester again. Good riddance, too. Nasty things!" Soran scowled. "And this is where we start to have our power problem. You're looking for something specific – which, by the way, is at least six months of hard work for me and Unwen, since we two are the ones who have to tell the ship's brain what to look *for* in a language it might begin to understand –"

Unwen smiled sarcastically and opened his mouth to speak – to say something about Soran's real motivations at last coming to light – but a look from Maya made him close it again. Now was not the time.

"– and it's that search that will consume the additional energy. A task that will take almost every nanoprocessor the ship's brain has, working in parallel, searching through the millions of different possible species of mammal that might evolve over millions of years... an incredible energy drain." Soran shook his head firmly. "It would be easier to program in a genetic map from scratch –"

"Except programming genetic code from scratch requires a genetic library and programming software, which we do not have." Unwen scowled.

Soran ignored him. "And having taken this dreadful risk, we then do it over again, and again, and again, a hundred times – and when those hundred slaves die clearing the jungle of monsters, another hundred times, and another hundred after that. Even if we get lucky the first time – the first thousand times, the first thousand thousand – eventually, our number will come up, the xokronite will be corrupted and we'll be finished. The answer is no, Maya. I'm not helping you burn through our only energy resources for the sake of your obsession. Or Unwen's."

Silence descended on the group. Maya bit into another of the clear sacs, washing down what was in her mouth. Eventually, she spoke.

"Strictly speaking, it's only the first one that's the risk. Isn't it?"

Soran narrowed his eyes. "What do you mean?"

"Once we create that first hominid, we'll have the genetic map to create more, won't we?"

"Well –" Soran stuttered, looking uncomfortable. Maya didn't let him finish.

"Once we have that, these other thousand thousand slave-mammals you're so worried about will cost us practically no power at all. We'll probably be able to churn them out as easily as Unwen made his thumb-thing yesterday. Right?"

"Well... I suppose..."

"Just the one gamble, then. That's what you're worried about. You know what I think, Soran?" Her voice grew a hard edge. "I think you're trying to turn a small possibility of trouble into certain doom because you'd be happier doing nothing – spending the rest of eternity pottering about inside this field – and to hell with the rest of us."

Soran glanced at Munn for support, but he was quietly picking at a yellow disc, looking lost, his face ashen. He'd barely spoken since the #7C attacked the field the day before. Seeing no help there, Soran opened his mouth to defend himself, to try and convince Maya of the possible dangers, but –

– the earth shook.

Soran's mouth closed. Munn turned pale, looking as if he might be sick.

And again. Unwen stiffened, watching the mammals scampering and skittering away into the undergrowth and the trees. He heard Munn choke back a sob.

The fang-beast had returned.

This time, it did not attack the perimeter-field, or bellow its rage. It only stared at the four of them, through cold, reptilian eyes. The trickle of saliva from its jaws was a promise.

"We have to kill it." Munn whispered, his voice hoarse and cracked. "Whatever it takes. We have to kill it."

Maya nodded, turning to Soran.

"I think you're outvoted."

"THINK OF IT like this. We might be taking a small risk – *once* – but we've got no other options. Munn's already gone crazy in this bubble, and we'll all join him soon enough unless we put ourselves towards accomplishing something."

"Oh, shut up," Soran muttered, looking over at Maya petulantly. He'd tried to stop this from happening many times, refusing to work on the project, delaying things as much as possible, but he was a weak man at heart, and the pressure from the other three had been too much. Now his fingers gently tapped and danced over the display field, making the final connections.

The Power Room hummed, the blue stone inside the central pillar glowing and crackling with added power, and Unwen held one of the mammals in place inside a larger containment field – big enough to hold whatever it might become.

The experiment was ready to begin.

"Where *is* Munn?"

"Outside, staring at his three-horned beasts. Or at the jungle line, waiting for our regular visit from the big #7C. I'm sure he'll be overjoyed to meet our new friend, especially if we can train him to use this." Maya hefted the portable field generator, a squat metal box with two handles, a dial on each to be operated by the thumb – a primitive thing, slapped together by Soran in the little spare time he'd had in between programming the ship's brain over the past few months.

Unwen smiled, crouching to look the small beast in the eye. "We'll have to fit him with something to keep him obedient first. And then teach him what's expected of him. It'll be a slow process, but I have a feeling we might be ready to bag our first #7C in three to six months, depending on how quickly 'our new friend' picks up the basics, like eating synthesised food and disposing of his waste." He reached out, running a hand over the field, and the creature skittered back, nervous and unsure. Unwen liked that. "Next year, we'll know more about how to teach them, how to equip them. The year after that, we'll make some real progress. A mass cull. Farmland. Perhaps a solid-matter wall to keep the smaller predators out. I predict that within twenty years – perhaps even ten – the bubble will be a thing of the past."

Soran shot Unwen a look. "Perhaps sooner yet."

"Now, now, Soran. Let's not be defeatist." Unwen stood, taking a step back. "How long do you think it will take?"

"A minute. Less. If anything, I'll be trying to slow the process down."

Unwen looked at Maya, who nodded. "All right, Soren. Let's begin."

Soran hesitated, as if considering a last attempt to make the others see reason – then he brushed his fingertips over the control field, and the stone trapped inside the cylinder hummed into life. Within the containment field, the creature began to squeal, paws scrabbling against nothing, the blue glow invading its flesh.

"It'll work quickly," Soran murmured. "The power flow is a little higher than we expected... in fact..." His voice trailed off, and then his fingers began to move, jabbing at the field.

"What is it?" Unwen murmured, watching the animal jerk and twist in the field. The muscle groups were shifting, growing in size, the spine warping, legs elongating – but it seemed to be happening spasmodically, without rhyme or reason, as if some parts of the beast were evolving faster or slower than others. And all the time, the stone in the cylinder was glowing brighter, ever brighter. "Soran?"

"We have to shut it down! *Now!* The power drain is growing exponentially, it's as if –" He froze. "Oh. Oh, no, no, no, you *fools* –"

"Soran?" There was an edge in Maya's voice now. Inside the field, the animal began to scream.

So did the machinery. The stone glowed almost white now.

"We're taking genetic information from the thing's descendants, aren't we?" Soran's voice was trembling.

"Yes, but –"

"Except this animal is destined to die fighting a #7C! A fang-beast! We're going to send it out to be killed! It's not going to *have* any descendants! The machine's trying to resolve the paradox, and it's bending the universe out of shape to do it!"

Unwen turned, staring at Soran. "That's impossible –"

"Possible or not, it's happening! I have no idea what kind of kinks this is putting in the probability of events... we could be warping the whole structure of time, distorting the whole future..." He wiped sweat from his brow.

Maya grabbed his shoulder. "Concentrate on the here and now, Soran –"

"Shut up!" Soran shrieked. "You caused this! You and that... that egomaniac with his delusions of godhood! Look at the stone! Look at it!" He waved his arms at the glowing white xokronite. "It's beyond unstable now –"

"Just turn it off!" Maya shouted to be heard above the shriek of the machinery and the humming of the stone.

"I can't. The controls aren't responding!" Soran raced towards the containment cylinder, shielding his eyes as he placed a hand against it. "I think the xokronite is coming unstuck in –"

There was a bright, white flash, and a section of the containment cylinder simply vanished. Soran stared for a moment, then put his hand into the break, as if wanting to make sure of it.

His fingers brushed the stone.

Then it flashed again, bright enough to make spots dance in front of Unwen's eyes. When they cleared, the xokronite was gone. So was Soran. So was a large section of the flooring he'd stood on.

Unwen and Maya stared at each other in horrified silence. From outside the ship, they heard Munn begin to scream. "The field! The field is down –"

Maya moved first, grabbing hold of the portable field generator they'd been working on, leaping nimbly over the hole in the flooring and running down the corridor towards the exit. Unwen watched her go, then turned to look at the shattered containment cylinder, the thing that had been able to withstand a supernova.

A first for science, he thought.

He felt oddly calm – calm enough to theorise, even. 'Unstuck,' Soran had said. Perhaps the cylinder had not been destroyed, exactly, Unwen thought. Perhaps it was just that a large part of it was now elsewhere in the temporal dimension. Along with Soran, the xokronite, and, of course, the metal flooring. Perhaps one of the outlandish hypotheses he'd mentioned during that fateful conversation a few months previously had involved the xokronite becoming unstuck in time.

It was a marvellous theory, made more marvellous by the fact that he would die before even beginning to find a way to prove it. It might just as well be true, at least to him. Soran and his magic stone. It had a certain fairytale quality to it.

The earth underneath him shook.

Of course. The #7C, which he'd arrogantly attempted to tame by assigning it a number and a classification, had returned to show him the folly of all his ridiculous theories. How just.

Another tremor. He heard Munn's scream, mixing with a terrible roar. Munn got halfway through another scream, and then there were some loud, wet sounds Unwen didn't feel like speculating on.

Perhaps Munn's sacrifice would give Maya time to get away. He hoped so. Perhaps she would even survive.

He glanced over at the flickering spherical field, and the animal trapped inside it that looked so very much like a man.

It looked back at him with wet, blinking eyes, unable to comprehend what it had become. Unwen smiled, and reached out a hand to bless his creation. A God could do no less.

Then he walked outside the ship, to meet the Tyrannosaur.

THE PRINTER'S DEVIL

The Body of
B. Franklin, Printer,
Like the Cover of an old Book,
Its Contents torn out,
And stript of its Lettering & Gilding,
Lies here, Food for Worms.

> – Ben Franklin's self-penned epitaph,
> written in 1728. He was 22.

IN THE DREAM, *the kite flaps in a bitter wind, rain pelting the* *canvas...*

THE OLD SPRUCE in the yard no longer burns.

The tree was set afire by lightning towards the end of the storm, as if the Lord was signing the symphony of wind and rain and thunder with a final flourish, an exclamation point. *You may tame the earth,* He tells us in our hubris. *You may make a toy of fire. But the lightning is Mine, and there is no man who may tame or control it.*

Saul was able to quell the flames in short order by forming a human chain to ferry buckets from the nearby riverbank to the site of the blaze, composed of his fellow slaves and a smattering of indentured servants. If any of the big Germans felt umbrage at taking orders from a negro, they did not show it, and the fire was soon halted. My hat is off to young Saul, who is as much an asset to the plantation as his father was. Would that I had it in my power to reward him adequately, but my uncle has made it painfully clear that my opinions count for little in the running of things here. I am merely unwanted baggage, fed and housed out of a sense of obligation to a man I despised. Were I a man of spirit – had I any shred of self-respect at all – I would leave this place, where I am so clearly surplus to requirements, and make my own way in the world. But I am not, and I have not, and things are as they are.

Writing this, I am reminded that next week will mark the third anniversary of Abraham's passing. It is clear Saul misses him dearly, as do I. Would that my own father had been as gentle and kind a man as Abraham, or, for that matter, as steadfast and noble a man as Donato Scorpio, but, again, things are as they are.

One day I will have that inscribed on my tombstone.

Scorpio is long gone now, of course. He vanished from my life more than twenty years ago, and with Abraham dead and the state of Pennsylvania far behind me I suppose there is no harm in telling the story of how he and my father left my life on the very same night – if only here, in the pages of this journal. And yet a part of me hesitates at the thought of finally committing the tale to paper. Perhaps it feels too much like a confession written by a man condemned.

Well then, let it be a confession, for God knows I feel I have much to confess. My name is Robert James Steele, and in the year 1728, at the age of ten, I caused my father's death.

Is that too strong a manner of wording it? Perhaps. Mine was not the hand that struck him down, but he died so I might survive, and there are days when the guilt of that survival weighs heavy upon me, a black shroud that settles over my soul. During such times I find myself retreating from the sight of men to spend the day alone in my chambers. I find myself wondering, on those days, how my life would have gone had he lived. Eventually, I suppose, I would have inherited the farm, become an owner of my own land, rather than a guest on someone else's. Perhaps I would have sold it, and taken some other profession, though the Lord only knows what. Perhaps he would have killed me first, as he killed my mother. But certainly I would have stayed in Philadelphia. Alive or dead, I would have stayed.

I feel dead now. I feel as if something has left me, or left the world – as if a vital actor has been lost from the play, and the cast is ad-libbing desperately, hoping that they can please whatever looks down on them from the darkness of the balcony. Sometimes, I dream...

But I digress. This is the story of three deaths – my father's, my own, and the catalyst for both. In the middle of the night, he was abducted, bound, taken to the top field of my father's farm and stabbed nine times, in the throat, chest and gut. His genitals were severed and placed in his mouth, and he was then buried in a shallow grave. Too shallow by far – for coyotes unearthed the body, dragging it from its hole and gnawing on it until they had eaten their fill.

Whereupon they left the remains for me to find.

IN THE DREAM, there is the crack of thunder from far away, and the kite looks very small against the dark of the sky...

I REMEMBER ALMOST nothing of my mother; a smell, a smile, the light catching russet hair. She died when I was two years old. My first real memory is of a man with kindly eyes and a timorous smile looming over me, asking if I was all right: the Undertaker.

My father, soaked in liquor after a night carousing in the town, struck her for some imagined slight, and as a result she lost her footing, struck her head on the jutting edge of the fireplace, and stove in the back of her skull. The Sheriff, a gruff and hard-faced man named Landon Reed, declared the death a ghastly accident – perhaps he was unaware of my father's nature, though given later events I doubt it.

The incident was spoken of rarely, and until I was eight I had no idea of the specifics at all. (Even then it was Abraham who told me what had occurred, after much urging. He begged me to keep the knowledge to myself, lest he take the blame for spreading the grim particulars, and – knowing the depths of my father's temper – I gladly honoured his request.)

I suppose it is to my father's credit that my mother's death spurred him to give up use of alcohol entirely. However, for him temperance was yet another kind of intoxicant – his sudden adherence to the cause replaced the irrational rage of the drunk with the seemingly rational anger of the overly righteous. In particular, he became obsessed with moral philosophy and the proper punishment of crimes, holding long debates on the subject with whoever would hear him and publishing at least one pamphlet on the subject. Perhaps it was a reaction to the knowledge that he never answered for the drunken manslaughter he committed, although if he felt any guilt over Mother, he never admitted it to me or any other living soul.

While his philosophies never seemed to apply to his own crimes, I was not so fortunate. As I grew up I was perpetually aware that the slightest offence – real or imagined – would result in him ordering me to fetch the heavy leather strap that hung on a nail in his study, whereupon he would 'teach me my lesson,' as he put it. He spent little time with me as it was, being more concerned with the running of the farm and his growing reputation in the town as a man of letters, and this vengeful and unpredictable streak ensured that I avoided him as best I could.

My time was thus spent either in my studies – I was tutored by a stern man named James Newton, who has recently made a great noise on the subjects of education and, more controversially, the uniting of the colonies for better defence – or at play in the fields. Father would beat me for being too familiar with the field slaves, but he saw conversation with those indentured servants working our crops as being of benefit; perhaps he envisaged their rough and ready nature rubbing off on my own slight frame, so that, like them, I would eventually sprout broad shoulders and a strong back. It was not to be.

To the workers in the fields, I was mostly a part of the landscape, and they spoke to me with a forced respect that betrayed their contempt. However, a few did take to me, in particular a tough, quick-witted Italian named Donato Scorpio, who referred to me as 'Generalissimo' – some private joke of his own. He thought nothing of downing his tools for half an hour to join Abraham and me in a brief game of soldiers or a romp through the woods. His popularity was such that a blind eye was usually turned to this, provided he made up the time in some way after the others had finished their labour; no doubt had my father known of this kindness, Scorpio would have been whipped and the overseer who allowed it dismissed from his duties.

My more constant companion, in rain or shine, was Abraham. I have mentioned him several times in the course of this narrative, but it occurs to me that I have not yet offered the hypothetical reader any information as to who he was. Should any eyes but mine read these pages, let me humbly beg their indulgence.

Abraham was a house slave, and his nominal task was to keep me out of trouble, and if I were to get into any trouble, to report it – thus saving my father the troublesome duty of raising his offspring. Abraham had other duties, but his was the lightest load of any of the house slaves, and they rarely let him forget it; the field slaves, meanwhile, hardly spoke to him at all.

I suffered from a lack of friends also, being shy and withdrawn around other children in the town, who responded to my reticence by bullying and taunting me without mercy, until I withdrew to the confines of the farm and grounds; thus, we were lonely together. Still, I was a happy boy, knowing no better and content with my world, and if Abraham ever grew weary of spending his days looking after his Master's son, or yearned for better conversation or stimulation than I in my youth could provide, he was gracious enough not to show it.

I suppose, then, that I had three fathers – my natural father, a judgemental and remote presence that I associated with loss, Abraham, the protector who kept me from harm and made sure I ate what was put before me, and Donato Scorpio, the role model I looked up to and hoped somehow to emulate, despite my slight frame and quiet disposition. And in a sense, my story begins with him, for the day I found the body was the day Scorpio was to leave my father's employ. His four-year term was up, and in a matter of days, certainly no longer than a month, he would be leaving Philadelphia to travel across the country and find more rewarding work elsewhere. I was heartbroken, of course, and I'm sure I drove Abraham to distraction with my petulance, stomping sullenly around the outskirts of the grounds and calling him and Scorpio all manner of unpleasant names.

It was while engaged in this ugly activity that I saw something in the woods at the edge of the top field, which lay fallow and deserted: a hole dug in the earth, just beyond the treeline, with what looked like a large and mangled animal lying half-in and half-out of it. Against Abraham's shouted advice, I crept closer to investigate further, and saw to my considerable shock that the animal was wearing a suit of clothes.

That was my first sight of the printer, Benjamin Franklin.

IN THE DREAM, *the kite loops and glides, dances and spins. It is heavier than it should be. Something is tied to the end of the string, next to the tail...*

I SHUDDER NOW when I picture his corpse in my mind, butchered at the hands of man and the teeth and claws of nature. But perhaps in my youth I was made of hardier stuff, for mixed in with the shock, horror and nausea I felt at the discovery, there was a kind of wild excitement, a thrill at being the discoverer of this grisly sight, at seeing something not meant to be seen, certainly not by one my age. Abraham tremulously warned me away, but I crept closer, wanting to see everything despite myself.

I assumed at first that the printer had been attacked and killed by some group of large animals, like bears or wolves, but Abraham, looking over the corpse, divined the truth – the printer had been stabbed with a man-made knife rather than gored by an animal's fang or claw, and had been buried by his killer. After that, he had been exhumed from his grave by passing scavengers.

I went straight to my father, which was foolish of me. His first thought on hearing the news was to order Abraham whipped, as though he was somehow responsible for my discovery. I protested, and he ordered me to fetch the strap; I refused, and he brought it himself, and beat me until rivulets of blood ran down to my ankles.

After that, he hand-picked a couple of the field slaves to re-bury the body in a deeper hole. He swore them to secrecy, hinting darkly that if they spoke of the matter to anyone, they would hang for it to my knowledge, they took the threat seriously and kept their own counsel. As for me, Father forbade me from speaking further on the matter. The man, he said, was undoubtedly a drifter, murdered by another drifter, and that was all there was to it.

Perhaps I should have taken his heed, but I felt that I could not let the matter lie. Drifter or no, this was still a man, and in need of man's justice; thus, risking my father's displeasure, I decided to consult my tutor, the aforementioned Dr James Newton, telling him all I knew about the body, and asking if my father was right to react the way he did. I shall always remember his words to me then:

"Idle gossip, Robert, is something I do not and will not tolerate."

He went immediately to my father, who stormed into the room and bade me fetch the strap again. Father proceeded to thrash me until I bled afresh, welts landing atop welts, and this time he did not feel the need to stop, even when I passed out from the pain of the blows. The wounds I suffered were so severe that I was bedridden for several days.

I lay in a state of fever, pain-wracked and delirious – doubtless the result of an infection of the wounds, though Abraham cleaned and dressed them admirably. He stayed by my bedside as I lay, mumbling in the grip of terrible hallucinations, seeing the mutilated face of the body I had found floating at the foot of the bed, whispering terrible secrets to me that I can no longer quite recall – except in my dreams.

Occasionally, Franklin's grotesque, torn head would lapse into great oratories on taxation and similar political matters that I could not at the time comprehend and do not remember with any clarity now. On these occasions it would often be replaced in mid-speech by the face of Newton, and though the cadence changed, the subject matter remained. At other times, my father's bloodless visage would float above my head, the skull smashed, and it would stare at me accusingly even through closed eyelids. Occasionally, the dead face that haunted me would be my own, although no wound was apparent. This last apparition would never fail to make me scream until there was no air in my lungs; Abraham told me later that during these episodes he could not help but weep to see me so transported.

My father shed no tears, nor did he visit. When I was finally well enough to eat at the table, he acknowledged my presence with a curt nod – nothing more.

I, for my part, was grateful to have survived my illness and my visions, and thought nothing more of them. Now, I can only wonder what message those grim visitations were trying to impart.

IN THE DREAM, *the storm is getting closer, and the pull of the wind bids to tear the kite from its frail human mooring, but the man does not let go of the string...*

*   *   *

ABRAHAM, FEARFUL OF my father's continued wrath, urged me to let the matter drop; however, although my fever had broken and I was regaining my strength, the printer's face continued to haunt my sleeping hours, and I found my waking ones consumed by thoughts of who he might have been and how he came to such an ignominious end. Surely, I thought to myself, it was neither right nor Christian that a man simply be buried and forgotten like that, with no grave marker to signify his passing.

Plagued by these thoughts, I eventually persuaded Abraham to accompany me into the town to see the Sheriff, Landon Reed. I knew that talking to a man of such authority would create terrible trouble, for he would surely swoop down on our farm like all the angels of God, demanding to know why my father and my tutor had conspired to hide the murder of a man from the public record, and yet my young conscience would allow me no other recourse. The Sheriff, I was told, was not in his office, and so I decided, against Abraham's better judgement, that we should see him at home. Trembling, I knocked upon the door, and when it opened the whole story flowed out of me as if a dam had burst.

Landon Reed listened with a weary ear, his face drawn and haggard, and then quietly informed me that I was a very foolish boy, and I should pay attention to my betters and keep my nose out of what did not concern me. He would forbear from informing my father of my foolish excursion, since to his mind I had suffered enough, but I was to go home at once and forget the entire business, or at least speak of it to no other living soul. Having officiated at the death of my mother, I can only assume that he knew full well that were he to tell my father of my visit, the next beating would likely lead to another death in the Steele household.

As he closed the door on me, I caught a glimpse of Reed's daughter Deborah, a young and pretty girl and much admired about the town. She was crying inconsolably.

All my expectations had come crashing down around my ears, and I was left confused and stranded, seemingly without further recourse. I had no idea of who to turn to next, and when Abraham quietly suggested that we make our way home before my father noticed I was gone, as if such a thing were likely, I could only nod in dumb acquiescence.

It was at that moment that I saw Donato Scorpio again.

He was emerging from a hostelry with a wide grin, doubtless after some great gambling win or priapic exploit, and when he saw Abraham and me, he bounded over, shaking Abraham by the hand and tousling my hair. Glad though I was to see him, my spirits were still in low condition from my encounter with the Sheriff, and at first he assumed I was sulking because he had left my father's employ, and planned to leave the state of Pennsylvania entirely as soon as he had decided where to go; the Newfoundland settlements, he thought. He was relentless in curing me of my sour mood, allowing me the rare treat of riding atop his shoulders and telling stories of all the fishing he would be doing when he reached Newfoundland, but I retained my sullen demeanour and eventually the truth came out.

Scorpio reacted with disbelief at first, then astonishment, then anger at my father, who he had little respect for, and my tutor, who he considered firmly in the wrong on the issue. When I related the meeting I had just had with the Sheriff, his emotions circled again to open disbelief. He did not think me a liar, but such a reaction from a man ostensibly tasked with upholding the cause of justice seemed to him so bizarre as to defy all credibility. Surely I must have misunderstood?

I insisted that I had not, and gradually he came to understand that I was telling the unvarnished truth. I had up until this point assumed that it was I who was somehow in the wrong, for surely all of these figures of authority must know more of such situations than a young boy, but seeing Donato Scorpio so astonished by their behaviour brought home how right I had been. Something was rotten in the house of Denmark, and Scorpio declared that he would investigate to the best of his ability on my behalf, that we might all know the plain truth of the matter, starting with the assumption that Landon Reed, Dr Newton and my father evidently had some unknown reason to see this killing hidden from the eyes of men.

I thanked him profusely, feeling truly confident for the first time since the sorry business began, for I knew that Scorpio would not fail me, neither in this regard nor in any other. Abraham, likewise, seemed buoyed by the promise of some resolution to my private sorrows; however, on the trail home, his spirits fell, and he muttered darkly that such a path would lead to unforeseen consequences, and perhaps we had set things in motion better left alone. I refused to hear him. He was an uneducated slave, I told myself, and I put his qualms down to some innate superstition that I imagined was common to his race.

I was a foolish child, and Abraham a wiser man that I will ever be. I was delving into an open, festering sore that it was far beyond my power to heal; there would be precious little justice done as a result of my actions, and the price for them would be far, far higher than I would ever have chosen to pay.

IN THE DREAM, *the storm is coming closer and closer, and the man pulls down the string, carefully tying it to a wooden stake, firmly hammered into the wet ground...*

I SPENT THE next two days dividing my time between my studies and my usual leisure pursuits of watching the men in the fields and wandering the farm, though I was forbidden from the top field and knew better than to risk a further beating by disobeying my father's edict. The time seemed to pass slowly, agonisingly, as I waited for any word from Scorpio. It crossed my mind that he may have been simply humouring me, or that he had asked a few questions and then given up, and that thought made the time pass even slower. I languished in my studies, prompting stern lectures from Dr Newton, and in my playtime I would trudge morosely up the trail leading to the town and sit at the side of the road for long spells, greeting each passing rider with renewed hope, only to be disappointed again.

At the end of the Friday, after a seeming eternity of waiting, I sat in my room and stared angrily at the ceiling, listening to the sound of the wind and rain outside my window as a flickering candle picked out the shadows on the wall. The air all day had been uncomfortably humid, and the storm finally broke at sunset, a deluge unlike any in my short memory that seemed on a par with the Biblical flood; on another day, I would have listened excitedly to each crack of thunder, gasped in mingled fear and delight at each flash of lightning, but now I simply lay on my bed and sulked. My father had left the house earlier that evening to attend some meeting of philosophical minds, so I was free to stay up as I pleased; Abraham would occasionally poke his head into the room and see how I was keeping and enquire when I planned to settle down for the night, and each time I would simply scowl at him, as though he were the root cause of all my woes. He did not deserve such treatment from an ungrateful boy, and I bitterly regret it now, especially in light of that evening's events.

Just as I was about to blow out the candle and prepare for another sleepless night, there came a gentle tapping on the shutters, and I opened the window to see Donato Scorpio stood in the pouring rain, with a look upon his face as though he had ridden straight from Hell with all the devils of the underworld at his heels. Ashen, he whispered to me to let him in, and I did as I was bid.

And there, as the thunderstorm raged and the lightning arced across the sky, he told me the dreadful story of the printer, and of how his body had come to lie in that shallow grave.

IN THE DREAM, *the kite flutters and soars in the midst of the raging storm, and the man watches the glint of metal at its tail – the glint of an iron key, tied securely to the frame, the key to a new world, a bright future of light and power, the key that*

*will unlock doors to knowledge undreamed of, the key to the
future of the human race...*

DONATO SCORPIO WAS not a man used to the solving of mysteries,
but he did pay attention to local talk, and the recent chatter
in the town had concerned the Sheriff's daughter, the same
girl I had glimpsed weeping when I visited him at his home.
The local scandalmongers had it that the poor girl had been
involved in some dalliance with a printer named Benjamin
Franklin, and some gossips even claimed that he had left
her with child. Franklin had since vanished from the town,
apparently leaving his home unoccupied and his business in the
hands of his partner, Hugh Meredith, all without a backward
glance. There was talk that he had somehow learned of the
pregnancy and swiftly fled before he could be forced to marry
the girl; although the existence of the prospective child was
naught but rumour and hearsay, most had come to accept this
explanation as the gospel truth.

As Scorpio recounted this, I felt the blood run from my face
and my knees weaken with the shock. The gossip of adults
rarely reached my ears, and until that moment I had possessed
no inkling that the body was not that of a wandering drifter, as
Father had maintained. But now there could be no doubt that
the missing man and the corpse twice-buried on the outskirts
of our property were one and the same. For a moment, in
my childish innocence, I wondered how the Sheriff could have
remained so unmoved by my story, given that the vanished
printer was so closely connected to his own family; but then
the scales fell from my eyes and understanding dawned.

Was that the moment of my death? It was as if I, like Adam,
had bitten into the fruit of knowledge, for I had in that terrible
instant gleaned the hideous wisdom of adulthood, and the taste
was sour and bitter and reeked of corruption. Like Adam, I in
that moment saw humanity for what it was – a naked, rutting
animal! – and, like him, I would never know even the meagre
paradise my innocence had afforded me again.

I staggered back, sitting on my bed as my legs finally gave way, and though my mouth fell open I found I could not speak.

Of course Landon Reed had known.

He must have known from the start that the body I had spoken to him of was the same man who had lain with his only child; I was not too young to know that here was motive enough to leave the crime uninvestigated, if not to commit it. Stammering, I asked Scorpio directly: was our Sheriff the murderer? Had the man we entrusted with the keeping of the law committed this most grievous breach against it?

I should have known nothing could be so simple.

There was a long pause from my friend, as he weighed in his mind whether to leave me my illusions. But the world is cruel, and Donato Scorpio knew it better than most; so he took a breath, steeled himself, and told me of the Junto.

IN THE DREAM, *an arc of blue-white light streaks down from heaven to the kite and the key, and God's finger brushes Adam's, and Prometheus brings the first fire to mankind...*

BENJAMIN FRANKLIN WAS a man with a quick wit and a powerful mind. In his native town of Boston, he had written various amusing letters for *The New-England Courant,* the famed news-sheet, albeit via subterfuge; as his brother, the editor, would not take the work from his hand, he slipped them under his door while hiding under the pseudonym of a middle-aged widow, a ruse that ensured fourteen of the missives saw print. Would that I had possessed such spirit at the age of sixteen! However, I was already well set on my present course, journeying into lassitude and despair. Franklin fled his apprenticeship in the face of his brother's wrath; I cannot bring myself to quit a household I have grown to despise.

On arriving in Philadelphia, he spoke often of his desire to found a news-sheet in his new home, even colluding at one point with the Governor of Pennsylvania on the matter;

however, despite a sojourn in London ostensibly for the purpose, the idea came to naught, and he soon returned to Philadelphia and his old calling once again. Still, that mind hungered for debate, for discourse, for *ideas*. All who know Franklin agreed on the spark of intelligence that lit him from within; who can say what that spark might have achieved, had it not been freed so summarily from its mortal shell?

The spark did achieve one thing before being so brutally extinguished, and that was the formation of the Junto.

The Junto was a group dedicated to the mutual improvement of its members by means of weekly debates on matters moral, political and philosophical, and to begin with its members were selected by Franklin himself, including his colleagues in the printing trade and various local businessmen whom he had encountered socially. It was by all accounts a fine idea, and a means of discussing ways to improve the community; Franklin himself posited such ideas as a group of men tasked to put out fires, a collected repository of books, and a hospital for public use.

Or was that Newton?

I am, I fear, confusing the narrative. None of this was related to me by Donato Scorpio; these were details I found out later, through correspondence with many of the original members. So broken was I that while other boys my age were learning trades and courting their future wives and seeing the world, I was sat in a lonely room provided by a hated Uncle, writing letter after letter in an attempt to force the world to make sense.

And here I have the entire story, and it *still* does not make sense.

James Newton was the thirteenth member of the Junto, and I am convinced he should never have joined. But how could Franklin not invite him? Newton was an intellect on a par with Franklin's own, and quite possibly the only man in the town who could say such. According to Meredith's account, meetings would often last into the small hours as the two men sparred and jousted with words and concepts, always on opposite sides; for Newton seemed to lack the essential humanity of Franklin, the dusty tutor acting as a dark twin, a mirror-self...

When I say that Newton should never have joined, perhaps what I mean is that Newton should never have existed at all.

Still, he did. George Webb assured me in a long letter that it was Newton who first posited the concept of the neighbourhood watch, while Joseph Breitnall would have me believe it was Franklin; what is certain is that the ideas of the two men overlapped to an astonishing degree, and yet always with that crucial difference between warm and cool, a smile and a frown...

If Franklin had intended to create a philosophical Eden, Newton was the serpent. Although the Junto had no official hierarchy, Franklin was their *de facto* leader, and Newton swiftly made himself co-leader by virtue of his intellect and his powers of persuasion. Although there was no warmth in him, he had the power of cold logic on his side; that was often enough to bend his critics to his will, against their own best judgement. Having secured a place alongside Franklin, he began to force out Franklin's old friends and co-workers, recruiting others to take their places; my father was one of them, for Newton's cold demeanour appealed to his own stringency. Then there was the Sheriff, and eight others besides. Breitnall was the last to leave, unable to bear the increasing rancour of the discussions, or the puritanical element that had entered into the gathering; on the way out of his last meeting, he warned Franklin to watch himself, or better yet, end the Junto as was and let the newcomers be what they wished under their own name. On learning of Franklin's disappearance, he assumed the printer had returned to London, throwing himself on the open ocean in sheer disgust at what his grand plans had come to; I had not the heart to disabuse him.

Donato Scorpio, suspecting Newton and my father were as much involved as he presumed the Sheriff to be, made the decision to discreetly follow my tutor on the night of the storm. It was one week after the murder, and the Junto convened to discuss the matter. Listening at the window, Scorpio heard it all. Some of the newcomers were shaken, and Landon Reed was disgusted with himself, while my father and Newton felt they had committed no sin, and they debated on the moral implications of their act long into the night, and in this manner Scorpio came to know everything.

The Friday previous, the Junto had convened, and Franklin had made his intention to disband the group clear; no longer would it continue in its present form. He would form his own society, with the friends whose company he had previously enjoyed, and allow Newton's icy version to continue as a separate entity. Newton agreed, in principle; but there was a formality to attend to first.

He had to ask the questions.

Every meeting of the Junto revolved around them; a list of twenty-four questions devised by Franklin to promote debate and discourse among the assembled company.

Question the sixth: *Do you know of any fellow citizen, who has lately done a worthy action, deserving praise and imitation? Or who has committed an error proper for us to be warned against and avoid?*

And the answer came back: *"Franklin! Franklin has committed the error!"*

Franklin protested, but the questioning continued.

Question the seventh: *What unhappy effects of intemperance have you lately observed or heard? Of imprudence? Of passion? Or of any other vice or folly?*

"Franklin! Franklin is intemperate! Imprudent! Franklin's passion is vice and folly!"

And on, and on, and with each new question the wrath of this circle grew. Veins throbbed, and hands clenched, and all the time, Newton watched, sinister as any serpent.

Question the nineteenth: *Hath any man injured you, from whom it is in the power of the Junto to procure redress?*

And at this, the Sheriff stood up quickly enough to knock over his chair, pointed a finger at the trembling Franklin, and screamed: *"He made of my daughter a whore!"*

At this point, Franklin tried to escape; but the door was

firmly locked, and the questions continued inexorably, despite his desperate, unheard pleas.

Question the twenty-fourth and last: *Do you see any thing amiss in the present customs or proceedings of the Junto, which might be amended?*

"*Franklin lives!*" came the cry from ten throats. "*Franklin lives! Franklin lives!*"

And as one, they fell upon him.

He was beaten senseless, and dragged in the dead of night up to my father's top field. The Sheriff, feeling unable when the moment came to involve himself directly, stood watch; Newton, for his part, merely looked on. The other nine – good, noble men of Philadelphia! – each plunged their knife up to the hilt into Franklin. I pray to God he was not awake for it! I pray to whatever God or Devil will hear it that he was not still alive when they severed his organs of generation and forced them into his mouth!

I pray he was not alive for the burial!

Scorpio did not stay for the full meeting, but slipped away to report back to me. He had agonised about whether or not to let me know the full truth, and I could not tell you to this day if he thought it was worthwhile; for myself, I would say that it was that awful truth that slew whatever force of life lay in me, leaving me the shell I am today. And yet, perhaps it is better to have the truth, and not a lie, no matter how painful the truth may be.

And it was a painful truth indeed. For my father had also left that meeting early, and he had returned home to hear Scorpio in the middle of his tale. He had silently listened himself, long enough to know that I had defied him a third time. He had listened, and the rage had built in him slowly, and now his face was a livid purple and his hands clenched so hard his knuckles were white.

And he stood in my doorway to kill me.

IN THE DREAM, *the lightning strikes the key and travels down the string, crackling like fire, proving a point, creating a*

future, and when it hits the wooden stake buried in the earth
it sets it alight, and the flames illuminate the face of Benjamin
Franklin, forty-four years old and only begun...

SCORPIO PUT UP his fists, but too late; Father hit him hard
enough to black his eye and send him crashing to the floor like
a sack of potatoes. Then my father's hands were around my
throat, squeezing my windpipe shut, and his eyes contained
nothing but fury and madness. Perhaps it was the poison
Newton whispered in his ear, or perhaps he had been drinking,
or perhaps this was my father's true face.

What did it matter? He had come too late to kill me, for I
had already died. All he could do was wring the life from a
corpse.

He sensed my lassitude, my apathetic refusal to fear him,
and it seemed to enrage him still further. I felt him prepare to
snap my meagre neck...

Then, abruptly, there came the sound of crunching bone,
his eyes rolled back in his head, his grip loosened and he fell
to the floor, quite dead. Abraham, hearing the commotion,
had run into the room and stove in his Master's skull with a
candlestick.

I feel grateful to him, even thought he only saved a husk;
for he must have known the penalty for such an act. Scorpio
said it first, upon regaining his full consciousness. Should
anyone find out what Abraham had done, he would instantly
be hanged.

I, in my shock and to my shame, was beyond caring, and
Scorpio did the only thing he felt he could. He took the
candlestick in his own hand, explaining that he would run
through the house and let the other slaves get a good look at
him. He would take the blame upon his own head, for he felt
he was more capable of running and hiding from the forces of
law, having done it many times before; in fact, it was a problem
with the authorities in Italy that had necessitated his journey
to Philadelphia. Abraham, to his credit, tried to talk Scorpio

out of it, but one of the maids walked in as Scorpio hefted the candlestick, and after that the plan was in motion whether it was agreed or not; Scorpio punched Abraham in the face for verisimilitude, barged past the maid, and was away.

The crime followed him. Four months later he was hanged for it in the port of New York, where he was living in sin with a negress; rumour has it she took his name after, and even bore his child.

Abraham, as I have said, died only recently. My father left his farm and his slaves to my uncle, Jebediah Steele, who sold everything off at a pretty profit, save for Abraham, who I insisted come with me. The two of us made the long journey down to Texas, where my uncle put Abraham to work in the fields; having been a house-slave all of his life, his constitution was not best suited to the work and he began to grow sickly. At the same time, his quick mind grew dull under the rigors of the work and the brutal treatment of my uncle. Where once his conversation was lively and his head was high, now he slumped and barely had a word to say. I soon stopped talking with him on any regular basis, though he will always mean the world to me.

The truth of Benjamin Franklin's death never came out, of course; nobody would have taken a boy's word and a slave's against the great James Newton. I have followed the latter's career with some dread, as he seems to be making increasing inroads into the political sphere. I cannot help but wonder whether Franklin, had he survived and somehow ended Newton – had he even known the nature of the strange, unholy duel Newton had fought against him – would have walked the same path. What would the course of our nation have been like? A shade warmer, certainly, which would be no bad thing.

Benjamin Franklin still lies in the soil underneath the fields that were once owned by my family, but his spirit is not entirely gone from Philadelphia. The town gossips were right, and Deborah Reed was with child, a fine boy she called Franklin; for she never stopped loving him, even when he vanished from her life so completely, without a goodbye. He is now twenty-two himself, and in matters of intelligence, the son seems likely to eclipse the father.

He has just invented a wonderful device called a steam engine.

Perhaps one day I will find the strength to hurl myself underneath it.

THE DREAM IS *coming to an end, and I will forget all but the vaguest impression of it. Benjamin Franklin has finished his show of magic, having harnessed the lightning with kite and key, and brought it down for man to play with; he does not speak, but he turns to his audience, gives a small bow, and offers the dreamer a warm, broad smile that speaks for him. The memory of the dream will fade, yes; but the dream goes on.*

The dream goes on.

"But the work shall not be lost;
For it will, as he believd, appear once more
In a new and more elegant Edition
Corrected and improved
By the Author."

– Ben Franklin's epitaph.

THE LONESOME RIDER AND THE LOCOMOTIVE MAN

Thomas stood atop the mesa and looked down at what was left of his hand.

Most of the flesh had rotted away from the fingers, so that the white bone peeped mockingly through. He felt no pain – just a tingling warmth at the end of his left arm, and then nothing beyond.

He could not let go of the stone.

He mopped the sweat from his brow with his good hand, licked his dry lips, and concentrated. Tiny bursts of galvanic power crackled over his skin, and his matted black hair began to rise slowly from his brow until it was standing straight up on his head. Almost against his will, he found himself smiling, a madman's idiot-grin. He couldn't help himself. The power running down his arm, across his chest, pulsing and throbbing in every part of his body – he'd never felt anything like it. No-one ever had.

When the soles of his worn-out shoes left the ground, he barely noticed.

He blinked the sweat from his eyes, looking up now, concentrating on the makeshift scarecrow he'd built, standing in front of him. The effigy. The target.

The power was building inside him, and that good, hot,

tingling feeling was growing more intense, a sensation of pins and needles across his arm and back, like some crawling insect or a lover's touch.

He held his breath.

After six seconds, perhaps a little more, the prickling sensation intensified, becoming pain, then agony, roaring over his flesh like fire and quickly becoming too much to bear. He held it as long as he could, gritting his teeth, until the stone glowed a bright white and the mesa below him seemed to fade and shimmer – and then he forced the power out of him with a high, thin scream, directing it through the stone, at the head of the dummy.

Lightning arced across the space between them, blinding him for a moment. When his sight returned, the scarecrow was on fire.

Slowly, he succumbed to gravity, his feet drifting back to rest on the rock. He realised that he was grinning again. He wanted to laugh, to laugh and laugh and never stop, but he just didn't have time. He had to make the long walk down into the town. He had a telegram to send.

He would send it that very day, and soon after that, the man who'd tried to destroy him, who'd treated him more cruelly than any of them, his enemy... his enemy would come to him. Come and be burned like the scarecrow. And after his enemy was dead, he would begin to build his new America.

Eyes dancing under a mane of wild black hair, Thomas Alva Edison licked his lips and spoke his enemy's name.

"*Westinghouse.*"

"HEY, BOY!"

The man in black finished securing his horse to the rail, giving no heed to the words. Jonah snorted, stamping his hooves – he was a fine horse with fine ears, a sagacious animal who knew a jackass when he heard one. The man patted his flank, gently, so as to calm him down some. A jackass wasn't nothing worth getting upset over, after all.

"Hey! *Boy!* I'm *talkin'* to you!"

Then again, it never did to let a jackass get away with being a jackass. He'd only be a jackass again.

The man in black frowned, looking over towards the office George kept in the town – he could see some young fella in a brown suit and round glasses in George's window, looking out at him. Some accountant or secretary, most likely.

"You *hear* me, boy? You deaf, or just yeller?"

Loud laughter.

Hell with it. Give the accountant a show.

The man in black turned around and took stock of the situation. Four men, a little drunk in spite of the early hour. Cowhands, by the look of 'em. Big fellas – the one talking was about a half a head bigger than he was, and he was a good six foot. Rounder, too, so that was all right.

The man lifted the brim of his black hat a tad and shot the jackasses a hard look. "Took four of you to say that?"

The ringleader – the big talker – sneered and looked around at his sidekicks for support. "Only takes the one of me to handle your kind, boy."

He spat. The man in black's eyes narrowed, and when he spoke, there was gravel in his tone.

"I got a name, mister. Figure you might know it."

"Aw, sure I do!" The big talker guffawed, sneaking another quick glance at his fellow rowdies to make sure they were with him, and a beat later they were laughing right along, sure enough. "Why, you're Jacob Steele, ain't you, boy? The famous Lonesome Rider of the plains, isn't that right? Well, we done heard *all* kinds of stories 'bout *you*, boy!"

Jacob Steele nodded curtly, pulling a cigar from the inside pocket of his black duster coat. "Is that right. Well, mister, I should tell you a lot of them stories the newspaper boys tell... they ain't entirely correct."

The big talker laughed again, turning back to his coterie. He didn't seem to be able to say a word without checking it with them first. Bad quality in a leader of men.

"Didn't I say so, fellas? Huh? Didn't I say there weren't no negro could outgun a hundred men?"

A small crowd was gathering. A couple of them nudged each other and grinned – jackasses in training. Steele shook his head, amused despite himself.

"Well, now. Is that what they say about me? That I done put a hundred men in the dirt? Well, don't that beat all." He chuckled softly, holding a flickering match to the end of the cigar.

His eyes narrowed.

"Truth is, it was a hundred thirty-six."

The men stopped laughing.

"And every single one of them sons of bitches drew first."

There was a moment of silence, and then the rightmost man – a mean-looking cuss with a ragged moustache and hate in his eyes – reached for the holster at his belt. Steele held off an extra split-second or two just to let him clear leather, and then he put a bullet through the varmint's hand.

"Case in point." He nodded to the owlhoot, who was screaming like a banshee, clutching what was left of his fingers and looking at Steele like he was the devil himself risen straight up out of Hell. "Go find a doctor 'fore you bleed to death, you dumb bastard."

The moustached man started off like a scalded cat, and the Lonesome Rider addressed the other three. "Like I said, them newspaper boys... they tone things down. They don't want it to seem like it's crazy talk. But there's two things about me you mighta heard, and them two are the gospel truth. First is, I never drew down on an unarmed man."

He watched a single drop of sweat trickle the length of the big man's face, and then all three of them unbuckled their holsters and let them drop into the dirt, guns and all.

Steele nodded. "Second thing is that I never suffered a damn fool my whole life. Never have and never will. Now, you folks got a choice. Either you can apologise for startin' this conversation off so ungentleman-like, or you can put up your dukes and fight. All of you."

The big man blinked, and the other two looked at each other, then all three of them seemed to recover some of the bluster they'd had a minute before. "Boy, you got to be out of your damn mind to make a challenge like that. There's three of us here —"

"That's right, fat man. There's three of you and there's one of me. And I am gonna beat you until your blood runs and your dead mama cries." He blew out a ring of smoke. "Make your choice."

They chose wrong. Jackasses always did.

The big man charged, swinging one arm like a mace. Steele could see he was way off balance — like as not it'd been a dog's age since he'd had to fight with a fella who could fight him back, and he'd gotten sloppy, if he was ever much good to begin with. Hell, maybe the big talker had been living off his size and his mouth since he was born. Waiting his whole damn useless life for this one moment.

The moment the talking had to stop.

Steele stepped to his left, grabbed the swinging arm and twisted it. There was a loud crack, and splintered bone tore through the big man's forearm and shirt, sending a gout of blood into the dust at his feet. Immediately the big talker went down to his knees, screaming — no, *squealing*, like a stuck pig. Steele shook his head sadly and stepped away. Then he spoke.

"Get up."

The big man looked up at Steele through tears, uncomprehending. The other two stepped back, looking white as ghosts, but the crowd pushed at them, refusing to let them leave. "W-what you mean, get up?" The big man whined, looking into Steele's eyes — maybe he was hoping to find some kind of mercy there, but there weren't no mercy to be had.

Steele's voice was like stone on stone.

"You bought yourself a whole mess of trouble today. You bought it and now you gotta pay for it. So get up, fat man. Get up and get ready."

He took a last drag on the cigar, then dropped it into the dirt and ground it out with the heel of his boot.

"I ain't near done with you yet."

*　　*　　*

"IT'S A BARBARIC display," Franklin Reed III breathed, shuddering. He took his glasses off, cleaning them with the handkerchief he kept in the breast pocket of his brown tweed suit. When he put them back on again, all three men were on the ground, bleeding. He leaned closer to the glass.

"If the sight offends your sensibilities, Mister Reed, then I suggest you step away from the window to prevent yourself gawking at it like a damned rooster." George Westinghouse leant back in the leather office-chair – not quite as fancy as the one he kept in his main office in New York, but certainly good enough for Fort Woodson – and grinned. "Those scofflaws knew the man they were dealing with, and so do I. Frankly, I'd be more than a little disappointed if he'd done otherwise."

Reed looked at Westinghouse for a moment, but did not step away. Through the murky glass, he saw that one of the cowhands had staggered back to his feet, only for Steele to land another sledgehammer blow to his jaw, sending a tooth flying. A man in the crowd caught it in his hand, gave a yelp of delight, and showed it to an older man he was with, just as if it were the winning ticket in a raffle. Reed stared for a moment longer before he realised that both the men wore badges.

He sighed and shook his head. "Well, I call this a disgusting spectacle, sir, on a par with the Roman circus. In my opinion, the man's made his point, and they won't soon forget it. He should let them walk away –"

Westinghouse snorted. "Walk away, you say? If they can walk at all, then in *my* humble opinion Steele ain't made his point well enough. And considering he'll be protecting your hide, and your creation, I'd have thought you'd be pleased to see him demonstrate the skills that'll keep you both in full working order." He chuckled to himself, as if he'd made some great joke, and indicated the ornate wooden box on his desk. "Cigar?"

Reed shook his head. "I won't be needing a bodyguard, sir, and neither will my 'creation,' as you very well know. And tobacco is a noxious weed," he murmured absently, "ruinous to the constitution and destructive to the tissue of the lung, which I will have no truck with."

Through the window outside, he saw Steele standing over the broken bodies of the men he had felled, once and then again, over and over until they could no longer rise and honour – or bloodlust – had finally been satisfied. Steele spat into the dirt and the crowd cheered for him, and Reed could not help but wince. "The bloody sport is over with, Mr Westinghouse. I trust Mr. Steele will not allow any other street brawls to delay our business further?"

The only answer Westinghouse gave him was another snort and a shake of his head. A moment later, the door to the office swung open and Steele was among them. Westinghouse stood, offering his hand to the man. "Good seeing you, Jacob. I noticed you got a little exercise before our appointment." He chuckled again.

"If that's exercise, George, I'm gonna get fat." Steele turned in Reed's direction and nodded once. Reed hesitated for a moment, then stuck out his hand. It was an opportunity to size up the man.

Steele had a hard grip, to begin with – hard, but not crushing. Reed had, in the past, met men who'd attempted to prove themselves superior to him by attempting to break the bones of his hand, and these were usually men desirous of concealing some defect or imperfection, possibly in the genital region. Reed next looked to the eyes, and found the man's stare as hard as his grip – not belligerent, but not willing to shrink from belligerence either. A hard man in general, then.

Reed scanned for other salient points. Age – mid-thirties or thereabouts, perhaps a little younger. A touch over six feet in height, taller than most men, and slim, but powerfully built. A small scar over his lip on the right side, and another over his eye, the ghost of some long-ago fight where a blade had gotten a little too close to blinding him.

And he was a negro, of course.

Reed realised the handshake had gone on uncomfortably long, and let Steele's hand go. "A pleasure, sir." It was not, but to admit the intimidation he felt would only lessen him in the gaze of all those present, including himself.

Jacob Steele had likewise used the long handshake to size up Franklin Reed III. He'd taken one good look at the eyes behind those round glasses and figured Reed for a lily-white jellyfish. He hadn't proved himself a jackass yet, though. Thank the Lord for small mercies.

Westinghouse leaned back in his chair. "Well now, I suppose introductions are in order. Reed, you've had a good look at Jacob here, and doubtless you know a little of his reputation as a bounty hunter. What you may not know is that I keep him on permanent retainer as a kind of trouble-shooter for the Westinghouse Steam and Signal Company. I won't bore you with the specifics of the arrangement, but he's worth every red cent I pay him and more besides. Saved my hide and my company more times than I'd care to admit."

He lit his cigar with practised confidence, puffed once, then used it to indicate Reed. "And Jacob, this tall drink of water is Franklin Reed III, scientific prodigy and the most able mind in my employ at twenty years of age. Started working for me when he was twelve. He's a little lacking in horse-sense occasionally, as young men often are, but I tell you now that *this* young man has the capacity to change our entire world. No joke."

Jacob gave the young man in question a sideways look. "Huh."

Reed blushed, looking at his feet. "I fear Mr Westinghouse is indulging in a little hyperbole."

Westinghouse shook his head irritably. "I don't believe in hyperbole, son, and neither should you. It's your inventive genius that's made this company what it is, these last few years, and that's before we bring up what you have sitting in that warehouse over yonder."

Reed shook his head, turning to Steele apologetically. "Really, I've only made a few small breakthroughs in the fields of –"

"Horseshit, son." Westinghouse stood up, stubbing his cigar out in the ashtray. "Hell with it – let's allow Mr. Steele here to judge what's a small breakthrough and what's not. Figure he should see what he's going to be travelling with." He grinned, looking Steele dead in the eye. "I remember when I first saw what you're about to see, Jacob. I went in there with that sceptical look you have on your face, and I walked out a true believer in the world that's coming."

His grin widened.

"I also walked out with shit in my pants."

TEN MINUTES LATER, in a guarded warehouse on the edge of Fort Woodson, Jacob Steele came face to face with the Locomotive Man.

At least, he would have done, if the damned thing had had a face to begin with. Instead, its head was a dome of smooth and expressionless brass, save for a pair of lenses – delicate-looking things – that took the place of eyes. The effect was a mite unnerving, not to say otherworldly, and Steele found himself leaning back a tad. He could feel that slight twitch in the muscle of his gun arm that signified trouble brewing.

For the Locomotive Man's part, it just sat there on a wooden block with its arms at its sides, like nothing so much as a crude statue fashioned from old train parts and iron boilers. It was slumped back a little, like a big, ugly puppet with no strings – a ten-foot-tall puppet at that. Steele couldn't help but wonder what kind of child might play with a toy like that, and the thought didn't exactly endear him to Franklin Reed much.

Reed smiled, opening the iron furnace-door in the thing's belly and feeding it a shovelful of coal. He yelled out above the clatter: "Just a prototype, you understand! I'm working on a system of microhydraulics that should allow me to reduce his dimensions a little. Of course, the firebox would also have to be reduced, which would mean shorter running-time unless we can dramatically increase fuel efficiency, but that's a puzzle I'm sure I can find a solution to..." He ran his mouth on in that vein while he added kindling and newspaper. The fella seemed more in his element now, tossing around a passel of forty-dollar words Steele didn't much feel like puzzling out. He couldn't help but feel a touch otherworldly himself – like he was watching some kinda ritual, some magic he didn't quite understand.

Pretty soon the flames in that firebox were roaring bright,

and to Steele's eye it looked like a glimpse straight into the fires of Hell. He shot Westinghouse a look, speaking almost under his breath. "I'll say this plain, George. I don't much like where this is headed."

Westinghouse just smiled, a little superior smile Steele didn't exactly appreciate. Kind of a jackass smile.

Reed slammed the furnace-door shut with a heavy clang, then walked around to the back of the thing. Around back of the Locomotive Man there were a whole mess of dials, switches and levers – a bank of them jutting from shoulder to shoulder. Reed ran his eyes over those, reading them and making what adjustments he found necessary. The chimney rising from the metal man's left shoulder was already belching out a thick black plume of smoke, which drifted up to a vent made for it in the ceiling, and presently the whistle built into its right shoulder gave out a shrill scream, like a train.

All aboard, Steele thought. He still felt like he was dreaming.

"All in working order!" Reed murmured, wiping a little of the soot from his hands onto an old rag. "A minute or two more, just to allow the furnace to reach the correct temperature for full operation, and then..." He smiled, in a proud and genial manner far removed from his earlier stiffness. It almost seemed to Steele as if only here, among the metal and brass and copper and rods and gears of his huge puppet, was he fully himself at last, comfortable in his own skin.

"Do you know," he continued, "I originally considered building the chimney in as a top hat. Can you imagine how that would have looked? But, of course, I had to leave room for the workings of the analytical engine."

Steele pricked his ears up at that. "The what now?"

"Analytical engine! A sort of thinking-machine, based a little on the work of one Mister Charles Babbage – have you heard of him? Dead nearly ten years now, God rest his soul, but he may yet be remembered as the father of the age... ah! There we have it!" He laughed like a boy, noticing some dial had finally crept up into the required temperature, and then yanked down the largest lever on the Locomotive Man's back.

The whistle sounded once again, and then the whole contraption shook and juddered for a second. From inside the brass dome there came an odd chattering sound. Jacob Steele remembered when he'd come across a deputy using one of Mr. Sholes' fancy new type-writers, and this sounded like nothing so much as a roomful of the damned things, all clattering and snapping away at once. The sound carried on for a couple of seconds more, long enough for Steele to convince himself that he'd guessed wrong. There was no way in creation this blamed contraption was going to move of its own accord.

And then – very slowly, as if only just working out how – it did just that.

The Locomotive Man stood up.

"By God!" Steele yelled, taking a step backwards, and the cold breath of fear ran through him. All of a sudden his knees seemed made of water, like they couldn't bear his weight. *I am dreaming,* he thought. *I am dreaming or going mad, having visions of some other place. Because that is not something that should be in this world.*

It was George Westinghouse's turn to smile now. "By God indeed. I had much the same reaction myself. Mister Reed, if you will please have your friend introduce himself to Jacob? I have a hunch they'll be getting along famously once he gets over the shock."

"If you insist, sir," Reed smirked, and he pulled and flicked the levers and switches, one after another. "I will add Mister Steele to the internal record..."

The thing took a lumbering step forward, heavy enough to make the floor shake underneath it. Then it slumped slightly, the lenses of its eyes gazing upon Steele's face, and just for a second the bounty hunter thought it might just reach out with its hands – them blunt mechanical claws it had – and grab a hold of him. And then? Why, he could see it bundling him into the firebox to burn alive like so much kindling while these two white men smiled their big happy smiles.

And then the damned thing reached out a claw out for him, and Steele very nearly shot it in the face.

It was only a split-second of fright, but he was halfway to his iron by the time he saw what it was really doing. Then he understood the gesture and forced himself to relax. "God damn it, George. Are you serious?"

Westinghouse just couldn't seem to get that grin off his face. He looked like a proud papa whose youngest boy had only just learned to walk. "Shake hands, Mister Steele."

"The hell with you, George. I ain't shaking hands with that." Steele found himself surprised at the venom in his voice. *Why not, damn it? No need to make trouble over it, these folks are proud of their toy, so why not play along?* Was it 'cause they'd laughed? That was part of it, sure, maybe a big part, but he was enough of a man to take that for what it was.

No, it was something else. The whole idea of the Locomotive Man just rubbed him wrong, somehow.

Westinghouse swapped his smile for a pained look, like he'd only just realised all the guests at the hoedown weren't quite getting along. As for Reed, the boy had a face on him like a kicked puppy. "It would be a lot better if you did, Mister Steele –"

"That a threat?"

"No!" Reed paled. "God, no! But it just... well, it helps it identify you as a friend... oh, hell." He bit his lip, looking miserable, then stepped forward and started flicking more of the switches on the thing's back. The metal man stared at Steele, almost accusing, while the cogs in its mechanical brain whirred and ground. "There," Reed said at last, "you're added to the record. No handshake required."

Westinghouse shook his head sadly, looking disappointed. "It's not something to be afraid of, Jacob. It's the future."

Steele turned away angrily. He was angry with Westinghouse and his damned disappointed look, like he was some schoolteacher talking to a child who'd got the answer wrong, and he was angry with Reed and his kicked-dog face and most of all he was angry with that cursed heap of junk that was still standing there like it was a man.

And he was mad at himself too, a little, for not playing nice with these overgrown kids and their overgrown toy – except he'd never gone against his gut yet, and in his gut he knew the Locomotive Man was bad news. Hell, it might just be the death of him.

He sighed, and pushed the feeling down. It was always good to listen to your gut, but you had to feed it occasionally too. And that meant money, which right now he didn't have a whole lot of.

"We can talk about that later, George. Right now, I imagine you called me in for more than showing off toys."

Westinghouse shrugged, and nodded. "I did indeed, Jacob. I have a job for you. Easy work, you'll find – you are to be an escort, if you're willing. A bodyguard. For Mister Reed here, as a matter of fact." He paused for a moment, looking away and scratching the back of his neck, as if he was working out how to broach some troublesome news. "And, um... also, for... that is to say, you'll be accompanied by..."

The Locomotive Man let out another shrill scream, and George had the decency to look embarrassed at that.

"God damn it." Steele said, and lit another cigar.

"THERE."

Steele watched irritably as Reed shovelled another heap of coal into the firebox. They'd made a stop at the side of the trail, so that Reed could feed his creation more of the coal and water it needed.

He had a plentiful store of both with him, in a great metal-and-canvas wagon that the Locomotive Man pulled along behind him. It was a hell of a thing in itself, with compartments for all the necessities, including food and water for the flesh-and-blood men on the expedition as well as for Jonah, and built-in bedding so a man might sleep in it at night, with the Locomotive Man standing guard – assuming any man could sleep through the night with the damned thing's whistle screaming out whenever it had a mind. Reed had gone so far as to paint his wagon with the legend 'FRANKLIN B. REED

III, OWNER AND INVENTOR OF THE ASTOUNDING &
ASTONISHING LOCOMOTIVE MAN,' just as if he was a
quack selling snake-oil or a blamed travelling circus.

He'd invited Steele to sit with him on the front seat of the
thing, but Steele had flatly refused. Now, as he watched Reed
load the firebox from the vantage point of Jonah's saddle,
he couldn't help but figure the astounding and astonishing
Locomotive Man was a mite more trouble than it was worth.

"About how long do you reckon this'll take, Mister Reed?"

Reed sighed. "Not much longer, I promise. Unfortunately the
current design means that, unlike in the case of the common
locomotive, we cannot load the firebox while the Locomotive
Man is in motion."

"Not unless we want to get ourselves stepped on."

"Yes. Quite."

Steele reached into his black duster coat and fished out another
of his cigars. "You considered putting the door in its back?"

Reed sighed as he hefted another shovelful of coal.
"Unfortunately, that would mean the control mechanisms
would have to go on the front, which again brings up the
problem of, ah..."

"Getting stepped on." Steele lit his cigar and took a few
quick puffs.

"Quite." Reed scowled, then slammed the furnace-door and
hung the dirty shovel on a hook jutting from the wagon's side,
where he could pick it up easy next time. Then he clambered
back up into his seat and started the Locomotive Man up – the
metal man gave out another shrill scream from his whistle,
and Jonah reared and bucked a little at that, and then the
thing juddered forward into a steady walking-pace, pulling
the wagon after it. Once Jonah had gotten over his fright, he
trotted gently alongside.

Steele listened to the Locomotive Man's slow, rumbling
clank, watching the landscape drift by slowly. "Can't help but
figure we'd make better time on horseback, Mister Reed."

Reed shook his head. "Ah, but then we would be without
the Locomotive Man!"

"Don't sound like such a disadvantage to me."

"And what if we run into trouble on our journey, Mister Steele?"

"I'll handle it."

Reed folded his arms, looking smug. "And if it's more than you can handle?"

Steele almost laughed. "No such animal, Mister Reed. No such animal." He took another puff on his cigar, then blew out a thick ring of smoke. "And I'll bet you a dollar to a dime it won't be the journey that gives us trouble. It'll be this Edison feller sittin' at the end of it."

According to what George Westinghouse had come out with back in Fort Woodson, after they'd finally gotten done looking at Franklin Reed's wonder, this Edison had been laughed out of most scientific circles, on account of his lack of education and some crackpot ideas about harnessing lightning for telegraph systems or lights or some such nonsense. After years of ridicule, he'd approached Westinghouse with his notions, although why the hell he thought that kind of crazy talk had a place in the Steam and Signal Company, George didn't know and Jacob couldn't tell him. George had treated the man as kindly as he could, but he'd shown him the door all the same, and maybe it was that small kindness that broke Edison at last. After that, he spent more than a year sending threatening letters, telegrams, smoke signals if he could – all promising war, a war George Westinghouse was just too sane to understand the meaning of.

George had refused to respond to the letters, or the impassioned rants on soapboxes in the middle of New York streets, or the full-page adverts taken out in newspapers with money Edison surely couldn't spare. Eventually Edison's propaganda war had tailed off, and Westinghouse forgot him, for he was a man used to dealing with colourful characters.

And then the telegram had arrived.

Steele dug into the pocket of his coat and retrieved it. He squinted at the words for a moment, then leant over in his saddle to hand it to Reed. "Here. Read it out. I want to hear it out loud."

Reed frowned, taking the piece of paper. "Why can't you read it?"

Steele shrugged. "I guess I could if you want, but it'd be a slow business. I didn't learn to read or write 'til I was fourteen, and even then I had to teach myself. Still ain't the best at it."

Reed blinked, and Steele could see the puzzlement on his face. Then he began to read in his soft, almost trembling voice:

```
GALVANIC AETHER A REALITY STOP SOURCE
OF POWER GREATER THAN ANY KNOWN STOP
MEET ME ON DEVILS EYE MESA IN COLORADO
IN  ONE  WEEK  FOR  DEMONSTRATION  OF
ULTIMATE POWER THAT WILL END DOMINION
OF STEAM FOREVER STOP YOU SHOULD HAVE
LISTENED TO ME STOP
                          THOMAS ALVA EDISON
```

Steele nodded grimly. "'You should have listened to me.' See, in my line of work, that's what we call a threat."

Reed shook his head. "I hardly think so. An 'I-told-you-so' at most. I'm more interested in this business of 'galvanic aether'..."

"I'm guessing that's that lightning-power George was talking about earlier."

"I'm not sure. From what Mr Westinghouse told me, Edison was always talking about galvanic *force*, or galvanic *current*. In the newspaper adverts, he described a great War of Currents – water versus lightning."

Steele scowled. "You'd think war between plain men was bloody enough. So what's aether in relation to that?"

"Honestly, I –"

"The simple version. Some of us didn't get your fancy schooling."

"The simple version, Mister Steele, is I don't know. In classical mythology, aether is the air breathed by the Gods

– the substance of a plane higher than our own, above the terrestrial sphere. If you ask me, his use of the term is ominous, very ominous." Reed bit his lip, looking towards his metal man, as if for protection. And, as if responding to his need, the Locomotive Man let out another scream from his whistle.

"You think he might be even crazier than last time – God damn it!" Steele tugged on Jonah's rains, keeping him from bucking. "Any way you can do something about that damned whistle?"

"Hmm? Oh, I'll work on it in the next iteration," Reed murmured. "Crazy... I don't know if I would call him that. Apparently he provided a couple of demonstrations that seemed to show he was onto something – some business with magnets and copper wire..."

"Well," Steele murmured, "George doesn't call me in to deal with peaceable types, and this feller sounds like his powder's about ready to blow."

"Ah yes." Reed sighed. "Now that, I can agree with. That's why Mister Westinghouse sent me, as I understand it – he thought if he went to see what Edison was doing himself, it might stir up old wounds..." He bit his lip, staring ahead at the road. "Or I might be wrong. It's possible he thought I might see something in Edison's ideas that he missed. Perhaps... if I saw what Edison was doing..." He paused a second, like he was about to say more, then shook his head and turned away.

That piqued Steele's curiosity. "What?"

Reed looked him in the eye for a spell, hesitating – then when he spoke, his voice shook. "Mister Steele... do you..." He paused again, then spat it out. "Do you feel as though the world should be *different* from what it is?"

Steele stared at Reed for a long moment. "Kind of a dumb question, ain't it?"

Reed blushed red, and looked back towards the unfolding road. Steele took another long drag on his cigar. "Tell you what, Reed, why don't you tell me how you think it oughtta be different, and then I'll tell you if I feel the same way."

Reed took a deep breath, not quite trusting himself to look Steele in the eye. This time, when he spoke, his voice was down to a whisper. "You must not think me mad, sir. Pray do not think me mad."

Steele shrugged. "You built a train with legs to carry you around like a damn caliph, Mister Reed. It's a mite too late to worry 'bout what I think."

Reed laughed despite himself, then his manner grew sombre again. "I... have had dreams, sir. Dreams in which the world is altered, almost imperceptibly. The differences are subtle, but..." He ran his tongue over dry lips. "Fireflies in glass bulbs. Automatic telegraphs festooned with wires. A system of lightning and wire spanning this country. The beginning of a world of wonders... you must understand, I would not trouble myself with such visions if... if they weren't so vivid. If it all didn't seem so real. So... so horribly plausible. So unlike..." He paused, staring into the distance. "So unlike *our* world, Mister Steele." He turned to Steele again, and now there was an almost feverish look in his eye. "Doesn't it seem strange to you? Doesn't it seem like we're missing something basic? Something we *should* have?"

He caught the look in Jacob Steele's eye, and looked away, composing himself. "I... I apologise. I must sound to you like some babbling half-wit. I just... I'm just trying to explain..."

Steele looked at him for a moment. "Let's just ride a spell, Mister Reed. Figure we'll both feel better once the sun's a little lower."

Reed swallowed, and nodded soberly, not trusting himself to speak further.

They didn't speak again until they reached the town.

DEVIL'S GULCH WAS a town about ten miles out from the mesa, and a good place to stop and re-fill the canteens with water and feed Jonah. Steele figured there'd be a place where the two of them could stay for the night, assuming those who ran it were happy keeping the Locomotive Man with their horses.

"We'll stop here a brief spell. Figure we can reach the top of the mesa 'fore sundown – can't be more'n an hour's ride from here." Steele said, tying Jonah to a rail outside the saloon. "Once we've talked to Edison, we can head back here and rest up."

Reed sighed. "If he allows us to."

"One way or another, he'll do that." Steele looked around at the townsfolk. A small crowd had gathered to stare at Reed's wagon and at the Locomotive Man, and a few wags in the crowd were already passing comment that whoever was inside it must be all-fired hot.

"C'mon, mister, y'all ain't foolin' nobody!" One of them called out. "Why don't you get whatever fella you got in there t'unscrew that dome o' his an' show his face?"

Steele couldn't help but crack a smile, but Reed seemed to take it personally. "The Locomotive Man is real, sir! And I will have you know it is the wonder of the age!" He yelled the words back, but the crowd only intensified their jeering.

"Y'all gonna sell us some snake-oil medicine, Mister? I could sure use some tonic!" One of the younger ones shouted.

"Yer too young for tonic, boy!" His father bellowed, and a ripple of laughter spread through the crowd. Steele couldn't help but chuckle himself, holding up his palms in apology when Reed turned his furious gaze on him.

"Now, now, Mister Reed. You surely must admit that wagon of yours looks the part."

Reed fumed, shaking his head. "By God, they'll learn. When there's a Locomotive Man in every town, on every street corner, they'll remember this day for the rest of their lives! The day they saw the first! They'll feel foolish then, I'll bet –"

"Hey, you! Metal man!" The boy yelled. "Why don't you do a trick fer us?"

Reed grimaced. "There'll be no tricks!" He shouted back. "This is a marvel of science! It's not a toy!"

Steele shook his head. "Could've fooled me –"

"*Steele!*"

The cry cut through the air like a thrown knife. By the time Steele turned to face it, his iron was already in his hand.

"Grey Owl. By God."

The man pushing his way through the crowd was an Indian,

an outcast from one of the Ute tribes, and a man whom Jacob Steele knew well. He walked with a slight limp, and that was the legacy of their last meeting, when Steele had put three bullets in him and watched him take the fall from a high cliff into a river. He'd always figured that if the day came when he ever saw Grey Owl again, it'd be in the next world – yet here he was, alive and well.

"Jacob Steele." Grey Owl's eyes were burning with hate. "I've had visions of meeting you again."

Steele slipped his firearm back in its holster. "Well, I can't say the same. We all figured you was a dead man. Hell, I collected the bounty on you. You've done a hell of a job of hiding yourself these last two years."

"Not hiding." Grey Owl's gnarled hands hovered over the pearl-handled revolvers he wore at his hip – the same guns he'd taken from Colonel Armstrong, after revenging himself for the massacre at Bitter Falls. "Waiting."

Steele's own gun-arm was twitching, and he found himself taking up a stance. Gunfights had their own cruel gravity, and he felt the two of them being drawn towards that irrevocable moment when one of them would kill the other. "Well, here I am," he said slowly, "but I don't much want to draw on you, Grey Owl. We done that dance once already. 'Sides... hell, I figure you had a right to do what you done. Lord knows that damn fool deserved worse."

"Did he? Is that why you hunted me across three states, then? Is that why you put three bullets in my hide?" Grey Owl spat, furiously, clenching and unclenching his fists in preparation for the draw. "Or was it for a fistful of white man's money?"

Steele stared Grey Owl in the eye. He didn't dare to blink. The baying of the crowd, Reed and his ridiculous metal monster – all that was forgotten now. It was just him and his enemy, a man skilled enough to drop him right here if he should falter. For an instant, he found himself thinking back to the big talker in Fort Woodson, and he realised it'd been a hell of a long time since anyone had given him a proper fight, at that.

"I hunted you 'cause I knew others were hunting you just as hard. Men like that evil son of a bitch Cogburn, or Butcher Terrill. I knew what they'd do, and you deserved better than bein' scalped or lynched or tortured for fun by the kind of man who'd look at you and see just one more damned savage in need of killing. Better a clean bullet from a man who understood. Least that's how I figured it." He licked his lips, feeling a trickle of sweat at his temple. "Was I wrong?"

Grey Owl hesitated a moment, then scowled. "Maybe not. But either way, I plan to repay that kindness here and now. Go for your –"

"Why?" Steele snapped. "For what? Why the hell do we need to kill each other today? Is it 'cause I shot you? You didn't know something like that was coming, you're a damn fool, and I never took you for that. Damn it all..," He paused a second. "You know I gave the bounty money to Red Cloud?"

"What?" Grey Owl blinked at the mention of his brother's name.

"To help raise your boy. I don't know what the hell he did with it. He might have burned it, for all I know. He seemed pretty mad at me at the time." Steele sighed and shook his head. "But there it is. And now here's you and me at the ends of each other's guns, and I can't think of a single reason why that ought to be so."

"There's bad blood between us," Grey Owl frowned, but his hands seemed relaxed now, no longer flexing.

"There's worse blood against us, and you know it."

Steele risked a glance at the crowd, who were looking angry and bored. A couple at the back were catcalling, "Draw, already! Ya yeller chickens!" Grey Owl frowned, turning his head as if noticing them for the first time. He paused for a moment, then spoke in a softer tone.

"These people..." He hesitated, then scowled. "They do not see men."

"They see a dog fight. And if one of us was white, they'd see a hero." Steele straightened. "I'm done talking, Grey Owl. Are we gonna do this, or are we gonna walk away?"

Grey Owl stiffened, and resumed his stance, hands flexing, poised once again over the twin revolvers. Everything in his stance showed he was readying himself to shoot, and Steele readied himself likewise, in case the other man should decide to slap leather after all. But when Steele looked in Grey Owl's eyes, the fire of revenge that had started the confrontation had been replaced by a weariness, a disgust with the whole business.

He relaxed. There'd be no gunfight today.

Then he heard the shriek of a steam whistle, and Reed yelling like a banshee – *"Forward the Locomotive Man!"* – and a ton of clanking iron and brass shoved past him, knocking him to the ground, making a beeline for the other man.

"No!" Steele shouted, as Grey Owl's eyes widened at the monstrosity. Up until now, like all the rest of the townsfolk, he'd seen it as another medicine show, a snake-oil demonstration that his enemy just happened to be riding with. Now, the terrifying reality bore down on him in all its cold, mechanical fury. He drew, firing at the Locomotive Man's centre mass, and the bullets pinged off the metal as if they were bee stings.

"Call it off!" Steele yelled over the din, drawing his own gun and aiming for the control mechanisms on the thing's back, trying to determine which might shut the damned monster off once and for all. *"Call it off, Reed, you son of a bitch!"* He fired, pulling the trigger again and again until the chamber was empty, and the bullets shattered dials and broke off switches, but nothing seemed to stop the Locomotive Man's charge.

One of the ricochets from Grey Owl's own pistols hit him in the chest, sending him staggering back, but the machine caught his head in its iron grip before he could fall. Steele heard him cry out something in the Ute language, and then the Locomotive Man crushed his head like an eggshell, sending a spray of blood and brains into the dirt.

It let what was left fall, and stomped back to its place at the wagon.

Not a soul in the crowd spoke.

"You god-damned son of a bitch!" Steele stormed over, grabbed Reed by the lapels and pulled him bodily down off

the front seat of his damn wagon and into the dirt, and then slammed him with a haymaker across the jaw for good measure. *"You miserable bastard, that was a man! That was a man!"*

"H-he was going to shoot you –" Reed stammered, and Steele's knuckles caught him again, sending his glasses into the dirt and blacking his eye.

"He was gonna walk away! Get up, you god-damn coward! Get up!"

The crowd rumbled, growing ugly. A small voice piped up from the back: "Why don't that metal man kill that boy already?" The rumbling grew louder, more insistent, and one of the men at the front of the mob picked a stone off the ground and threw it at Steele's head.

He spun around and shot it from the air.

Then he lifted his hat and let the crowd see what was in his eyes. "I never shot an unarmed man yet," he growled. "If I start, I can't promise I'm gonna stop."

The crowd scattered.

"Those jackasses are gonna grow their balls back soon enough," Steele growled. "On your feet, you lousy bastard. Get your damn metal man up and running."

Reed cowered in the dirt, scrabbling for his glasses. "I – you broke the controls – I need to check if –"

Steele hauled him up by the scruff of his neck. "Get it running and get the hell out of here! *Now!*" He pushed Reed roughly into the wagon, and the younger man scrambled up onto it, reading the broken dials as best he could and flipping what switches were left. Eventually, the Locomotive Man juddered into life. Satisfied, Steele untied Jonah and led him over to the spot Grey Owl had fallen.

As the metal man slowly began to trundle forwards, building up speed, Steele hefted Grey Owl's body up over one shoulder, then tossed it into the back of the wagon as it passed.

"You can't just throw a body into –" Reed protested.

"*Shut up*, you snake in the grass!" Steele spat, swinging up onto Jonah's back and spurring him to a trot. His eyes roamed the empty street, expecting trouble, but none came, and soon they'd left Devil's Gulch behind them. "There. Now, we got an appointment to keep up on that mesa, and I'm anxious to be done with it. After that, we'll bury this man best we can according to custom. Right now I'm of a mood to make you dig the rocks out with your own two hands."

"Steele, the man wanted to kill you –"

"Shut up, I said."

"For God's sake, he was a *savage* –"

Steele drew his gun.

"You say one more word. Just one. I will kill you where you sit."

Reed stared into the barrel of the revolver. He didn't say a word, and after a pause, Steele put his iron away.

"After we're done with the burial, I'm going back to Fort Woodson to tell that son of a bitch Westinghouse just where he can stick his damn retainer. I'm done with all you sons of bitches."

THEY WERE HALFWAY up the long spiral path to the crown of the mesa, and the sun was an angry red ball, low on the horizon.

The journey had taken longer than either man had expected, and the Locomotive Man seemed to be moving slower with every step. From underneath the brass dome, there was the usual whirring and clattering, but occasionally Franklin Reed would hear a fearful grinding sound emanate from the delicate workings within, which frightened him. Finally, he had to speak: "I don't like these noises..."

"I thought I told you to shut up." Steele's voice was weary, and his anger was gone. Reed considered the situation for a moment, then took his courage in his hands.

"I don't believe you are going to shoot me, Mister Steele."

Steele sighed. "Well, maybe I'll just shoot some unnecessary part of you, such as your pecker. Or bind and gag you and stick you in the back of your own damn wagon to pass the time with the man you murdered."

Reed bristled, and anger crept into his voice. "I would not call it murder, sir. From where I was sitting he was ready to murder you, at least until I intervened –"

"Shut up, God damn it." Steele shook his head, looking more tired than ever. He gestured at the Locomotive Man as it sluggishly toiled up the slope, dragging its burden behind it. "What the hell possessed you to build that damn thing anyway? What's it even for, aside from pulling you around?"

"I designed it to ease the burdens of life, Mister Steele." Reed's tone was frosty. "Once the Locomotive Man is mass-produced, it will remove the difficult tasks and drudgeries from life. Ploughing a field, for example, or digging a mine –"

"Or killing a man."

Reed blinked. "Excuse me?"

Steele had a disgusted look on his face, as though Reed's stupidity was a noxious substance that he's stepped in or got on his hands. "What is it like living in that head of yours, Reed? That damn metal man of yours ain't for pulling wagons or planting seed. If you'd swapped your monster out for a good horse we'd have been there and back by now. No, I've seen the one thing your fancy Locomotive Man's good for, and that's killing folks. You honestly think the world ain't gonna pick up on that too?"

The Locomotive Man picked that instant to offer another grinding, agonised whine from inside its brass dome. Steele winced. "Hell, that does sound ugly. I guess it is time you gave the poor bastard a break."

"It's not a 'poor bastard,' sir." Reed snapped, "It's a machine for performing difficult and dangerous chores –"

"Like killing folks."

Reed clamped his lips tight together, biting his tongue to keep the anger in. *How dare he? He dare he judge me, when he's killed a hundred men or more? The man's clearly nothing but a brutal, degenerate n –*

He pushed the thought away and leaned furiously forward, flipping and pushing at the remaining switches furiously, trying to coax life out of the machine.

"Kind of vulnerable for a killing machine, all them levers and switches on its back," Steele commented, dryly. "You might want to do something about that."

Reed scowled. "Well, they won't be there for long. I plan to do away with most of them entirely, in fact – I foresee future models with a simple starting lever, no more than that." He turned to Steele. "The more we – *scientists*, I mean – study these analytical engines, the more improvements we're going to make. I won't bore you with some of the breakthroughs they're making in London, but with what I know now... well, the second Locomotive Man will be able to make complex decisions on its own. It will, in a very limited sense, be able to think for itself."

"And then you'll have the perfect war machine, huh?"

"I've told you, Steele, it's for performing tasks unfit for human beings –"

"Right." Steele shook his head. "So when these machines of yours can think and decide like a man, what makes you think they'll want to do your chores for you? Hell, what makes you think you'll have a right to tell 'em to?"

Reed frowned. "I don't understand you, sir."

"No, you don't, do you? Four years of bloody war and a country built on pain and sweat and blood, and you jackasses still don't understand a damned –" Steele's voice suddenly trailed off. Reed turned to see what he was looking at and turned pale.

"By God," Steele breathed, "what... what is that, Reed?"

Reed licked dry lips. "I don't... I don't know," he whispered. "God help me, I don't know what I'm seeing..."

They had reached the top of the mesa.

Edison was waiting for them.

HE WAS SUSPENDED in mid-air, a foot above the ground, surrounded by a halo of rocks and stones that floated around him like the moons of some mysterious planet. His eyes glowed a gentle blue, and his flesh was a pale, ghostly white, corpse-like and dotted with great drops of sweat. One of his arms, Reed noted with dawning horror, had actually rotted away, leaving only the bone from the elbow down.

In his skeletal hand, he held a chunk of glowing blue stone.

Steele stared for a moment, as if wondering whether to turn back and leave the whole business behind, but then he swung himself down from Jonah's saddle. The horse turned and made its way back down the trail, away from whatever was happening, and Steele did nothing to prevent it. Perhaps he thought Jonah was making the wisest choice.

Reed climbed off the front of the wagon and exchanged a wary glance with the bounty hunter. Then the two stepped forward, approaching Edison slowly, like a pair of skittish deer. Neither man said a word.

"*Where's Westinghouse?*" Edison's voice was distorted, oddly hollow, as if it was coming from somewhere very far away. He nodded to a small pile of charred straw lying nearby. "*I've been conducting experiments. I thought he'd want to see for himself.*"

"What..." Reed swallowed, shaking his head. He couldn't form the words.

Steele scowled. "What the hell is that?"

Edison stared at him for a moment, then looked down at his skeletal hand, still wrapped around the glowing stone. "*This?*" Another stone floated up from the mesa's surface as he turned the thing over. "*I'm sorry. It's... it's hard to think.*" He closed his eyes for a moment, as if calling the memories back over some immense mental gulf. "*I was wandering in the desert. I was drunk. I drank a lot, after... after everything...*" He concentrated, rubbing his temple with his good hand. Another stone drifted up from the ground near Steele's feet.

"*There was a man. Foreign, I think – he called out to me in some language I didn't understand. He was dressed strangely... I took him for a vision at first, or a hallucination born of the bottle. I think... I think he tried to tell me his name... Sorren? Does that help?*" A pause. "*He died.*" Edison shook his head. "*I couldn't do anything. He was burning up with fever,*" *and he'd been baked alive in the desert sun. He died in my arms. He was trying to tell me something about the stone. Trying to warn me away from touching it, maybe, but I didn't understand... and then it was too late."* He stared into the blue glow of the stone for a long second, and then he raised his head and stared at the two men with narrowed eyes. *"It's mine now. Where's Westinghouse?"*

There was a note of anger in his voice, and the stones spinning and orbiting around him spun faster. Steele took a step back, hand hovering over his holster.

"Where's Westinghouse? He was meant to –" Edison froze, the blue glow of his eyes fixing on Reed, and suddenly it did not seem quite so gentle. *"Wait."* He scowled. *"I know you. You shouldn't be here."*

Reed blinked. "W-what?"

"It's the stone. It shows me things. You shouldn't be here." Edison's anger seemed to be building, and now tiny sparks and crackling lights danced over his exposed skin. *"I should be here. So should Westinghouse. But not you."* He pointed the stone towards Steele. *"Or you."*

Steele drew his gun.

Reed didn't know if Steele meant to fire it, but he never got the chance. A bolt of blue-white energy leapt from the surface of the glowing stone to the barrel of the gun, and Steele cried out, dropping the revolver and clutching at his hand. Reed saw to his amazement that the flesh of his hand was badly burned.

Edison smiled. *"Don't do that again."* He turned back to Reed. *"Have you ever heard of Alessandro Volta?"*

Reed took a step back, looking over his shoulder for a moment at the Locomotive Man. Could he get to the controls in time? Would the Locomotive Man even stand a chance against whatever Edison had become? "No," he heard himself say, "I don't think I have."

"You wouldn't have. He was stabbed by a robber in the street. Michael Faraday was knocked down and killed by a horse before he had done anything of consequence, although he had theories. Benjamin Franklin was murdered by a man

who should not be here." He tailed off for a moment, and his eyes were burning like miniature suns. *"Is this coincidence? Is this enemy action?"*

"I don't..." Reed swallowed, cursing his dry throat. "I don't know what you mean."

"The stone knows. The stone remembers. It's... it's difficult for me to think with my own mind... to talk in three dimensions..." He grimaced, and his matted black hair rose up, crackling with static. *"Where... is Westinghouse? He should be here. You shouldn't be. Neither of you."* He lifted the stone again, pointing it at Reed. *"Now... now I'll have to start again."*

The stone crackled with power. Reed stared into its depths and saw what was to happen. Edison would use the power to annihilate him, burn him like kindling, and then he would walk – no, float – down from his mesa, and first he would kill everyone in Devil's Gulch, and then Fort Woodson, and if he did not find George Westinghouse there, he would travel to New York, and everywhere he went he would leave scorched earth and burning bones...

Reed closed his eyes and prayed to a deity he did not quite believe in that the end would be quick. And then, just behind his left shoulder, there was an ear-splitting sound.

The shriek of a steam whistle.

Then everything happened very fast.

Reed was suddenly on the ground, and the Locomotive Man was thundering past him, belching smoke, gears grinding in his brass head. The orbiting rocks bounced off his metal body as he swung a blood-stained claw towards Edison, and Edison had just enough time to bring the stone to bear –

– and Reed was almost blinded by the blue-white light that flew from the stone to the Locomotive Man's chest, stopping the deadly charge and tearing the furnace-door from its hinges, then moving to the shoulder joint to rip one great iron arm clean off its body –

– and then Steele was reaching with his good hand for his gun, grabbing it from the dirt while Edison was engaged, and firing twice, all in one smooth motion, aiming for the exposed ulna and the radius, hitting both –

– and when the bones snapped clean in two from the force of the bullet impacts, it was Edison that fell to earth and the stone and the hand that held it that continued to float, the centre of a cosmos of rocks –

– and Steele scrambled to his feet, making a grab for the floating blue stone, catching hold of it while it was still crackling with all manner of strange, unfocussed power –

– and then he was gone.

Reed blinked. Jacob Steele and the blue stone had simply vanished into the air, as if they had never existed. Edison lay on the ground, coughing weakly, and the Locomotive Man stared down at him with its expressionless glass eyes. Then, quite casually, it reached down with its good arm and grabbed hold of Edison's head.

"No –" Reed cried out, but it was already far, far too late.

"GOOD GOD. WHAT happened then?" George Westinghouse asked, pouring a brandy.

"I switched it off. It's standing there still." Reed rubbed his temples, then reached for the glass.

"You left it there?" Westinghouse seemed incredulous.

Reed sighed. "It was too heavy to deal with."

Westinghouse shook his head, frowning. "And Edison? What happened to his body?"

"I buried him as best I could with the coal-shovel. The Indian too." He shrugged, remembering the hard ground and the shallow graves. He hoped some predator hadn't dug them up again.

Westinghouse scowled. "Very convenient."

Reed shook his head and ignored the comment. "Anyway, Steele's horse let me ride on his back as far as the town, and they let me telegram from there. And here I am. If you'll allow me to retrieve the Locomotive Man at the earliest opportunity, I can look into what went wrong in the mechanism that made it act without orders..."

"Now that, I'm interested in." Westinghouse poured a glass for himself. "This is something you were working towards – the Locomotive Man acting alone. If that part of your story isn't..."

"Made up? None of it is."

Westinghouse took a long sip of the liquor. "Well, I'm not saying you're lying, exactly, but it sounds like your account might be a little confused. The important thing is what your Locomotive Man did."

"Killed a man." Reed took the brandy and swallowed it in a single gulp. Westinghouse ignored him.

"It acted autonomously, based on earlier instruction. I understand that's the direction they're going in in London. I'd like to get there first, and this might be the key."

Reed lowered his glasses and looked into Westinghouse's eyes. "Steele was right. The Locomotive Man's nothing but a killing machine. I'll have no further part of it." He sat back in his chair and folded his arms.

Westinghouse winced. "Now, Mister Reed, you've obviously had a shock. I'd go so far as to say your recollections might be –"

"I'm not insane, Mister Westinghouse. I might have been when I thought up the Locomotive Man, but not now. It was a childish fantasy, and if I wasn't worried about some fool building another, I'd leave it to rot on top of that rock." He shook his head, reaching down to rummage in a canvas bag at his feet. "Having it pull a wagon was... imbecilic. Why not infuse the technology into the wagon itself? Powered vehicles, sir. A revolution in transport. If that's what you want to do, I'm behind you all the way – but I'm done with mechanical men, and that's the end of it. Let the fools in London take the blame for what's coming."

Westinghouse looked sceptical. "And the money with it? Well, we'll discuss that later. Right now, I want to talk more about what happened up there. Now, as I said, I'm not going to call you a liar, but –"

Reed interrupted him by pulling a heavy mahogany box out of the bag, slamming it on the table. "It's a cigar box. I picked it up in town for the weight."

"I'm not sure I understand."

"You will."

Unceremoniously, Reed opened the box, and a smallish stone drifted up out of it to hang in the air in front of Westinghouse. For a full minute, the older man was unable to speak. Then he reached out with a fingertip to touch the stone, watching it bob away from him. "Good God," he whispered at last.

"Every word of my story is true, Mister Westinghouse. I believe some trace mineral present in this stone, and in the others I took with me, was affected by the object Edison was carrying in such a way as to... well, eliminate its susceptibility to gravity. I'd like permission to correspond with certain mineralogists of my aquaintance, with a view to duplicating this faculty. I've been in conversation in the past with a Dr. Herbert Cavor, who I think might..." He paused. "Sir?"

Westinghouse grinned like a boy. "Good God. More of this, you say?"

Reed smiled. "Well, we'll see. It might take a century or more before we can actually synthesise it, but... it's nice to think I might have been instrumental in the creation of something that won't end in death." He looked down, as if embarrassed. "I even thought of one interesting application of an anti-gravity alloy on the way here – something that couldn't possibly be used to kill..."

"Hell, I'll bite. What did you think up?"

"Wings, sir." Reed grinned. "A pair of steam-powered wings."

THE EVE OF WAR

(Excerpt from *The New York Clarion*, dated August 27th, 2000.)

FORBIDDEN ECSTASY

Jason Satan, the Man With The Touch Of Death, gazed hungrily on a beaker filled with his own blood, and hissed like a cat!

"What wonderful poison flows in my veins!"

The oozing liquid had the colour and consistency of spoiled milk and a sour and sickly smell, that seeped into the air and filled every nook and cranny of the warehouse. Satan breathed it in, shuddering in depraved, forbidden ecstasy at the unholy scent!

What horror did his unspeakable pleasure portend for the citizens of New York?

HE LIVED ONLY TO KILL

(For the benefit of readers new to the most action-packed news-paper in the five boroughs, there follows a brief description of this noted enemy of mankind.)

Jason Satan was a tall man – six and a half feet – and rail-thin, with the appearance of a skeleton wreathed in skin the colour and texture of office paper. His hair was as fine as cobweb and as white as his face – in fact, there was almost no part of his body that held colour. When he ran his bloodless tongue over his thin lips, it was as if a grey slug was emerging from some sunless cave. When he fixed you with his pitiless, inhuman gaze, his pupils were tiny black dots in a sea of wet, white jelly.

The only exception was his smile – for his teeth were yellow, rotting gravestones poking from grey gums. That devil's rictus was the last sight hundreds of innocent victims had ever seen – for Jason Satan had a love affair with Death, in all its varied forms, in all its horrors and brutalities. He was happy only when Death was near, when he could taste it on his tongue, feel its awful power working through him. *He lived only to kill.*

CATALOGUE OF HORRORS

"How beautiful." The Prince Of Poisons purred the words, his eyes glittering with unholy light! "My blood – the source of my killing power! Were a single drop to fall on your exposed skin, my friend..." – his eyes narrowed suddenly, a trace of anger showing in his skeletal features, and a discordant note of malice entered his voice – "...had you not inoculated yourself *against* my gift... why, you would be dead before you hit the ground! Were I to shake your hand, or kiss your cheek, you might have time for a few last seconds of horror before that final end claimed you -- for all time!" He brightened at the thought, his sickly yellow smile springing to life like a jack-in-the-box. "And now... now you say you will translate the deadly power of this perfect ichor to the very air itself?"

He addressed his question to the other man in the room -- though 'man' was hardly the correct term.

For Mister Murder, The Master Of The Murder Chair, was much more – and much less – than a human being!

VAST, BALLOON-LIKE HEAD

(Again, for the benefit of new readers, we will attempt a description of this most hideous of master-fiends.)

Mister Murder was, in truth, not so much a man as a vast, balloon-like head, criss-crossed with pulsing veins. The diameter of his skull measured a touch over four feet, and as if in compensation, the body that hung from his neck was almost vestigial – tiny and withered, as if it had barely grown since emerging from the womb. His face was a hideous, cracked mass of wrinkles, grotesquely magnified in proportion to his gigantic cranium, and his bulging eyes possessed a secondary, nictitating membrane, like a bird's – so that a murky green film flickered occasionally over them as he spoke. Otherwise, his gaze was utterly fixed and unblinking, an endless stare that seemed to penetrate deep into the soul, worming out all hidden secrets. There were whispers that the hideous experiments which had given him his gigantic brain had also blessed him with telepathy, for he often seemed to know exactly what an enemy or ally was thinking – a talent which made him all the more dangerous.

Some said he possessed the power to control a man's very soul – though none who might have seen it had lived to confirm its use!

Such qualities were bizarre enough to earn him pride of place in any catalogue of horrors. *But the evil scientists of the Ultimate Reich had not stopped there!* They had created a means of transport as dreadful as the creature it was designed for – *the terrifying Murder Chair!*

BEHOLD THE MURDER CHAIR

Reader, if you dare -- *behold the Murder Chair!* The

man-monster sat awkwardly, like a doll, on a brass and leather seat, with metal straps to hold his gigantic head in place and prevent the weight of it from snapping his neck. The back of the chair, meanwhile, was composed entirely of Babbage machines and analytical engines, constantly ticking and clicking, and connected to large gold-plated pipes – and here the true horror of the apparatus began, for those pipes extended from the back of the chair through the skull and into the tissue of Murder's living brain!

The workings somehow fused with the criminal's nightmare intellect, increasing his terrible mental powers beyond measure and providing him the means to control and propel the Murder Chair by thought alone – for instead of four legs, it scuttled on eight, like some unspeakable insect, each mechanical leg ending in a fearsome point suitable for gutting enemies in a single stroke! Attached to the two frontmost legs were a pair of nozzles, through which the diabolical master-brain could direct sheets of searing flame – meanwhile, the arms of the chair ended in a pair of crude robotic hands, allowing Mister Murder to do the work of his fiendish Nazi masters without assistance. In the past, he had been content to be a mere weapon of Untergang – that malign organisation created to serve the mad dreams of the seemingly immortal Fuhrer and his sinister Ultimate Reich! But, following the shocking events of the past few days, our paper can reveal that this inhuman monstrosity had been selected by the Fuhrer himself to fill the vacuum of power, and become the newest and most horrific leader of that devilish terror group!

And his first act as leader was to partner with the diabolical Jason Satan! Had there ever, in the history of mankind, been so unutterably dreadful a pair of arch-fiends collected together in one place? *Never!* And now their evil alliance had borne fruit – *in a plot to poison the very air New York City breathed!*

SLOW, AGONISING DEATH

"Tell me," purred Satan, running his grey tongue over his yellow teeth, "will the gas we propose to create act quickly? Or... *slowly?*" He shuddered as his evil mind savoured the dreadful thought!

Mister Murder allowed his obscene face to crack into a grotesque smile, and the analytical engines burrowing into his skull made a soft, satisfied *clack*. "According to my calculations," he said in his hollow, high-pitched voice, "death should occur within twenty to thirty hours of inhalation. During that time, the organs will rot and soften, starting with the lungs, until finally they simply melt like wax, pouring out through holes in the skin as it, too, rots away. Total liquefaction of the organs and muscle tissue will occur perhaps five or six hours after death – and finally, after no more than forty hours, the bones will crumble and desiccate. Two short days, *mein herr*, and New York will be a mausoleum! The streets will run with blood and powdered bone! *And you and I will be the only human beings left alive!"*

Jason Satan's eyes seemed to flash, almost glowing with pleasure! "How wonderful! Oh, how perfectly perfect!" He giggled. "Although to call either of us *human* seems... somehow insulting."

Mister Murder's cracked lips stretched wider, the grin seeming to split his head in two, and his massive eyes narrowed to vicious slits. "Quite so. We are *übermenschen*, you and I. And may I say how pleased I am that you have finally chosen to, ah... *join the winning team,* as you Americans say."

Satan giggled again, swirling the beaker of white ooze around and around before setting it down on a long table and turning to look around the room - *at the machinery that would swiftly bring a nightmare reign of horror to the greatest city on Earth!*

LETHAL POISON GAS

The room was a large, ostensibly disused warehouse, long ago commandeered for the purpose of terror by Untergang, and the best part of it was taken up by a massive network of copper and brass piping, feeding in and out of various distilling tanks and stills. This was the machinery that was even now slowly chugging and hissing, clanking and fuming, as it went about the business of transforming the blood of Jason Satan into lethal poison gas!

Soon, they would have enough to blanket the entire city – at which point they would load the tanks of gas onto the short, squat rocket that sat in the centre of the room, underneath the dust-covered skylight. The rocket, fuelled by hydrogen peroxide purchased on the black market, would shoot into the sky above the city like some firework of the damned – *then explode and blanket the whole of Manhattan with a poisonous fog of pure, unstoppable death!*

And that was only the start of their devil's scheme! After the initial airburst, if the wind forecasts were accurate, the cloud would drift inland, bringing death to the boroughs, to the suburbs, to the small towns...

Jason Satan shivered again, hugging himself. He imagined the crowds of panicked people rushing to and fro on the sidewalks, coughing and spluttering up gobbets of their own blood and tissue! The dogs howling! The fathers trying to explain the horror to their dying children! And after that -- the corpses, stacked like cordwood in the streets!

So many corpses!

His face suddenly fell into a parody of a frown. "Oh, but what of the Frenchman?" he mused, in a mock-tragic tone.

There was a clatter of cogs from the Murder Chair, followed by a high, rasping chuckle. "Perhaps I will decide

to inoculate *him* as well, before the end. Or perhaps – *not!*
He is a mercenary, *mein herr* – If he were to remain alive,
we would eventually have to pay the bill."

His chuckle became a laugh, a high-pitched squeal of
devilish mirth, and Jason Satan could not help but join
his own voice to the cackling chorus – a tolling bell of
terror for the city that never sleeps!

Who would save us now?

MASTERS OF TERROR

The answer – a shadow falling across a filthy skylight!
A sudden crash! The air filled with shattered glass! And
at the centre of the rain of razor shards – *a man!*

And what a man! Blond and bearded, with piercing
blue eyes and skin the colour of bronze, and a familiar
lightning-bolt insignia splashed across his blue shirt –
the flag of *Doc Thunder, America's Greatest Hero!*

Neither the shards of glass nor the twenty-foot drop
seemed to trouble New York's premier he-man, as he
landed, cat-like, on the stone floor, mere feet from the
deadly missile. In a voice of cold steel, he addressed the
cowering villains: "You'll pay the bill, all right."

*Those deadly masters of terror now knew fear
themselves!* For the hero standing to defy them was no
ordinary man – this was Doc Thunder! The scientific
superman born from the Ultimate Reich's own strange
science, and devoted to crushing their power wherever it
might raise its merciless head!

A man capable of leaping an eighth of a mile in a single
bound – so powerful that nothing less than a bursting
shell could penetrate his skin! Even with their ignoble
forces combined, would the malicious mind of Mister
Murder and the deadly death-touch of Jason Satan be
enough to subdue the hero of New York? Were even odds
of two against one enough against such a powerhouse
of heroism?

They thought not! *And a fair fight was the last thing on their minds!*

MURDERER OF MILLIONS

Satan ran to a speaking-tube dangling from the wall and screeched into it. *"Savate!"*

A moment later, a lithe, powerfully-built figure dressed in an orange jerkin burst in from an ante-room! Their ace in the hole – Savate, the deadly mercenary and master of the French martial art whose name he had adopted as his own!

The mysterious Man Of A Thousand Kicks had clashed a dozen times or more with America's Greatest Hero, and always escaped to fight another day! Savate was usually hired to delay Doc Thunder and other champions of the law for the crucial moments necessary to complete some heist or scheme – yet his strange code of honour forbade him from taking the lives of those uninvolved in the struggle between the forces of law and the criminal underworld.

But to delay Doc Thunder's victory now would be to doom thousands to slow and painful extinction! Was Savate an unwitting dupe of the sinister forces of Untergang? *Or had he finally crossed the line that separates the dashing rogue from the callous murderer of millions?*

The answer will astound you! Turn to page five for more of the incredible front-page scoop this reporter *had* to call -- *"The Fearful Fate Of Doc Thunder!"*

(Note: The bare facts of this account may have been dramatically embellished in parts by ace reporter Stan 'Scoop' Mann in order to increase the pulse-pounding verisimilitude of this incredible story – in the mighty Clarion manner! However, we maintain that the awesome action presented herein remains true to the spirit of the original events.)

* * *

"MAKE ME ONE with everything."

"Sure thing, buddy." The hot dog vendor narrowed his eyes, frowning. "Hey, uh, aren't you that El Sombrero fella?"

El Sombra grinned. He was dressed in his usual style – a pair of ragged trousers from a black tuxedo, stained with dust and blood, and nothing else, save the mask over his eyes. "What tipped you off, amigo?"

In truth, the masked swordsman had become altogether too famous for his liking after the business with Donner, Crane and Lomax; he was used to being a figure of mystery, hiding in the shadows and alleys – or better yet, out in the desert, away from all human company. Now, everyone in New York seemed to think of him as some kind of masked hero, one of the many the city had produced. It was fun, but it was distracting him from his real mission, which was why he'd taken to lurking around the docks: as soon as he found a boat that would take him across the Atlantic, he'd be on his way.

In the meantime, there was always room in his belly for another hot dog.

"Ha!" The vendor smiled, loading up the hot dog with the works. "I guess there ain't many fellers like you walkin' around, right? This one's on the house, pal."

"Muchos gracias." El Sombra speared the hot dog deftly on the end of his sword and took a bite, and it tasted meaty, watery, decidedly unhealthy and absolutely delicious. Hot dogs, he thought to himself, were probably the single thing about New York that he'd miss the most. Maybe when he hit Berlin, he'd enjoy a quick bratwurst or two before he killed Adolf Hitler. But it wouldn't be quite the same.

"You know, those things are gonna kill you."

The swordsman turned to see a tall black man standing in a nearby alley. He was greying at the temples, with a patch over one eye and a large, luxuriant moustache. He was dressed outlandishly – a bright, almost fluorescent blue trench coat worn over some sort of close-fitting white jumpsuit, dotted with pouches, holsters for a knife and pistol, and an insignia El Sombra didn't quite recognise. A pair of steel-capped combat boots completed the ensemble – not quite jackboots, but El Sombra felt himself tensing anyway. He wondered how it was he hadn't noticed the man before. "Let me guess – you're a nutritionist?"

The other man held up a silver badge – that insignia again, a mandala inside a five-pointed star, like an old west Sheriff's badge, with a letter at each of the points. "Not quite. Jack Scorpio. Agent of S.T.E.A.M. Special Tactical Espionage And Manoeuvres." El Sombra gave the badge a careful examination, looked into Scorpio's eyes for a moment and then relaxed – a little.

"Sure, I've heard of you." El Sombra nodded. "Spy guys, right?" The journal he'd stolen from Donner, the ex-head of Untergang, had mentioned them several times, and never favourably – there were rants about a *degenerate organisation of addicts, sexual perverts and nonconformists* that went on for whole pages. Reading them, you'd never believe this same organisation was taking down Untergang threats all over the globe, but somehow, there it was.

Frankly, they sounded like El Sombra's kind of people.

Scorpio smiled. "Yeah, I've heard of you too, true believer. Let me see if I got my story right – Mexican village, evil Nazis, brutal massacre, lone survivor. Spends nine years out in the desert grooving on some kind of way-out psychedelic scene and ends up as a living weapon. Hey, you ever hear of the Fourth Earth Battalion? My outfit back in the late 'sixties, before this whole international superspy gig."

El Sombra shook his head. Scorpio grinned.

"Really? I could have sworn you'd read the manual I wrote. Check it out sometimes – some of the training techniques in there might look familiar. Anyway, desert, mind expansion, develops second personality of El Sombra in order to offload extreme combat stress, blah blah blah – and nine years later, to the day, our hero blows right back into that village and gives those Nazi assholes some instant karma. As in wiping them off the face of the earth. As in destroying giant robots, traction engines, Luftwaffe battalions and scientific research the Ratzis have been working on for *decades* – with nothing but a *sword*." Scorpio looked El Sombra right in the eye, as if daring him to deny it. "You know what? That's the kind of story I like to hear." He opened up one of his pouches, took out a long cigarette and lit it. "Want some of this?"

"No thanks." El Sombra wrinkled his nose at the strange scent of the smoke. He wasn't happy with having his past summed up so casually.

"That's fab, fervent one. More for the rest of us." Scorpio took a long, deep drag, holding it in his lungs for a moment before exhaling. "Anyway, turns out this mystery swordsman decides cleaning house back home ain't enough – he's gonna take out the big bad voodoo daddy Mr Adolf Hitler himself. You do know he's a giant killer robot now, right?"

"I know."

"Cool. Where was I? So along the way our hero stops over in the city that swings – New York, natch – and puts the whammy on a whole nest of Nazi spies and a decidedly un-hip mad scientist who's been giving the long-underwear crowd hassle for years. Then it's right back to the mission, right?" He took another puff on the cigarette, breathing out slowly. "You know, effendi, I do find myself digging that story. You know what I love about it? It's believable. It's all stuff that could just about actually happen. Right up until the ending." He shot El Sombra a look.

El Sombra rolled his eyes. "Don't tell me, amigo. I hate spoilers." He frowned. "And I'm not sure about taking advice from an undercover spy guy you can see from six blocks away. Isn't that a little... noticeable?"

"Funny man. Take a look around, funny man."

El Sombra looked around. The two of them might have been standing just off the street, but they weren't exactly invisible, and New York's docklands were a busy place at this time of day. Yet not a soul passing by was looking in their direction. Even the hot dog vendor was acting as if they just weren't there.

Scorpio smiled. "Anti-camouflage. Draws the eye and reassures on a subconscious level. It's all in the right shade of blue." He took another long toke. "Day-Glo Ops are the new Black Ops, brother. You're living in the S.T.E.A.M. age now."

El Sombra raised an eyebrow. "It's your world, I just live in it?"

"You got it. So, you want that ending?"

"Why not?"

"Well, it's kind of a downer. This El Sombra cat thinks he can go straight to Berlin and take on Mecha-Hitler and the whole Ultimate Reich by himself, and he ends up six feet under – just like everyone else who tried it. And there have been many." Scorpio took another drag. "Just having a little trouble suspending my disbelief on that one, you dig? Like, when there's a whole country just itching to paste the paper-hanger once and for all – why would a cool fool like El Sombra try to go it alone?"

El Sombra shrugged, but there was an edge in his voice. "Maybe he thinks America is a little slow, amigo. If you people had scratched your itch a little sooner, my family would be alive now."

"I can dig it." Scorpio nodded. "But to start the kind of war we're talking about, you'd need the cats in Magna Britannia to turn a blind eye. They got a vested interest in things in Europe staying just the way they are, which is why our friend the freaky Führer ain't rattled any sabres lately – except in places the Brits don't give a damn about, like your home town. And mine. Likewise the Italians, who are grooving on our kind of frequency, politics-wise – they would love to hit Hitler where it hurts. But up until now, the rule's been that if one country starts a party" – he dropped the remains of his cigarette on the concrete and then crushed it out with the heel of his boot – "Britain's gonna be the one to finish it."

"Up until now?"

"You been reading the London papers, pilgrim?"

El Sombra shook his head. "I've been a little busy."

Scorpio grinned. "We got our blind eye. I won't bore you with the details – although they are deeply *yvoorg*, true believer – but Victoria just got hit smack in her ugly face on a scale nobody never saw before, even counting that Martian jazz from last year. Britannia is reeling with the feeling right now, and – assuming they survive this – they are not gonna to be able to say boo to a goose any time soon."

El Sombra blinked. "If they *survive*? Magna Britannia?"

"Could go either way. Obviously, if they don't, it's a whole other ball game, but I'm a glass-half-full kind of cat, dig?"

"So..."

Scorpio nodded. "So right now, there's everything to play for, and if we don't take advantage our buddy Adolf definitely will. Which means sometime in the next month or so – as soon as we negotiate how down the Italians and Russians want to be with this happening – America goes to war." He pointed a finger at El Sombra's chest. "And America wants you."

El Sombra couldn't help but laugh. The idea of him dressing in a helmet and flak jacket and parachuting into the forests with a hundred other men, weighed down by some heavy machine gun, seemed somehow far more absurd than the thought of sneaking half-naked across the border with his sword in his hand. "I don't know, amigo. I think I might prefer to be my own man."

"You would be, baby. In the squad I'm building, there's no room for anything else." He grinned.

El Sombra blinked. "You're a very strange man, Jack Scorpio. Why all this... *cool, cat, baby, groovy*, all that. What is that? Spy talk?"

Jack nodded. "Kind of. It's dream language – focuses the trained mind, distracts the untrained mind. Right now, it's futzing you up a little, am I right?"

"Well..."

"It's cool, I'll tone it down, let you think straight. If we work together, I'll teach you how to do it – Jim Channon turned me on to the concept when we were in the First Earth Battalion. It's basically a mixture of lucid dreaming and... well, it's kind of hard to explain without, uh..." Jack tugged idly on his moustache for a second. "Okay, have you seen what Andy Warhol's been up to lately?"

"Ow!" El Sombra winced, feeling his other self bubbling painfully up. He rubbed the knot at the back of his mask, forcing the thoughts back down. "Djego has. He enjoyed 'Cellphone' – the sculpture."

"Yeah, he's just finished a new one called 'Pod' – it's similar, only instead of the grid of numbers, there's a perfect ceramic circle. I was meditating on that earlier today. Anyway, it's connected to that – dream logic, dreamworld thinking. There is another world. There is a better world." Jack smiled, and El Sombra felt suddenly ill – faded and washed out, as if he was no longer quite real. "Well, there must be. Right? See what I did to you there?"

He was grinning, as if he knew some secret El Sombra didn't. The masked man's guts turned over, and he felt the sudden urge to throw up. Scorpio laughed. "Weaponised cosmic awareness. Welcome to the big leagues."

"Let's... change the subject." El Sombra said, quietly. "Why don't you tell me more about –" he tailed off suddenly, noticing Jack's eyes widen at something just behind his left shoulder. In the distance, he heard the crash of shattering glass.

"What?" El Sombra turned, and saw that one of the disused warehouses now had a broken skylight. A cloud of disturbed dust lingered in the air. "What happened?"

Scorpio breathed out. "Doc Thunder happened. Damn."

"What?"

"He just fell out of a clear blue sky and into that warehouse." Scorpio reached for his holster, drawing a large revolver – a Magnum of some kind – with three chambers, arranged on some sort of revolving drum. "Didn't look like an accident, either. Want to see for yourself?"

El Sombra blinked. Well, why not? He had nothing better to do. "Groovy, amigo."

SLEDGEHAMMER BLOWS

"En garde!"

That was the war-cry on the lips of Savate, The Man Of A Thousand Kicks – as he leapt into astounding action! Few men alive could hope to avoid the hammer-blows of Doc Thunder for long, but the wily Frenchman was perhaps the most agile fighter ever to take on the forces of law and order – and in addition, he was the veteran of a dozen previous duels with the super-scientific powerhouse, and thus knew his every move almost before he made it.

Meanwhile, Doc Thunder fought under the handicap of his own heroic conscience – for he knew that if he struck his enemy with his full strength, strength enough to punch a hole in a brick wall and bend solid steel girders into pretzels, Savate would die – as surely as if he had been hit by a cannon shell! Thus, he pulled his punches, which only made them easier to avoid, and all the time the dread machinery was continuing to distil the blood of Jason Satan. Every second spent in battle brought closer that fatal moment when the deadly poison gas would be ready!

If he could only wreck the machine before it finished its terrible operation, but no! The mercenary was determined to force him away from it, and from the rocket that would deliver the hideous payload into the skies of New York!

Savate knew all of Doc Thunder's weak points. Every second, another flurry of kicks like sledgehammer blows slammed into Doc Thunder's eyes, blocking his sight. He swung a fist out at his side in a wide arc, hoping to knock the rocket over, but struck only the empty air!

And the next moment, twin jets of fire engulfed him in an aura of flame!

For the stumbling combat had driven America's Greatest Hero into the firing-line of Mister Murder's Murder Chair!

And as readers of the *Daily Clairon* well know – *mayhem is the Murder Chair!*

FIERY HOLOCAUST

The insect-like front legs of Mister Murder's fiendish contraption bathed Doc Thunder in a blazing inferno, burning the world-famous t-shirt from his back – but it would take more than that to ignite the Man Of Might! Judging that the Frenchman had leapt to safety rather than risk being consumed by the fiery holocaust, Thunder turned towards the source of the flames – grabbing hold of the Murder Chair's incendiary legs and crushing them in his super-powerful grip as if they were tissue paper!

"*Nein! Nein!* You cannot do this!" screamed the balloon-headed Nazi, as Doc Thunder lifted the Murder Chair from the ground, the six remaining legs scrabbling furiously at his naked chest – but the razor points could do little more than scratch at his near-indestructible skin. Doc Thunder turned his head and saw Savate, already tensing to dodge what he knew was coming. But Savate wasn't the only one who knew how to predict an old foe.

With a mighty heave, Doc Thunder hurled the Murder Chair, with the screaming head of Untergang trapped within it, not at the place where Savate was – but where he would be!

Wha-a-amm!

The French mercenary was treated to the head-butt of a lifetime – and he was lucky to get it! *For had Doc Thunder used any less skill in aiming one enemy at another, the razor points of the Chair's insectile legs might have speared Savate through the chest and ended his life in one agonising instant!*

As ever, Doc Thunder made pains not to take a human life if he could possibly avoid it. But against the deadly killing power of Jason Satan, The Man With The Touch Of Death, would even America's Greatest Hero have the luxury of choice? Did he dare to leave this maddest and deadliest of criminals to live another day?

No!

Not now that this most monstrous of men had stumbled upon the deadly secret contained within his own blood! Jason Satan was a living weapon of death, a ticking poison-bomb that would end the lives of millions were he to escape that room!

But could even Doc Thunder subdue the grinning albino without succumbing to the foul ichor that coursed through the insane murder's veins? Could even his mighty constitution survive a single touch from the lunatic's hand?

The choice was kill – or die! Which would it be?

THE TOUCH OF DEATH

The two combatants circled warily. Jason Satan's arms were spread wide, the venom in his fingertips ready to strike as he blocked Doc Thunder's path to the clanking machinery that was even now completing the distillation of Satan's blood into deadly poison gas!

Doc Thunder considered wrapping his bare knuckles to strike the death-blow and perhaps ward off the worst of the fatal effect – but with his clothing destroyed by the Murder Chair's flame-cannons, he had nothing to wrap them in. He would have to hope that he was strong enough to touch Jason Satan and survive – *though no man ever had!*

The super-scientist's eyes narrowed – his enemy's did likewise! Like gunslingers of old, they were judging the moment to unleash the deadly forces at their command! Concentration was total! The slightest distraction now could mean the difference between life – and death!

And at that moment the warehouse door crashed open – and Jack Scorpio, Agent of S.T.E.A.M. burst into the fray! Joined by Mexico's Greatest Hero – the masked swordsman known as El Sombra!

Fate can be cruel! For Doc Thunder allowed his attention to be drawn to the smashing entrance of these two incredible heroes for the split instant his foe required – *to land the fatal blow!*

Jason Satan leapt forward – to plant his open palm

square in the centre of his opponent's bared chest — inches from his beating heart!

The touch of death had been delivered – to Doc Thunder!

(CONTINUED ON PAGE FOLLOWING.)

"This doesn't look good, amigo," El Sombra muttered.

It didn't.

Doc Thunder was on the floor, convulsing. His skin had turned a hideous, waxy yellow, and as Jack Scorpio watched, a clump of hair came loose from his scalp and drifted to the floor. His bowels had let go, a rivulet of blood ran from one ear, suggesting some terrifying haemorrhage in his brain, and white foam oozed from the corners of his mouth. His eyes stared blankly at nothing at all.

Jason Satan stood over him, fixing the two intruders with his milk-white eyes and his ghastly yellow grin. Doc Thunder had fought The Man With The Touch Of Death several times over the past few years, always careful to wear protective clothing in their battles. This time, he hadn't expected Satan's involvement – but then, Satan was generally a solo operator. He'd never been part of the world of Untergang before.

Not that Doc Thunder had suspected Untergang's involvement either.

Before he began his vacation in the forbidden kingdom of Zor-Ek-Narr, he'd been cleaning up the loose ends from previous cases – including the theft of a large quantity of high-test hydrogen peroxide, stolen from a rocket research facility out in Brentwood by a gang of inexperienced heist artists. Peroxide was expensive and difficult to synthesise, but it worked well in attitude jets, and wasn't half so expensive as cavorite – in fact, there was talk of using it to send rockets into space without the benefit of the gravity-defying alloy. Presumably the crooks had read one of the reports extolling its virtues and figured it'd be easier to steal than cavorite, too.

In the planning stages, it had sounded like a three-man job, but they'd needed to bring in a couple of inside men at the facility, and, after all their efforts, the peroxide they stole was only worth fifty grand as opposed to the hundred they'd assumed they could get. In the end, they just didn't have the experience or the contacts to get a good price, and the resentment had simmered, with each member thinking they deserved more than their meagre share.

The gang had planned to split the cash after fencing the H_2O_2, but greed prevailed, and Doc Thunder – having easily tracked the gang to their hideout – found himself bursting in on a pitched gun battle. Too small a payoff between too large a group – it often turned out that way.

After he'd picked up the pieces and found out from the surviving thieves who their fence was – a man named Winston F. Keeler – he wasn't that shocked to find the man apparently dead of a heart attack. He was a good thirty stone, and clearly didn't take much care of himself. He did take good care of his records, though, and Thunder found a notebook in a wall safe – along with a hundred thousand dollars in cash – detailing exactly where the peroxide had been delivered; some kind of insurance, presumably.

It hadn't helped him. Winston Keeler's death had not come naturally to him; he had been assassinated by an injection of digitalis. Had Doc Thunder known, he might have had second thoughts about crashing into the abandoned warehouse the peroxide had been delivered to.

As it was, he assumed it was a fairly simple scam of a type he'd seen before – concentrated peroxide would be stolen, then diluted depending on the target market. Laboratories and water treatment plants would buy it at concentrations of 30% without looking too hard – with further dilution, the same stuff could be bottled and sold as hair bleach. Keeler had bought for fifty grand and sold for ninety – an enterprising businessman could turn that into as much as three hundred, depending on supply and demand. A large, seemingly abandoned warehouse most likely meant an operation of that nature.

Undiluted, high-test peroxide also made for excellent bombs, of course. Doc Thunder thought that was possible, but unlikely. He definitely didn't consider that it might be used for the purpose originally intended: rocket fuel.

More fool him.

"I honestly didn't know if that would work." Jason Satan grinned. "Isn't it wonderful when your secret dream comes true?" He sniggered, taking a step closer, his fingers flexing eagerly.

Scorpio levelled his gun. "Hold it, slick. One more step and I put a hole in you the size of the Brooklyn tunnel."

"Go ahead," Satan cackled. "Shoot me. Send my beautiful blood hissing and spraying from my veins. Drench yourself in it." He took another step. "Make my day."

Jack Scorpio's finger squeezed the trigger, but the gun refused to fire. He just couldn't seem to squeeze hard enough.

Behind him, the Murder Chair hissed and clanked as Mister Murder righted himself and scuttled forwards. He chuckled, a high-pitched giggle that echoed obscenely out of his cavernous mouth. "Herr Scorpio. How wonderful to see you again. Especially now that I've learned to counter your... unique mental defences. Please, tell your trigger finger to move. You'll find I am fully in control. And if I can control one finger..." – Scorpio felt his mind lurch as his arm suddenly swivelled, aiming the gun at El Sombra's head – "...there. Good soldier."

"Make him fire." Satan ran a wet grey tongue over his yellow fangs. "I want to see the Mexican's head burst."

"Why not?" Mister Murder twitched his shoulders in something almost like a shrug. "I've grown so much more powerful since the last time we fought, Herr Scorpio. You should have made sure of me then. Now... my mind is powerful enough to wear you like a glove. Like a puppet." The wrinkled, egg-like head cracked into a malevolent smile. "You will make a fine agent of Untergang."

"Excusez-moi?"

Mister Murder froze, then scuttled slowly around. Savate stood behind him, arms folded, brow furrowed in anger.

"Did you say... Untergang?"

CREED OF HATE

Mister Murder's eyes blazed with sudden rage! *Curse the luck!*

Up until now he had used his strange mental powers to fog Savate's mind, so the Frenchman accepted any story he was told without thinking. Thus, he did not question why the World's Most Evil Brain should no longer be working for Untergang, nor why two such accomplished killers should be wasting their time preparing 'knockout gas' to use against the city. In his mind, the three of them had been planning some great caper, to rob a sleeping city blind – but now, with a single unguarded word, Mister Murder had torn the scales from his pawn's eyes!

Could he reassert his mental domination and retain control over Jack Scorpio at the same time? It would be a supreme effort – but he was *ubermensch!* Created in the laboratories of the Ultimate Reich to annihilate free will and spread the Fuhrer's creed of hate across all the continents of the globe! Not only could he do it – *it was his destiny!*

Savate froze, feeling a prickling sensation running down the nerves in his arms. Suddenly, he was rooted to the spot, his limbs refusing to obey him. Jack Scorpio was likewise helpless, unable to do anything but keep his weapon pointed directly at El Sombra's head. Doc Thunder, meanwhile, was still insensate, struggling in the terrible grip of Jason Satan's poison – and despite his superhuman physiognomy he found himself inching closer to death with each passing second!

OOZING GOBBETS

Glistening beads of sweat trickled over Mister Murder's horrifically enlarged brow as he concentrated on keeping the tableau in place. It was all he could do to keep two minds under his control – three was quite impossible. Thus, the time for El Sombra to die was now – *and at Jack Scorpio's hand!*

The hideous mutant supermind gritted his teeth as he tightened his mental hold. There was some vague fuzz gathered around Scorpio's thoughts – the vestiges of the S.T.E.A.M. brain-training that had thwarted Mister Murder in the past – but still, the deranged telepath forced the agent's finger to tighten on the trigger of his incredible multi-ammo magnum... squeezing it... *until –*

– until the gun clicked uselessly in Scorpio's hand... and El Sombra seized his moment and leaped forward – *for the kill!*

His razor-sharp blade – which this reporter can exclusively reveal was inherited from his dead brother in a furious battle against the forces of the Luftwaffe – sliced directly thru Mister Murder's obscene cranium, transforming the Untergang abomination's gigantic head into a gruesome cauldron, open to the world, filled with oozing gobbets of bloody, sundered brain matter! *A fitting end for the arch-Nazi!*

Jack Scorpio felt the mental pressure ease, and breathed a sigh of relief before once again aiming his gun between Jason Satan's near-luminous white eyes.

But this time, he flipped the safety off.

AGONISING STRUGGLE

"Nothing has changed, Scorpio," Satan sneered, hissing the words through his rotting teeth. "By all means, shoot me, stab me – I'll take all of you with me! I'll shower you with my beautiful bleach-white blood and drag you down with me to the lowest pit of Hell!"

At his words, El Sombra backed away! *Had Mexico's greatest hero turned coward in the face of a man who could kill with a single touch?*

"Very sensible, masked man. Just turn your back and let me slip away. You have business in Germany, I understand. You'll be far away from the action, I guarantee." Satan giggled, his eyes flickering between Savate and Scorpio, then looking down at the pale, jaundiced face of Doc Thunder, savouring his triumph!

Once Thunder had been a veritable superhuman – now he shivered feverishly on the cold ground, blind and deaf to the struggles above, every breath an agonising struggle for his very survival! *How long did America's Greatest Hero have left to live?*

"Your turn now, Scorpio. Lower the gun and walk away. Perhaps you can get the good Doctor to a hospital before it's too late." He giggled again, but Jack Scorpio refused to lower his weapon. "No? Then we all die – here and now!"

The madman tensed, readying himself to spring! All his attention was focussed on the leader of S.T.E.A.M. – and delivering the one touch that would end his life! The time for talk was over – *now was the time for action in the mighty manner only the Daily Clarion can deliver!*

It was time – for Savate to strike!

PURIFYING FIRE

He leaped forward, aiming an expertly-delivered kick to Jason Satan's jaw, hard enough to split the monster's lip! A single drop of noxious white blood flew past Scorpio's ear, deadlier than a bullet – then the Man With The Touch Of Death crashed to the ground, the force of his momentum sliding him across the dusty floor – *and underneath the exhaust of the rocket!*

Savate turned to El Sombra and yelled: "Yours, mon ami!"

"Gracias, amigo!" El Sombra shouted back. Then be reached to the wall of switches he'd been backing towards – and pulled the lever for launch!

"Noooooooooo!" Jason Satan's inhuman scream was cut off by the roar of engines – *and then the hydrogen peroxide ignited, consuming Satan and all his toxins in a pillar of purifying fire!*

The rocket soared up through the shattered window before detonating high above the city – but without the deadly payload of poison gas, Untergang's deadly firework proved no more than a damp squib!

With two merciless master-villains dead, and Savate rumoured to be working closely with the American government to pay off his debt to society, New York can finally breathe a sigh of relief. *Or can we?*

Untergang's latest foul plot may have been smashed – but their Uncle Adolf is still waiting for his turn! *And America's Greatest Hero is still lying at death's door!*

Buy the Clarion tomorrow for a pulse-pounding front page special on Doc Thunder's fight for life – and the looming conflict receiving unanimous support in Congress! It's all under tomorrow's heart-stopping headline – *"If War Be Our Destiny!"*

"WHY ZE HANDCUFFS, mon ami?" Savate grinned as the police pushed him into the back of a waiting van. "Surely you do not think ze great Savate will perform ze daring escape?"

"Not if ze great Savate knows what's good for him." Jack Scorpio flicked the wheel of his lighter, sparking up another of his special cigarettes. "And by good I mean profitable. Stay cool, Savate. I'll be in touch." Savate stared at him for a moment, and nodded, and then the van doors closed and he was driven away.

Doc Thunder had already been taken away in an ambulance. Most of his hair had fallen out, and he seemed somehow shrivelled, as though someone had opened a hidden valve somewhere and let a little air out of him. The paramedics wondered privately if he'd last the night.

Scorpio took a long drag. "That's what happens when you just blunder in without backup, true believer."

El Sombra raised an eyebrow. "Alternatively, that's what happens when someone blunders in on you."

Scorpio shrugged. "Either way, if we'd all been together, things might not have gone the way they did. Stolen hydrogen peroxide's something S.T.E.A.M. should have known about from the start. Folks like us need to hang together, or we'll sure as hell hang separately."

"Who said that?" It sounded to El Sombra like a quote from somewhere. For some reason, the thought disturbed him.

"Someone in a dream," Scorpio said, and smiled that infuriating secret smile. El Sombra had a feeling he'd be learning to hate that soon enough. Scorpio was right, he knew. The USSA was going to war, and he'd have a better chance of killing off the Ultimate Reich and all their bastards if he took advantage of that. Which, for the time being, meant joining whatever team Jack Scorpio was forming.

Scorpio sighed heavily, breaking El Sombra's train of thought. "God damn it."

"What?"

"Untergang finally won one, even if they hadn't planned it. We figured we had Doc Thunder on board for the war effort, but that didn't look like a man who's going to be storming any bunkers any time soon." Scorpio tapped a little ash out onto the ground. "So much for it all being over by Christmas. Except maybe for him."

"You think he's really going to..." El Sombra couldn't bring himself to finish it. The idea seemed too outlandish. He'd only met Thunder recently, but he'd been under the impression you could throw just about anything at him and he'd walk right through it. To see him shrivelled up and going bald like that – it seemed almost sacrilegious.

"Maybe. Unless we can find an antidote. Even then..." He shook his head. "Well, at least I've got a line on Savate now. I was wondering when I'd get a chance to bring him on board."

"Wait, you're recruiting *him*?" El Sombra blinked. "A guy who kicks people for money?"

"Well, I already got a guy who stabs people for free. I like variety. Anyway, you guys seemed to work pretty well together back there..."

El Sombra had to admit that. "I suppose. So who else have you got lined up in this merry band of yours?"

Scorpio inhaled, held it for a second, then blew out a ring of smoke.

"Trust me, true believer. You ain't seen nothing yet."

THE LAST STAND
OF THE YODELLING
BASTARDS

OFFICIAL RECORD CONCERNING EVENTS OF 07/12/2004:
"OPERATION FALSE FLAG." THE FOLLOWING FILE
CONCERNS THE FINAL MISSION OF THE EXPERIMENTAL
COMMANDO UNIT YANKEE BRAVO SEVEN AND IS THUS
CLASSIFIED ABOVE TOP SECRET.

"GENERAL ZITRON, SIR!" Major-General Allen marched up to
the desk and snapped into a salute almost vigorous enough
to knock his hat off. Matt Zitron rolled his eyes and tried to
suppress an irritated sigh.

"At ease, Hal. Take a load off." He indicated a chair with
his pipe.

"I prefer to stand, General, sir." Allen clicked his heels
together for emphasis, then threw in another salute for good
measure. Zitron thought about chiding him for his failure to
stand at ease – but then, for Allen, this was at ease.

Well, so be it. The USSA needed men like Hal Allen – he
might be wound tighter than a termite's *tuchus,* but he was a
good man for admin work and he did possess a certain gift for
strategy. Just so long as nobody was ever dumb enough to put

him in the field, that was all. He belonged right here in sunny Italy, in the rear with the gear.

"That's fine, Hal. You go ahead and stand." Zitron blew out a long plume of smoke and nodded towards the office door. "You got Jack Scorpio out there?"

Allen winced. "Permission to speak freely, General, sir."

Zitron knew what was coming. "Go on, Hal, let's hear it."

"In my opinion, sir, Colonel Scorpio is completely wrong for this mission." He licked his lips nervously. "Now as you know, sir, I cannot quite bring myself to credit the, ah, *otherworldly* elements involved in the mission brief –"

Zitron nodded stoically. "You don't believe in time travel, mysterious portals or Leopard Men. Duly noted."

"– but I respect that this could be a pivotal operation. One that – if even half of what we've been told is true, as opposed to some bizarre fantasy – could possibly turn the tide of this whole war. And, to be quite frank with you, General, sir" – Allen scowled – "I just don't believe Yankee Bravo Seven can do the job."

"You don't, huh?"

"No, sir. They're just not soldier material, sir."

"Seems like they've done all right so far. Ask Von Hammer," Zitron grinned, dropping the name of the enemy Luftwaffe commander – one of the most feared names in the war – who Yankee Bravo Seven had captured alive, and in possession of the latest top secret Nazi wing-pack design, the previous week. Cavorite was still in short supply on the allied side, which meant they were stuck with Rocketeer squadrons for now, but it was still a hell of a coup.

"Sir..." – Allen drew in his breath, as if trying to control his temper – "...regardless of any... flukes of performance, these men do not and cannot possibly function as a proper military unit. I mean, the organisational structure alone – it makes no sense. In the same squad, we've got a Colonel, a Captain, an OSS Captain, a *Navy* Captain, a French mercenary, two civilians, one of whom is still wanted for crimes against Magna Britannia and the other of whom is a *conscientious objector,* for Christ's sake, and a... a... I don't know what he is, but he's *naked* –"

"Half-naked. His junk's covered."

"That's hardly the point, sir! He's an escaped lunatic from Mexico on a revenge mission! He's about as far from being an American soldier as you can *possibly get!*" Zitron couldn't help noticing how red Allen's face was getting. Yankee Bravo Seven had a habit of causing that reaction in him.

Well, at least it loosened him up a little. "Major-General, since you're actually standing at ease for once, how about sitting down?"

Allen snapped back to attention. "No, thank you, sir. Since I brought up the nudity issue –"

"Half-nudity."

"– I should say that I find it abhorrent that these men do not understand the simple concept of a uniform. Even Colonel Scorpio refuses to dress in a manner befitting his rank – and this is a man who used to wear a *skintight white jumpsuit* to command a top-secret Black Ops division –"

"Anti-camouflage. That's another thing you don't believe in, right?"

Allen fumed for a moment. "What I believe, sir, is that as a leader, Jack Scorpio seems completely incapable of controlling the men under his command."

"Colonel Scorpio," Zitron gently reminded Allen, "led S.T.E.A.M. for forty years."

Allen took a deep breath. *"In a skintight white –"*

"Anti-camouflage. If I had my way, we'd be using it in the field." He leant back in his chair, fixing Hal with a stern look. "And try moderating your tone a little, huh? The day you get your fifth star, that's the day you get to raise your voice to me."

"Sir..." Allen forced himself to calm down. "S.T.E.A.M. under Scorpio was practically a one-man operation, and an irresponsibly expensive one at that. I am given to understand that a significant portion of his operating budget was used to... for the purposes of" – he flushed a deep shade of scarlet – "of smoking reefer and copulating with fetish models. There, I said it."

"Not reefer, Hal. Some kind of special herb from the mountains of Zor-Ek-Narr. Keeps him young, or so I'm told."

Zitron watched Hal turn a deeper crimson, almost purple. "It's a Leopard Man kind of thing. And that 'fetish model' you're talking about is a respected member of the Yankee Bravo team with over fifty confirmed kills to her credit. Not to mention one hell of a driver."

Allen took another deep breath. After a moment, his face made some progress back towards a normal colour. "Sir – he is simply not capable of the degree of command necessary for this man's army. Yankee Bravo Seven is... Sir, I hate to say it, but it's a *terrible* unit. They're undisciplined, anti-authoritarian and at least three of them have recognised mental problems."

"You're exaggerating, Hal."

"Sir, Cohen is under the delusion that he's Blackbeard the pirate."

"Well, perhaps he is, Hal. We're living in interesting times." He leant forward and whispered. "Leopard Men."

"Sir, I do not believe in Leopard Men. I never have believed in Leopard Men." A manic tremble was creeping into his voice. "If a Leopard Man were to walk in here right now and offer me a cigarette made of 'special herbs' – I would *still* not believe in Leopard Men."

Zitron smiled. "Well, you don't have the clearance to anyway, so it's probably for the best. Is that everything, Hal?"

"Just... please, sir. Give me one platoon of real soldiers. We can still do this the right way. The *Army* way."

"Mmm... no, I don't think so." Zitron shook his head. "This one's a little too crazy to try it the Army way, Major-General."

"Sir –"

"No, I think this one, we do the Yankee Bravo Seven way." He smiled. "You're dismissed, Hal. Send Jack in on your way out."

Allen stared at him in fury for a moment, then saluted sharply. "Sir!"

Zitron watched him storm out of the office, and wondered when exactly Allen would have his heart attack and be done with it. Ah, well. Right now he had bigger fish to fry.

A moment later, Jack Scorpio entered the room.

PERSONNEL FILE: JACK SCORPIO - COLONEL (FOURTH
EARTH BATTALION, STRATEGIC TACTICAL ESPIONAGE
AND MANOEUVRES) - SKILLS: LEADERSHIP, ESPIONAGE,
UNCONVENTIONAL WARFARE, ELONGATED LIFESPAN -
PREFERRED WEAPON: S.T.E.A.M. ISSUE COLT X-007
MAGNUM CALIBER HANDGUN WITH MULTIPLE AMMUNITION
CAPABILITY - WEAKNESSES: SEX, DRUGS, MAGICAL
THINKING

Jack's uniform had changed since he'd left S.T.E.A.M. to
form Yankee Bravo Seven. The white jumpsuit was gone, as
well as most of the gadgets – his only concessions to the secret
agent life were his S.T.E.A.M.-issue multi-ammo Magnum
pistol, and a pair of shades which he never removed. The left
lens was simple smoked glass, functioning as a replacement
for his eyepatch, but the right lens had – allegedly – been
specially treated to perceive human auras. Like a lot of things
about Jack, it was hard to say whether or not that was on
the level.

When you came right down to it, Jack was a very strange guy.

These days, he wore fairly standard military combat trousers,
albeit a little baggy in the hem, a flak jacket – usually open to
the waist – and little else. Instead of wearing the steel-toed
boots of old, he walked barefoot, and the soles of his feet had
developed a hard layer of callus. Where the S.T.E.A.M. insignia
had dotted his old uniform, he wore tattoos of pentagrams and
other more mysterious symbols – images of bats and circled
lightning, serpents coiled inside heraldic shields.

There was a scorpion branded into the skin at the base of
his skull that hadn't been there before. Matt Zitron had once,
in the mess after a particularly gruelling mission, asked what
it represented. "My nature," Jack had said, and smiled his
unsettling smile.

Jack had originally trained with the First Earth Battalion,
before taking Jim Channon's ideas into newer, weirder
directions. His offshoot, the Fourth Earth Battalion, had
eventually mutated into S.T.E.A.M. in order to find favour

with the establishment; now it seemed as though Jack had gone back to his roots.

It was no wonder someone like Hal Allen didn't like him. Hell, it was a wonder Zitron liked him, but he had to admit he had a soft spot for the creepy bastard.

If they were going to win this war, it was Jack that would do it.

Zitron stood, offering Jack Scorpio his hand. "Jack. Good to see you."

"Matthew." Jack gripped the General's hand as though he was about to arm-wrestle, squeezed tight, then let it go and offered his fist. Zitron looked confused. Jack smiled. "Greetings from the dream world. Go on, bump your knuckles."

Zitron looked at him for a moment, then gingerly bumped his fist against Jack's. For a moment, he felt strange, insubstantial. Jack's occasional 'dream world' talk always made him feel weird.

"How's the boy?" Jack asked, smiling widely.

"Isaac? Oh, he's doing great. Growing like a weed."

"All part of the circle of life. So, I hear you've got some action? Something regular army can't handle, is that right?"

"Oh, yeah."

Zitron took a long puff on his pipe.

"It's one for the Yodelling Bastards."

"AHEM. FIRST SLIDE, please."

Jack Scorpio sparked up another joint and inserted the next slide – a photograph of a bearded, nervous-looking man in round spectacles. The flickering of the oil lamp that projected the image onto the wall made him seem even more frightened, as if he kept some secret that horrified him.

Standing in front of the photograph, Captain Richard Reed puffed gently on his pipe. "Thank you, Corporal."

"*Aaar*," snarled Lev 'Blackbeard' Cohen, in the broad Cornish accent he'd had ever since his ship was sunk from under him by a Nazi U-boat in the Atlantic. "What's this lily-livered son of a swab have to say to us? *Captain,* he calls himself! Yet he's never stood on the deck of a ship in a ragin' storm o' cannon-fire, urgin' his lovely lads on to th' work o' plunderin' –"

Reed rolled his eyes. "Not this again. Cohen –"

"*Captain Teach, dog!*" Cohen leapt out of his chair, sending it rattling backwards, and drew his cutlass in one savage motion. "*I'll have ye dance a hornpipe at the end of me rope, ye scurvy bilge-rat!*"

"Put it away, fool," Mike Moses growled in his deep, rumbling bass. "Save it for the Ratzis." Cohen turned to him, scowling through blackened teeth, then re-seated himself with a grudging *aar.*

"Honestly," Marlene Lang sighed. "Boys and their swords." She flashed El Sombra a contemptuous look, and he flashed her a grin in response. Savate, sat in the row behind, rolled his eyes.

"Zere eez an Eenglish phrase... ah, oui, I have eet." He smiled, leaned forward and patted them both on the shoulder. "Get a room, mes amis."

In the corner, Johnny Wolf raised an eyebrow. He didn't speak. Ever.

Scorpio looked his team over as the banter continued. Seven specialists, each one the best there was at what they did – and right now, what they were doing was wasting his precious time. Calmly, he drew his multi-ammo Magnum and fired a dum-dum round into the ceiling.

That shut them up, all right.

"Captain Reed." Scorpio smiled. "You have the floor."

The six seated members of Yankee Bravo Seven grudgingly turned their attention to Reed. "Thank you, sir. Now, to answer Cohen's – I'm sorry, 'Blackbeard's' – idiotic question, the reason I'm giving this briefing is that I'm the best equipped to understand what we're facing and translate it for you... laypersons." He took a puff on his pipe. "Or *'morons,'* as we in the scientific community call you."

Mike Moses groaned. "Aw, man. This is gonna be all kinds of crazy-ass mad science, ain't it?"

Reed smiled. "My dear Michael... is there any other kind?"

```
PERSONNEL FILE: RICHARD REED - CAPTAIN (OFFICE
OF STRATEGIC SERVICES) - SKILLS: CODEBREAKING,
ENGINEERING, SCIENTIFIC GENIUS, TECHNOLOGICAL
SAVANT - PREFERRED WEAPON: NONE - WEAKNESSES:
LOW COMBAT SKILLS, IS A CONDESCENDING ASSHOLE
```

"So! First slide – here we have Magna Britannia's own Professor Philip Hawthorne. Fact: fourteen months ago, Hawthorne attended a scientific conference in Switzerland to give a lecture on Parallel Universe Theory and the I Ching. Fact: shortly before he was due to deliver his lecture, he vanished from his hotel room without explanation. Nobody knows why."

El Sombra shrugged. "Kidnapped by the bastards, amigo. It's obvious."

"If by 'bastards' you mean Nazis – and you usually do – then yes, it was deeply obvious, but neither Magna Britannia nor Switzerland want to enter the war. Which is good for us. Right now, it's the USSA versus Nazi Germany, with our various European friends – and theirs – providing moral support, staging posts and deniable resources like Savate here. If Switzerland and Britannia got involved, we have no idea which way they'd go..."

Reed took a puff on his pipe, and Jack Scorpio broke in. "Doc Thunder's the big factor there."

"*Arrr,*" Cohen growled. "How fares he 'gainst the ravages o' the black spot?"

Scorpio shrugged. "He's out of danger, I hear. In a couple of months, maybe he'll even wake up." He shook his head. "Anyway, as long as he's recuperating in Zor-Ek-Narr – and who knows how long it'll be before he's back to his old self – we're a lot weaker. Meanwhile, Magna Britannia know they can control Hitler when he's at full strength; they've been doing it for decades, and apart from occasional Untergang agents like Dan Dashwood, they've had no problems. So do the math. If they enter the war, it'll be to do a nice little deal with the Führer and get their old colony back. Then they'll throw a bone to the Nazis – Italy, maybe – and get back to business as usual."

"They'd do that?" Very little shocked Marlene Lang, but she seemed nonplussed at that.

"Sure. Britain wasn't exactly friendly even before all their shit hit the fan. Anyway, back on topic..." He nodded to Reed and changed to the next slide.

Reed smiled. "Back on topic – here we see Phil Hawthorne and Alexander Oddfellow having a drink in the Eagle in Cambridge, in happier times. If you've been reading your Above Top Secret files, you'll remember Oddfellow as the man who accidentally discovered time travel. Which, funnily enough, was Hawthorne's specialist subject and the focus of most of his theorising. The two of them corresponded until Oddfellow got caught in his own matter transporter back in '97 – which we're not supposed to know about, of course. After that, the British government was a little more careful about who he talked to, but it's my understanding that they managed to meet up once or twice. In addition to his correspondence with Oddfellow, Hawthorne also wrote to me regarding the Devil's Eye Incident of 1888, which my great-great-grandfather was the only surviving witness of. He theorised that that was also caused by a temporal anomaly. You see where I'm going with this?"

Savate shrugged. "*Non.*"

Reed sighed. "The world's greatest living expert in time travel has been kidnapped by the Nazis."

Johnny Wolf leaned back on his chair, lifted the brim of his stetson and looked Reed straight in the eye. Reed caught his meaning and nodded.

"As a matter of fact, Wolf, we do know where he is. Or rather, we've got a pretty good idea. Next slide, please." The picture of the two men was replaced by that of a German *schloss* – a great stone castle in an eccentric and forbidding style, complete with two massive flat-topped turrets. "Castle Abendsen. Situated about ten miles from the ruins of Castle

Frankenstein – also rumoured to have been the scene of a temporal anomaly in 1943, which I find significant. Recently, some of our spies operating behind enemy lines have spotted deliveries of vacuum tubes, microhydraulics and industrial cavorite being ferried to the castle by traction engine, and it's rumoured that that's part of a supply line running straight from Berlin bringing some worryingly high technology into the area. It's also rumoured that Castle Abendsen is home to a VIP – that's as in *very important prisoner*. Anyone want to have another go at putting the pieces together?"

Savate nodded. "Ze Bosche are holdeeng zees Hawthorne een zeir castle and forceeng heem to build zem... 'ow you say... *une machine a voyager dans le temps.*"

Reed scowled. "You're making your accent even more ridiculous just to annoy me, aren't you?"

"*Oui, oui, mon petit chou-fleur.* Do you suppose zey weel attempt to go back een time and change ze course of ze Second Great War?"

Scorpio broke in. "I doubt it. Current thinking for folks who know what went down back in 1943 – including the Führer – is that you just can't change the past. All you can do is have shit happen the way you remember it happening, only it turns out that was you all along. Not much use in a military situation." He finished his joint and stubbed it out on his flak jacket. "But from our point of view here in the present, the future's still mutable, until someone comes back and tells us otherwise. So we could – according to those in the know – bring stuff back from there, like weapons, or troops. There's nothing theoretically stopping the Nazi army of next week from coming back, joining up with the Nazis of today and kicking our asses, so long as the Nazis of today remember to keep their diary free next week. Try not to think about it too hard – I don't need any of you getting a migraine before the mission – but be aware that on this op, there's literally no time to lose. They could be throwing the switch right now, and the first we'd know about it would be when we suddenly had to fight five Ultimate Reichs at once."

"Crazy-ass mad science. I knew it." Mike Moses groaned, holding his head in his hands. "So the mission is to bust in, grab Hawthorne and bust right back out?"

"And destroy anything that even smells like a time machine." Scorpio grinned. "Oh, by the way, Castle Abendsen's in the heart of enemy territory and so heavily guarded on the ground that you can't get inside a mile of it without coming down with a lead overdose. Rumour had it they've even got a King Tiger patrolling the area."

Marlene let out a low whistle.

El Sombra looked over at her. "King Tiger?"

"The largest, toughest, most powerful traction engine in the world. It's like driving a battleship, so they say. I've been itching to get behind the wheel of one..." She purred, savouring the thought.

"Well, you won't on this mission," Scorpio informed her. "It's way too dangerous to approach on the ground, and we've got the Luftwaffe patrolling the area from the air. Castle Abendsen's sealed up tighter than a drum."

"Also not to mention all the heightened security inside," Reed murmured. "The place is crawling with SS, and I'd be very surprised if they hadn't been assigned a Zinnsoldat or two to help tidy up any unwanted human beings breaking in."

"I see. A King Tiger, the Luftwaffe, the SS and a couple of Zinnsoldats. And a time machine." Marlene raised an eyebrow. "Jack, dearest, would you say this was a suicide mission?"

"Like the man said." Jack Scorpio grinned. "Is there any other kind?"

IT REALLY IS *a beautiful day for killing*, Emil Farber thought.

He'd led his squadron south, for a sortie over what had once been Austria, and they'd run into a platoon of Rocketeers escorting a troop carrier on the ground. Farber couldn't help but smile at how easily his men had out-manoeuvred and out-gunned the Americans in their clumsy jetpacks and helmets. The socialists just couldn't afford the cavorite necessary to maintain a proper flying corps, and their experiments with hydrogen peroxide were only good for creating gangs of human fireworks, exploding with a single bullet in the right place. What sort of moron would send their men out wearing their own deaths strapped to their backs?

The best the Rocketeers could have done was bought time for the troop carrier to get to safety, but they didn't even manage that – it only took half of Farber's squad to destroy the American fliers, their cavorite-infused wing-packs flying rings around them, while the other half calmly machine-gunned the soldiers from above. Farber counted a good forty Americans killed, at the hands of a mere eight men. A good afternoon's work.

He chuckled to himself as his men landed on the tarmac at the Staffel. As long as the Fatherland had the vital advantage in the air, the Americans were doomed. Sooner or later, he knew, his Führer would realise how weak Magna Britannia was and finally give the order to attack the French and Italians. One by one, the countries of Europe would topple like dominoes, and then – finally – Britain and all her resources would fall before the might of the Ultimate Reich.

After that, mopping up the Americans and their fireworks would be child's play.

Behind him, Pfeffer, the newest member of the squadron, piped up shrilly. "Herr Major? Where *is* everyone?"

Farber looked around the Staffel. It was a small area, with a barracks, an officer's mess and a couple of administrative buildings, and usually it was crowded with guards and clerks – at the very least, the engineers should have been rushing out to check over their wing-packs. And yet, nobody was there at all.

"Have we been attacked, Major?" Ludwig Richter this time, ever ready to jump to a pessimistic conclusion. Farber shook his head, although he found himself unable to think of any other explanation. And then, just as he was about to order the squadron to split up and conduct a search, the door to the Officer's Mess opened.

Standing in the doorway was a strikingly attractive blonde woman, wearing a suit of some figure-hugging black material

– from a distance, it seemed like leather, but surely it couldn't be – along with a pair of red gloves, and red high-heeled ankle boots. Farber seemed to remember seeing girls dressed like that during pre-war furloughs in Milan – 'swinging Milan,' as the British called it. As the blonde flashed him a dazzling smile, he began to wonder if perhaps this was some star of the cabaret stage, here to raise the morale of the troops? No, he would have been informed. A working girl from nearby Feldkirch, then, smuggled in by the ground crew to help one of his young charges celebrate a birthday and a coming of age? No, nobody in Feldkirch looked like that – and again, he would have been informed. Wouldn't he?

In his confusion, he almost didn't hear the sound of seven bodies hitting the ground behind him. He turned around – and saw all his men splayed out on the concrete, a tranquiliser dart jutting from the neck of each one. How... how did...?

He turned back, wide-eyed, to see the blonde aiming a pistol directly at him. He had time for one thought before the dart buried itself in his neck: *this is how the Rocketeers must have felt.*

Then everything went black.

Marlene smiled, and spoke into the communicator at her wrist. "Blood Widow to King Sting. Snake Eyes got seven of them, I dispatched the last. Over."

Jack Scorpio's voice crackled in response. "Only seven? He's slipping."

"He's a gentleman. He knows how much I enjoy shooting commanding officers – I always think of you when I'm pulling the trigger."

"You're going to hold what happened in London over my head for the rest of my life, aren't you?"

"At the very least." Marlene said, and blew a kiss towards the roof of the barracks.

If a man spent an hour poring over that roof with a pair of high-powered binoculars, he'd see nothing but roof tiles in the sun. And then – ten seconds after he'd given up – the pattern of the tile would shift almost imperceptibly, or the shadow of the chimney would lengthen by a fraction...

...and Johnny Wolf wouldn't be there any more.

```
PERSONNEL FILE: JOHN STALKING WOLF - CAPTAIN
(MARINE CORPS) - SKILLS: SNIPER (ULTIMATE
CLASS), STEALTH, EXTREME SURVIVAL, NON-VERBAL
COMMUNICATION - PREFERRED WEAPON: DRAGUNOV SVU
GAS-OPERATED SNIPER RIFLE (ADAPTED FOR MULTI-
AMMO CAPABILITY) - WEAKNESSES: HAS NEVER SPOKEN
```

He unfolded himself from his hiding place on the roof, and Marlene couldn't help but note that he'd taken his shirt off.

How delightfully decadent of him.

"I AIN'T STRAPPING on no wings, fool!"

```
PERSONNEL FILE: MICHAEL MOSES - CIVILIAN
(PREVIOUS OCCUPATION: CIRCUS STRONGMAN) - SKILLS:
UNARMED COMBAT, EXTREMELY HIGH NATURAL STRENGTH,
INTERMEDIATE MEDICAL TRAINING - PREFERRED WEAPON:
FISTS - WEAKNESSES: CONSCIENTIOUS OBJECTOR,
SUFFERS SEVERE AVIOPHOBIA
```

"I will steal a damn tank if I have to!" Mike Moses bellowed. "I will *walk!* I will *hitch-hike!* But you are *not* getting me into no damn wings!"

"Oh, for goodness' sakes, Michael." Reed sighed theatrically. "Statistically, wing-packs *are* the safest form of travel."

"Like hell! You shot a damn missile at one last week!"

Reed shrugged. "I can't argue with that logic."

"They're the safest for what we're about to do." Scorpio said, buttoning his coat. "Now get your damn clothes on." Apart from Moses, they were all dressed in the uniforms of the Ultimate Reich fliers; the fliers themselves were bound and gagged in the Officer's Mess, with the ground crew and the guards. "We need to be in the air in five minutes if this plan's gonna work."

Moses scowled, struggling into a uniform a size too small for him. "Well, it's a crazy-ass plan, Jack. I mean, we fly up to that castle, what the hell are they supposed to think? 'Aw, hey, two black guys wearing our clothes! That look suspicious to you, Hans?' 'Hell, no, Fritz, 'cause the Nazi party's all about equal opportunities and also it's German Opposite Day –'"

"*Es ist Gegenteiltag,*" Reed murmured.

Scorpio sighed. "I've done this before, Mike. We'll be too far away. Nobody on the ground is going to see what colour we are."

"How about when we land on the turrets? Those guards are gonna shoot us like pigeons –"

Marlene smiled, adjusting her cap. Out of all of them, she was the only one who didn't look out of place in the Reich's uniforms; El Sombra in particular was scratching himself as if afflicted with the shirt of Nessus. "Not if we shoot them first, darling," she purred.

"What's this '*we,*' lady?" Moses scowled angrily. "I don't kill fools. You *know* I don't kill fools. Hell, I *pity* the fools ain't their fault they got all indoctrinated, y'know? But you don't have to worry about me not killing fools, because I *ain't* strapping on no god-damn *wings* –"

Marlene shot him with a tranquiliser dart.

"What?" she asked, as the others looked at her.

Jack sighed. "One of these days I'm getting him a therapist. Reed, you got that doohickey you told me about?"

Reed smiled, removing a large piece of clockwork from the backpack he wore and clipping it onto the controls of the largest wing-pack. "This little brain will keep him flying with the rest of us while he sleeps. Just wind it up when you want us to take off."

"Excusez-moi, mes amis," Savate piped up. "But, ah, what do we do with..." He indicated the Officer's Mess.

El Sombra shrugged. "They're bastards, amigo. We kill them." He hefted his machine-gun.

Savate laughed nervously. "Well, I am not wishing to sound like Monsieur Moses, but to machine-gun two dozen men in cold blood... it seems so... wizzout honnair, n'est-ce-pas?"

El Sombra drew in a breath, and the Officer's Mess picked that moment to explode.

Once the rubble had settled and the myriad pieces of smoking meat that had once been men had hit the ground, Scorpio turned to Lev Cohen. "Blackbeard. That was you, wasn't it?"

PERSONNEL FILE: LEV 'BLACKBEARD' COHEN - CAPTAIN (US NAVY) - SKILLS: NAVAL STRATEGY, BLADE COMBAT, DEMOLITION VIA EXPLOSIVE DEVICES - PREFERRED WEAPON: CUTLASS, EXPLOSIVE DEVICES - WEAKNESSES: BELIEVES HIMSELF TO BE HISTORICAL PIRATE BLACKBEARD, RESULTANT AGGRESSIVE BEHAVIOUR INCLUDES CONSTANTLY LIGHTING FUSES IN BEARD, HAIR, EXPLOSIVE DEVICES

"Aaarr."

"HOW'S IT COMING, *mein herr*?"

Herr Doktor Diederich looked around Castle Abendsen's massive dining room, squinting through his monocle at the maze of copper piping and clockwork. In the centre of it, Professor Hawthorne fiddled nervously with one of the Babbage arrays, occasionally winding it with a key and running slips of paper through a slot in the base, then examining the figures that emerged. "It'd be coming a little easier if you didn't have me under such damned pressure." He shook his head. "I shouldn't be doing this at all. It's insanely dangerous – for God's sake, think what happened to Alexander, and he was only attempting transportation through space! For that matter, think what happened to your own man, Dashwood!" He shuddered. "I personally have no desire to end up a skinless monstrosity, thank you. If it was up to me, I'd stop everything here and now and tell your Führer to... to get knotted!"

"You'd do no such thing, Hawthorne. You're too much of a coward. If you were even in the same room as our glorious Führer, you would... what is the English expression?" Diederich considered for a moment. "*Es lag mir auf der Zunge...* ah yes. You would shit yourself." He chuckled to himself. "Anyway, it is not up to you. You have no choice in the matter, *ja*? You work for us now, Herr Professor. Get used to it."

Hawthorne bristled for a moment, then sighed and bowed his head. "Of course, of course. I work for you. All I'm saying is that you need to be aware of the danger, that's all."

"That is your opinion as a scientist?"

"Yes."

"Well, I am a scientist as well, *mein herr*, and I have my own ideas. Keep working."

Hawthorne stared daggers at Diederich, then finished his tinkering and ran another set of numbers through the array. Having finally come to a result he found pleasing – or at least not displeasing – he slotted the clockwork in amongst a group of its brothers, then stepped back and ran his eyes over the whole contraption.

An immense host of Babbage arrays, logic engines and analytical mechanics had overtaken the room, a maze of connections fed by a gigantic furnace built into the stone wall and constantly supplied with fresh coal by two muscular Aryans. The clattering noise as the machine thought was like a thousand chirping crickets – but it was only standing by, waiting for the key to turn that would set it to its real task. In the very centre of the room was a cylindrical column, three feet tall and six in diameter, made of several dozen wafer-thin discs – copper and zinc, interlaced with discs of purest cavorite. Steel clamps secured the column to the stone floor below, to stop the whole thing rising up to the ceiling and yanking the vital connections with it.

"It is an impressive beast, Herr Professor." It was. Diederich could not entirely conceal his awe at the scale of it. "The question is, will it do what you have claimed?"

"I never claimed anything," Hawthorne muttered, bitterly. "I posited that it *might* work. It still depends on the absence of human error. In fact, for your own safety, you should stay out of the room when –"

"Don't be foolish, *mein herr*. I must remain to make sure the experiment is a success." He snapped his fingers, and two of Standartenführer Ackermann's burly stormtroopers marched over and gripped Hawthorne by the arms. "You, on the other hand, are too valuable to risk. Your brain will perform many great works for the Fatherland, Professor Hawthorne. Who knows? Perhaps we will give it a nice new home."

"Now, wait a second! Let go of me at once!" Hawthorne struggled helplessly, beard quivering with indignation at the rough treatment. "You need me here! If the machine goes wrong, you'll be smeared through time like ink on blotting-paper!"

Diederich narrowed his eyes for a moment. "I see. Perhaps I will make a few last-minute checks of your work, *ja*? And make sure I have the sequence fully memorised. In the meantime, you can return to your quarters... in the dungeons." The SS men frogmarched him away, still protesting.

Diederich watched him go. There was something about Hawthorne he didn't like. He seemed so hunched and cowardly, such a miserable and unkempt little Englander... but then again, there was something sinister in his manner, as if he knew more than he was letting on. Best not to have such a man close by during the final stages of such an important experiment, even if he was the driving force behind it; Diederich doubted he could count on Hawthorne's loyalty to the Führer.

He shook his head, then looked over the maze of copper and iron around him, wondering if he dared to set it in motion. He'd hidden his own fears from Hawthorne, but the Englishman's nervousness was rubbing off. He thought of nearby Castle Frankenstein, destroyed decades ago; when they woke this monster from its noisy slumber, what would it do to them?

In the end, it didn't matter. Yes, he would wait, check for himself, make absolutely sure... but there was never any question that he would eventually throw the switch. He was afraid of bringing the machine to life, but more afraid by far of not doing so.

After all, the Führer was waiting.

He turned around, smiling to the groups of SS men hovering

on the edge of the room, watching him intently... and the two Zinnsoldats, the immense steam-powered robots, standing to attention and gazing on him with their terrible red eyes.

Yes, it would not do to keep the Führer waiting much longer...

PRIVATE METZGER LOOKED at the minute hand on his wristwatch, willing it to turn faster. He and Vogt had spent eight hours on this miserable detail, guarding the top of the east turret – a double shift, as punishment for pilfering a bottle of *landwein* from the castle cellars. It wasn't even good wine, and Vogt had argued, convincingly, that it wouldn't be missed, and didn't they deserve a little luxury, being stationed in such a boring, stifling hole, so far away from the front?

Vogt's convincing argument had bought them both double shifts on guard duty, from now until that pompous oaf, Unterfeldwebel Trommler, decided they'd learned their lesson. It could have been worse – Trommler had taken pains to point out that had those thugs in the SS caught them, they would likely have been shot, and he was probably right. Those bastards didn't care about the ordinary soldier – they'd shoot a hundred Metzgers if they thought it would win them a kindly look from their precious undying Führer.

All in all, it hadn't been Vogt's finest hour, and Metzger was quite justified in refusing to speak to the light-fingered little rodent. But that decision did make the eight-hour shifts pass so terribly slowly.

Twenty minutes left. An eternity. Well, at least Metzger had a good view.

From his place up on the flat roof of the east turret, he could see for miles, giving him a spectacular vista of the various troops moving to take up their positions. The ground units far below seemed to be constantly buzzing to and fro, like ants, or hornets, endlessly setting up new defensive positions to counter attacks that never came, from American soldiers that were twenty miles away, being pounded down by armoured units and the Luftwaffe. Perhaps they were as bored as he was.

"Speak of the devil," Metzger muttered, as he noted the Luftwaffe squadron on the horizon. Every so often, a pair of wingmen would buzz the castle, waving to him or to whoever was stationed on the west turret, but occasionally a full squadron would fly past on the way to the next point on their regular patrol. It was hardly an uncommon occurrence.

But there was something different about this squadron – about the way they flew, like amateurs, wobbling through the sky. Not just those in the middle of the formation, either – the ones who might have conceivably been on their first flight – but *all* of them, even the Squadron Leader. As if they hadn't been doing this every day for years...

Metzger squinted at the winged specks as they closed in, and pursed his lips in a disapproving frown. One of them even seemed to be asleep, although of course that couldn't be possible.

Metzger opened his mouth, but some lingering trace of resentment prevented him speaking to Vogt – just yet, anyway. The last thing he wanted to do was look like a fool in front of that idiot. It was probably nothing, anyway – after all, what did he know about flying? It wasn't as if he'd ever strapped on a wing-pack himself.

Still, something about these fliers, as they came closer and closer... he felt a sudden wave of panic and found himself scrabbling for his binoculars, even as the wingmen came close enough to confirm something was terribly wrong. The uniforms didn't fit. Now he could see – mein gott, was their Squadron Leader a *schwartzer*? A chill ran through him as the awful truth struck him.

Americans!

Now he *had* to talk to Vogt, to warn him, and yet somehow he still could not speak. To admit to Vogt, the idiot, that he had been a greater idiot, and now it was almost too late, and what if he was *wrong*? Desperately, he raised the binoculars to his eyes, to make sure of what he thought he'd seen –

– and a Magnum bullet ploughed through the right lens, his

eye and his brain, bursting out through the back of his skull in a red fountain, and that was that.

Another magnum bullet hit the back of Vogt's head an instant later. Vogt had had no idea of Metzger's anger and resentment. He'd assumed the two of them were still fast friends.

He had been busy thinking of recipes for stuffed carp. He died happy, absorbed in idle musings upon the topic of whether carp was a freshwater or a saltwater fish.

Another instant later, Jack Scorpio fired off another two shots, expertly dispatching the sentries on the western turret before they could raise the alarm. "Lang! Blackbeard! Wolf! Grab Moses and land there! Everyone else, eastside! Go! Go! Go!"

The two groups of four crashed down onto the hard flagstones, releasing the secure clips on the wing-packs immediately and letting them float slowly up into the air, unguided. Scorpio's team ran for the steps into the Castle immediately, while Marlene gently manhandled Moses' clips; once the wing-pack was off, she opened a small glass bottle under his nose, then took a few quick steps backwards, out of his reach.

It was a worthwhile precaution. Moses came awake with a sudden start, and his massive hand immediately snapped closed around Cohen's neck.

"How'd I get up here?" He roared. *"Huh? How'd I get up here, you son of a bitch?"*

Cohen drew his cutlass in a flash, pressing it to Moses' throat. *"Avast, ye dog! Unhand me or I swear I'll slit ye from stem to stern –"*

"You put me in the damn wings, fool! You took me up there and I wasn't even awake! I oughtta tear your head off and play dodgeball with it!"

"I be not afraid of ye, ye swab! I'll grind ye up for sharkbait and save yer bloodless head for a cannonball!"

Marlene drew one of her .45s and fired into the air.

"That. Will. Do."

Moses and Cohen looked at her, nonplussed, Moses' hand still clamped about Cohen's neck. Behind her, Johnny Wolf couldn't help but smile.

"Michael, much as we'd all love to see you pull Cohen's head off and use it as some sort of improvised bomb, I seem to remember you don't actually kill people, so you might as well stop making empty promises. As for you, Cohen –"

"Arrr!"

Marlene sighed and rolled her eyes. "I'm sorry, *Captain Teach*... you know perfectly well how testy Michael can get if we don't indulge his little phobia. Next time, stand further back."

Moses scowled. "Hey –" he began, and then Marlene flashed him an icy look, and he found himself opening his hand to let Cohen fall. Marlene had a habit of getting what she wanted.

"You know, if God had meant man to fly, he'd be a sadist, right?"

"He may not be, Mister Moses, but I most certainly am." Marlene smiled coldly. "Now, why don't we go and complete our half of the mission before Professor Hawthorne dies of old age?"

Moses and Cohen exchanged an angry look, then stalked towards the stairwell leading down into the belly of the castle. Johnny Wolf turned to Marlene, and the corner of his mouth twitched, almost imperceptibly.

Marlene sighed. "I know, darling." She grinned, offering her arm. "Isn't it all too, too fabulous for words?"

JACK SCORPIO TOOK a moment to double-check the three chambers of his S.T.E.A.M.-issue multi-ammo Magnum. He'd selected his three ammunition packs carefully: dum-dums to pack a hard punch, tranq-darts for stealth – and the third category, the one he knew for sure he'd need before the day was over. The experimental round.

The four of them were inching along the cold stone corridors of Castle Abendsen, taking out troops as they found them; so far, the alarm hadn't been raised. Scorpio wanted to keep it that way. The deeper they could penetrate into the building without raising the alarm, the easier it'd be to smash whatever insane scheme was being built here once and for all.

He turned to the other three men and raised a finger to his lips – *silent running*. Then he flipped open one of the pockets of his flak jacket and took out a shaving mirror, angling it so he could get a look around the corner at the next corridor. Two stormtroopers were walking towards them – SS men, not the usual guards. These two weren't bored and feckless after weeks cooped up in here; they were fresh, rested and itching to find four American spies, and in another half a minute they'd turn the corner and do just that. And then they'd suddenly find a use for those Sturmgewehr 88 machine-guns they were carrying, which would probably mean raising the alarm if nothing else. Sturmgewehr 88s made a hell of a racket.

Scorpio took another look at the Magnum, and winced. Out of tranquilisers again; how come the non-lethal ordinance was always the first to go?

Hell, no time to beat himself up over it now. He looked at his men; Reed was just about useless for this kind of situation – it just wasn't in his skill set. El Sombra would deal with the soldiers effectively, but Scorpio couldn't be certain if he'd do it without a burst being fired. He *probably* could, but 'probably' just wasn't good enough right now. Scorpio needed a sure thing.

He needed Savate.

And Savate knew it, the arrogant son of a bitch.

PERSONNEL FILE: JEAN-PIERRE "SAVATE" BEGNOCHE – MERCENARY (ON RETAINER TO US GOV'T) – SKILLS: UNARMED COMBAT (ULTIMATE CLASS), SAVATE, PARKOUR – PREFERRED WEAPON: FEET – WEAKNESSES: SERVICES FOR SALE TO HIGHEST BIDDER, HIGH LEVEL OF ARROGANCE

Scorpio held up two fingers, then three, then an 'O' with his thumb and forefinger. *Two of them. Thirty seconds.*

Savate nodded, and assumed a ready stance.

Scorpio noticed El Sombra's hand twitching next to the hilt of his sword, and he shook his head once. *No.*

By now, they could hear the approaching soldiers talking to each other in brisk, clipped German. Savate closed his eyes, judging the moment.

Then he jumped.

Five feet, straight up. He didn't even seem to tense his legs first.

Scorpio had lost count of how many superiors had read the reports and proclaimed them a gross exaggeration of the facts – a string of acrobatic feats surely impossible for a human being to achieve. They'd never seen the Frenchman do the impossible in front of them, on command.

With a cocksure grin, Savate folded his legs up, pushing off one stone wall, then the other. He seemed to become a human pinball, ricocheting effortlessly from wall to wall high above the heads of the approaching men. Despite the steel-grey uniform he wore, and the jackboots that surely constricted his ankles, he was almost completely silent; by the time the two Germans became aware of the creak of leather that signalled him sailing over their heads, or the flash of grey at the upper edges of their peripheral vision, he was already somersaulting down behind them.

On the way down, he lashed out with the tips of those creaking leather boots, each foot striking twice in a single second at the point where the spine meets the skull. Neither of them felt a thing; it was like a candle being blown out.

Another impossible feat; although this time Scorpio didn't get to see it happen. He heard the muffled *crack* of their necks breaking at the same instant, and then Savate strolled back around the corner, grinning like a cat, and gestured dramatically to the bodies. "Observe," he murmured, keeping his voice low. "The trick, she eez done, n'est-ce-pas? Notheeng up my sleeves, mes amis – or my trouser-cuffs."

He took a stage bow, to Reed's silent, pantomimed applause. El Sombra rolled his eyes, trying not to look bitter and failing miserably. "You're a show-off, amigo."

"Oh? Or could it be zat perhaps I am simply... 'ow do you say... *better* zan you are, mon cher ami. Oui? Maybe zat is why I was picked to –"

"That's enough." Scorpio hissed sharply, before leading the three men further down the corridor, creeping past the bodies as he went. "We're not here to compete. Come on – the closer we get to wherever this experiment's happening, the easier it'll be to find. Something like this is going to need a lot of computing power, and that means they'll need a lot of room and they'll make a lot of noise. You boys ever been in the room with a top-of-the-line analytical engine?"

Savate and El Sombra shook their heads. Reed smiled. "It's like fifty typewriters all clattering at once, or a roomful of crickets. An endless clicking, even when it's just standing by. If they start performing any serious calculations, it'll only get louder. We'll know it when we hear it."

El Sombra nodded. "Okay." He cocked his head for a moment, listening. "So, when you say a clicking noise... would it sound anything like what's at the end of the corridor, amigo?"

The four men stared at each other for a moment, then started moving forward, in the direction of the sound.

ROLF BAUMGARTNER WAS getting thoroughly sick of his post in the castle dungeons.

He would have preferred to be up guarding one of the turrets, enjoying fresh air and a little sunlight; instead, he was stuck in the very depths of this miserable ancestral pile, trapped in a dank stone cul-de-sac with only a flickering candle for light, babysitting one of the most depressing men he'd ever met. He couldn't decide if the post was worse when Hawthorne was around or when he wasn't.

During those times Hawthorne was absent, having been dragged away from his cell by the SS for whatever nonsense he was helping with upstairs, the dungeon was a deeply boring place. Baumgartner wasn't allowed to read a book to pass the time, or bounce a ball off the stone walls, or anything that might let the endless hours drag by a little faster. There were various speaking tubes through which he could speak to his fellow guards in different parts of the castle, if he wished, but the penalty for misuse was strict, and there were little sneaks like Ehrlichmann around who'd jump at the chance to report him for some minor infraction if it meant scrambling a little further up the greasy pole to the officer class.

When Hawthorne was in his cell, as he was now, that was a little better. He and Baumgartner could play a word game, if they chose, or discuss what the weather might be like outside. Or they could sit in dreary silence, as they were doing at the moment, since Hawthorne had decided to sulk for some reason. Baumgartner sighed; it wasn't that much better, after all. Hawthorne was such an astonishingly pitiful specimen.

It was the way he was constantly cringing, as if expecting to be hit, or found out for some unimaginable crime. And he never smiled or looked you in the eye – just sat there, hunched over and trembling. Baumgartner often found himself wanting to grab Hawthorne by the throat and shake him like a rag doll, just to give him something real to cry about.

Part of it, surely, was that Ackermann and his SS thugs refused to allow Hawthorne a proper room. Anyone would start to go a little mad if they were forced to eat and sleep in a dingy cell without a single creature comfort. What harm would it do to give him a real bed, for goodness sake? Or a window? What was he going to do, squirm through the bars like an eel and make a mad dash for freedom? He'd surely earned a degree of trust at this point.

No, if Baumgartner was ever put in charge of the SS, the first thing he'd do would be to allow Herr Hawthorne a proper room, and a good night's sleep, and some decent food – a little bratwurst would probably do wonders for him. After that, Baumgartner, in his role of Reichsführer – or at least Oberstgruppenführer – of the entire, nationwide SS... would make some changes to the uniforms.

Get rid of the skulls, for a start. The skulls were just tacky.

Baumgartner looked over at Hawthorne, huddling in his cell, and thought about bringing up his ideas for the new SS uniforms. Best not, he thought. It didn't pay to voice one's private thoughts on the subject of the SS; they had a habit of finding out, somehow, and after that your position in the Ultimate Reich could get very tenuous indeed. Baumgartner had no desire to end his career as one of the lobotomised 'human robots' in Berlin, thank you very much. Or was it Fortress Berlin, now? The wall was more than half-built, after all. Baumgartner wondered idly if any of the allied spies had had a chance to see it yet. *It'll put the wind right up them,* he thought. *It does me. Pray God I never end up in there.*

He shivered. The silence was growing intolerable. Hawthorne was in one of his moods, Baumgartner could tell – one of those spells where his frown was a little deeper, the slope of his shoulders a little more profound, his eyes even more eager to avoid yours. He hesitated, struggling to remember the English, and then spoke.

"Cheer up, Philip, *ja*? It might not ever happen, you know."

Hawthorne scowled, and turned away. *Be like that, then,* thought Baumgartner. *We'll just sit here in silence and die of boredom.* He let out a loud, melancholy sigh, tinged with a hint of bitterness. Surely, thought Baumgartner, he was the unluckiest man in the entire Ultimate Reich!

In this, he was mistaken. Rolf Baumgartner was a very lucky man indeed.

If, when Marlene and her team had crept up on him through the shadows of the dungeon, anyone other than Mike Moses had reached him first, he would have died without even knowing about it. As it was, his jaw and nose were shattered when Moses slammed one of his outsize fists into his face, he lost several teeth, and he suffered minor brain damage from the extended concussion, but at least he wasn't killed. Mike Moses, for reasons his team-mates could never quite grasp, made it a point of principle not to kill his fellow human beings.

Luck takes strange forms.

"Professor Hawthorne? We're here to help." Marlene smiled, as Moses took hold of the iron door of the cell, braced himself, and began to pull. Slowly, under Moses' incredible strength, the metal bars warped – then tore loose from their moorings altogether, leaving a hole big enough for a man of Hawthorne's size to walk through.

Hawthorne only sat, looking bewildered. "I... I don't understand. Help me? In what way? Are... are you here to help with the experiment?" His eyes narrowed. "Or are you with *them?*"

Marlene's smile lost some of its warmth. "It's been quite a while since you were kidnapped, Professor. It's understandable you might have lost all hope of rescue..."

Hawthorne blinked. "You're not with them at all, are you? Or perhaps they're just using you. They use everyone. They used *me*..." He shook his head, chuckling darkly. "Kidnapped, you say?"

"Yes, Professor," Marlene said, suddenly unsure of her ground. "You were kidnapped in Geneva, don't you remember?" She looked over at Wolf, and then at Moses, and both of them seemed suddenly as worried as she was.

Professor Hawthorne began to laugh.

Marlene took a step back. The sight of the man wearing a smile was so incongruous as to make her feel slightly ill.

"Professor Hawthorne –" she began, hoping there was another explanation for her looming dread than the one that came uncharitably to mind. Deep down, though, she knew exactly what was coming.

"You honestly think I was *kidnapped?*" He shook his head, trying to control the fits of giggles. "Oh, my hat! They *really* know how to string their agents along these days. Kidnapped indeed!"

"You weren't?" Marlene asked.

His eyes narrowed. "Of course I wasn't. I *defected,* you silly girl." He smiled. "In fact, if you want to get technical? I defected for show, and then I decided to defect for *real.* Because *nobody* uses me! Not even Hitler, not even..." He stopped, as if aware that he might have been about to say too much. Then, quite suddenly, he made a mad lunge for the speaking tubes, grabbing one from the wall and screaming into it.

"Help! Help me! The Americans are in the dungeon –"

A moment later, his head, looking shocked, was bouncing across the cold stone floor, and Cohen was sheathing his cutlass.

"All hands on deck, me hearties!" He growled, as he struck a match to light the fuses in his beard. *Stand by to repel boarders!"*

Marlene looked around for Johnny Wolf, but he was nowhere to be seen; either he'd already melted into the shadows, looking for cover to attack from, or he'd left them to face the music alone.

She honestly wouldn't blame him.

EL SOMBRA SHOOK his head.

"This... does not look good."

"I am so *sick* of you *saying* that!" Reed hissed. "Is that your catchphrase now? Every time we come across something out of the ordinary, we get a statement of the obvious from a half-naked swordsman! Of course it *doesn't look good!* We're an elite commando unit tasked specifically for abnormal operations – we handle things that *by definition* do not look good! If they looked good, do you know who'd be looking at them? *Private Normal and his Tedious Boredom Platoon!"*

El Sombra blinked. "I was just saying, amigo."

"Where's your shirt, anyway?"

"It itched."

"Quiet, both of you." Scorpio hissed. The corridor had led to some sort of balcony overlooking the dining room; perhaps at some point in antiquity it had been used by musicians, or actors, to entertain the nobility and their guests. The important thing was that it gave them a perfect vantage point to watch Herr Doktor Diederich tinkering with his experiment.

He wasn't alone. Scattered around the room were SS troops of various ranks, from the Standartenführer himself on down, there to meet their own future selves as they stepped through from next week, or next month, or next year. In addition, a pair of immense brass and steel robots flanked the Doktor at all times, the furnaces in the bellies glowing with fires akin to

Hell's own. Occasionally, one of them would stomp over to a coal bin in the corner of the room, take a large handful and tip it into the great furnace-doors that formed their mouths. *Zinnsoldats,* they were called, and El Sombra knew them of old; he knew that, should they ever run out of coal, the next thing to be forced into those doors and burned for fuel would be a human being.

"Last time, I smothered its flames with sand..." he muttered, then looked furtively around. "Has anyone got any sand?"

"Quiet. What are we looking at here, Reed?"

Reed frowned. "Analytical engines. Lots of them. Still in standby mode, until the good Doktor starts to flip some of those switches over there – see that bank of levers over on the far side? That's the input. I'm guessing that disc there is supposed to be the gateway they'll bring things through from. I'm not sure quite how it all links up... I wonder, is that an Omega field?"

"A what?"

"Omega energy. The 'cursed science,' according to legend. People who go looking for it have a habit of ending up dead."

Scorpio nodded. "I seem to remember Doc Thunder harnessing it for some machine of his..."

"And look at him now. Makes you wonder, eh?"

Scorpio frowned, and changed the subject. "We're going to have to stop this from –"

And then the voice of Philip Hawthorne filled the room.

"Help! Help me! The Americans are in the dungeon –"

The words echoed from one of the speaking tubes on the wall – then the voice went dead.

"Was that Hawthorne?" Scorpio couldn't believe it. What the hell was he *doing*?

Immediately, the SS troops sprang to attention, six of them running for the exits. "Bring Der Zinnsoldat! Bring both of them! The Americans must be stopped!" The robots, following the new orders, turned and stomped out of the room.

"It seems we are out of time," Herr Doktor Diederich sighed, moving towards the bank of levers. "The experiment must begin slightly ahead of schedule. Cross your fingers, my friends, and wish us luck, or at least a quick and painless death, *ja*?" He chuckled humourlessly.

El Sombra frowned. "We need to make our move now."

Scorpio shook his head. "Not yet."

"What?" El Sombra looked incredulous. Diederich was already flipping the switches, and the chittering of the clockwork crickets in his gigantic maze of arrays was growing louder and louder. "Amigo, in another second it's going to be too late –"

"Wait for my signal, I said! Damn it, I need you to trust me!" Jack Scorpio reached up to brush the back of his finger across his forehead, and realised he was sweating. Through his special glasses, El Sombra's aura was glowing an angry, pulsing red, like a throbbing vein. "Just... *trust* me. I'm asking you to hold back for just five minutes. Reed and Savate will back me up on this – there's more going on here than you know."

El Sombra just stared at him, his lips pulling back from his teeth in a cold snarl.

"Trust me. That's all I ask." Jack Scorpio looked into the blazing eyes behind the bloodstained mask, and spoke softly, soothingly, almost desperately. "Can you just hold back for one minute?"

The eyes behind the mask narrowed.

"Can you?"

PERSONNEL FILE: DJEGO 'EL SOMBRA' (LAST NAME UNKNOWN) – ??? – SKILLS: UNARMED COMBAT, BLADE COMBAT, PARKOUR, HIGH PAIN THRESHOLD, STEALTH, DISGUISE, GUERRILLA WARFARE, UNCONVENTIONAL WARFARE, (CONTINUED ON SEPARATE SHEET) – PREFERRED WEAPON: SWORD – WEAKNESSES: UNIQUE PERSONALITY DISORDER (SEE MEDICAL FILE #ES1007, 'DJEGO SYNDROME')

EYES ONLY: THIS INDIVIDUAL IS HIGHLY DANGEROUS. IT IS STRONGLY RECOMMENDED HE NOT BE INCLUDED

IN ANY OPERATIONS CLASSIFIED ABOVE TOP SECRET
OR HIGHER.
(I'll take the risk - J.S.)

El Sombra spat in Scorpio's face.
"Chinga tu madre."
Then he drew his sword and leaped down into the fray.

THE SOUND OF Mike Moses punching Der Zinnsoldat was like
Big Ben striking the hour – a heavy, ringing gong that echoed
right through the walls of the dungeon. The metal buckled
with the force of the blow, and inside the robot's head, the
complex clockwork that made it function slipped its gears,
cogs and wheels coming loose as the machine tottered a step
to the left before crashing to the floor.

"Now *that's* what I'm talking about!" Moses bellowed, turning
to backhand a stormtrooper who'd been getting too close.

"Mike! Are you okay?" Marlene yelled over the roar of her
automatics, as she aimed a hail of bullets down the bleak tunnel
before rolling back into cover. The SS answered with a fusillade
of machine-gun fire, their bullets chewing great chunks out
of the stonework. Lev Cohen, snarling unintelligibly, pulled a
stick of dynamite from the recesses of his borrowed uniform,
bellowed something about the Spanish Main, and lit it from
one of the fizzing fuses threaded into his beard. Marlene threw
herself down on the ground, covering her ears as Cohen hurled
the stick overhead – the explosion was enough to shake the
whole castle, but it didn't seem to do more than buy them a
moment's respite against the waves of SS pinning them down.

"Mike!" Marlene screamed, over the ringing in her ears.
"Are you okay?"

"I think I broke my hand and I might be deaf!" Moses yelled
back.

"Well, how's your other hand? They've got another one of
those things back there –"

Moses grit his teeth. "Gimme a damn gun, I'll take care of

it!" He scrabbled around for the machine-gun the stormtrooper he'd knocked out had been carrying, but it was lying out of his reach; if he broke the cover of the alcove he was hiding in and went for it, he'd be gunned down in an instant. "God damn it! I need a *gun* here!"

"Arrr, I thought ye were a man of peace, matey?" Cohen grinned, before switching his voice to a parrot's high-pitched squawk. "*Aharr, I be Mike Moses! I pity the fools! Pieces of eight! Mikey wanna gun!*"

"Leave your damn invisible parrot outta this, fool! You can't kill a damn robot! Now quit your jibber-jabber and gimme some of that dynamite before I come over there, pick you up and throw *you* at it!"

"Too late for that, me brave bucko! 'Twas the last gunpowder in me hold!" Cohen spat, then grinned savagely. "Let 'em come, me fine lads! *The noose holds no terror for Edward Teach!*"

Marlene winced as her own guns clicked empty. "I'm down to my last clips!" She looked up as she reloaded – and saw the SS troops pulling back, clearing the way. Behind them, the remaining Zinnsoldat snorted, great clouds of steam and smoke coming from its horrifying maw. It looked like the Minotaur roaming the ancient labyrinth.

"Wait a second." Marlene frowned, concentrating. She nodded to the dead-end wall behind them. "What's behind this?"

"Who cares?" Mike yelled, "It's gotta be a foot thick! Hell, maybe if Captain Crazy here hadn't shot his load we coulda blasted it, but now? The only way out is through these fools and their crazy-ass man-eating robot –"

"Maybe not." Marlene took a deep breath. "Maybe it's the other way around." She stepped out, standing in front of the dead-end wall, and raised her twin automatics.

The Zinnsoldat charged.

"*What the hell does that even mean?*" Mike yelled, as the twin .45s roared into life again, bullets bouncing off the oncoming robot. Marlene was aiming for the robot's eyes, but they were thin slits in its nightmarish head, and she just couldn't make the shot.

It was getting closer. She had to take out the viewing slits *now,* before it slowed. If it reached them intact, it would kill her instantly, then start on Mike and Lev and Johnny. She couldn't allow that to happen.

Marlene frowned.

Where *was* Johnny?

And then Johnny was behind her, stepping out of nowhere as he always did, and his hands were on hers, guiding the guns upwards just a fraction, inwards just the tiniest amount... and when she pulled the triggers, the bullets chewed through the glass lenses of the robot's eyes and into its clockwork brain, and even though it was dead now, just mobile junk, the momentum of the charge kept it ploughing on blindly, even as Johnny and Marlene threw themselves to the side and out of the way.

The blind robot hit the back wall with a sound like a wrecking ball. The room shook.

Marlene looked back at Johnny and grinned. "You too?"

Johnny just smiled.

"We got our way out! Move it!" Moses bellowed, as Marlene raised her guns again, this time to lay down covering fire as her team ran through the hole in the wall and into the next room.

Which, it turned out, was being used as a garage.

For the King Tiger.

The largest, most powerful, most indestructible traction engine in the world, just waiting for someone good enough to take it and drive it away.

Marlene's grin widened. "Face it, Tiger..."

PERSONNEL FILE: MARLENE 'BLOOD WIDOW' LANG – CIVILIAN (PREVIOUS OCCUPATION: VIGILANTE) – SKILLS: PROFICIENT WITH ALL LAND-BASED VEHICLES, COMBAT DRIVING (ULTIMATE CLASS), VEHICLE THEFT (ULTIMATE CLASS), AMBIDEXTROUS, STRONG LEADERSHIP SKILLS – PREFERRED WEAPON: DUAL .45 CALIBER PISTOLS – WEAKNESSES: UNKNOWN

"...you just hit the jackpot."

* * *

STANDARTENFÜHRER ACKERMANN TURNED white, then purple. For a moment, the scream was trapped in his throat, as if locked there by the angry vein pulsing at the side of his neck.

When El Sombra landed on one of his men, sword first – the point slicing vertically down his belly, spilling his guts out onto the floor in a pool of blood and bile – the scream finally burst free.

"Kill him! Kill the American!"

El Sombra grinned, turning in a circle, facing each of the SS troops in turn as they closed around him, guns drawn.

"Who are you calling *American,* amigo?"

He darted forward, kicking one man backwards and stabbing another through the heart as the bullets began to fly.

"God damn it!" Jack Scorpio cursed, leaping after the masked man. "Reed – stay where you are! Savate – with me!"

Savate vaulted the balcony and immediately went to work, dispensing lightning kicks to soft tissue and vulnerable bones, crushing windpipes with the ball of his foot, snapping necks, driving nasal cartilage deep into brain tissue. Scorpio spun around in a circle, the Magnum exploding with brutal thunderclaps as it spewed chunks of hard metal that fragmented on impact, blowing great, ragged holes in what had once been men. The stormtroopers outnumbered them ten to one, and there seemed to be always more arriving, rushing in from every corner of the castle, converging on the slaughter until the floor around the chattering arrays was awash in gore, and the whole room seemed to have become a storm of bodies and blood, an infinitely complex chess match with every move carried out at the speed of a bullet.

And in the eye of the storm, there was El Sombra.

He was in his element now.

He was no longer part of Jack Scorpio's elite team. He was no longer part of any human structure. He was a creature of vengeance, without ties to man or country.

El Sombra had spent the past four years trying to force

himself to fit in, to align his war with America's. He'd mistakenly thought they were the same conflict. But there was one vital difference.

Someday, America's war would be over.

Herr Doktor Diederich, meanwhile, continued to flip switches, the sweat trickling down his face as he tried to ignore the bloody battle going on all around him. A bullet whined past his ear, breaking the handle off one of the levers a second before he reached for it. He grabbed hold of the jagged metal left behind, cutting his palm open as he pulled it down. He had very little choice but to carry on.

In a gun battle, he could be killed. That was a risk he understood. But if he left the experiment half-finished, there was a risk of worse. Some terrible combination of death and undeath, perhaps – frozen in time for eternity, or stretched across millenia, screaming in agony for thousands upon thousands of years...

What on earth had possessed him to play with the fabric of time like this? How much of this had been his own idea, and how much was Hawthorne? He racked his brain to think of any part of the process that had not been subtly suggested by the Englishman – and nothing came.

Mein Gott, who was working for who all this time?

There was no time for such thoughts now. This was the fatal moment. He threw the last switch, and prayed.

The metal dais began to spark and crackle with strange blue-white energy, the pure cavorite layered into it glowing and pulsing with its own mysterious forces. Diederich closed his eyes and winced, and then the glow of the dais stabilised to a steady, throbbing pulse.

"I've... I've done it!" Diederich smiled, suddenly delighted. "It's begun! It can't be stopped now! Oh, this is a marvellous day! Hawthorne was right – the armies of the Reich will double in size, and the Americans will be –" He turned in mid-flow, to look at the formidable armies of the Reich.

They were all dead.

El Sombra, Savate and Jack Scorpio stood amidst a sea of

corpses. Standartenführer Ackermann was still barely alive, on his knees with El Sombra's blade sticking through his throat. As Diederich watched, he coughed up a thick wad of blood, and then his eyes rolled back in his head and he slipped backwards off the sword, slumping to the floor.

"Ah, well. It seems the human error has defeated us after all, *ja*?" Diederich smiled ruefully. Then Jack Scorpio put a Magnum bullet through his brain.

With the last of the bastards dead, El Sombra found his eyes drawn to the dais. Slowly, a column of blue light was rising up from the centre.

"So," he said softly, "I guess this is some big science, huh?"

"You guess right." Reed said from the balcony, "And if you think I'm coming down there, you're crazier than I thought. It's Scorpio's job now."

El Sombra frowned. "Your job, amigo? Here I thought it was a team effort. What haven't you been telling us?"

Jack Scorpio shook his head. "What you didn't need to know. The Yankee Bravo mission is over. The S.T.E.A.M. mission starts right here, and if you interfere with it, I *will* kill you. I'm working on a scale you can't possibly understand, and you just proved you can't handle it." He shot El Sombra an angry look. "I'd take a step back if I were you."

El Sombra didn't move.

Inside the column of blue light rising from the dais, there was a man. He was indistinct – barely visible – but he seemed to be dressed in some sort of duster coat and what could only be a cowboy hat. In one hand, he was carrying a stone – a large, blue, glowing gem that was the only distinct thing about him, almost as if it was the only part of the strange scene that was real.

He had something else in his other hand, but El Sombra couldn't make it out.

Scorpio aimed his gun.

"Drop the rock."

The man in the blue column turned to face Scorpio. He seemed to be moving at half speed, as if the blue light had the consistency of molasses.

Scorpio spoke slowly and carefully, as if taking this into account. "This is your only warning. The bullet in this gun is made from the same copper, zinc and cavorite structure as the dais under your feet – the one that drew you here. It's an Omega bullet, and make no mistake, it will kill you whether you've materialised fully or not. So either way, you're going to give us the rock."

El Sombra looked around at Savate. "What is this?"

"I could tell you, mon ami," Savate whispered, "but zen I would 'ave to keel you. *Comprendez-vous?*"

Reed grinned, up on the balcony. "It's the man from the mesa, 'amigo.' The Keeper of the Stone. You're watching the future happen."

"Last chance, pilgrim," Scorpio barked, and pulled back the hammer. "I want the stone. Drop it and kick it over to me – *now* – or I'll sh –"

The figure in the blue column of light moved, and El Sombra heard what sounded like a gunshot, slowed down to half speed, and then Jack Scorpio staggered back and fell to the floor, with a neat round hole in the dead centre of his forehead.

Even at half normal speed, a bullet was still a bullet.

And Jacob Steele, the Lonesome Rider of Time, was still the best shot there had ever been.

El Sombra stared at Scorpio's body, then up at Steele. The Lonesome Rider slowly reached up to touch his hat-brim, then faded away, as though absorbed into the swirling energies whence he'd come.

For the first and last time, El Sombra saluted.

"No," Reed croaked, his voice hoarse. "Bring him back. *Bring him back!* Without the Stone –"

He never finished his sentence. With a tremendous crash, the King Tiger smashed right through the wall and rolled over the bank of levers, and the column of blue winked out for good.

"I'VE BEEN ACCUSED of acts of treason against the United States, and that's probably true." Reed smiled genially, lifting up the handcuffs he wore. "I mean, as a covert agent of S.T.E.A.M. I definitely took part in missions that didn't line up with the goals of the war. We were playing the long game – Jack Scorpio, Savate and myself, I mean. Thinking about America's interests, post-war. The world's interests." He looked up to the military policeman standing at his elbow. "Where did Savate vanish to, anyway? Does anyone know? Oh, well, I'm sure he'll turn up where you least expect him."

On the other side of the one-way glass, General Zitron listened carefully, making notes. He couldn't help but wonder if he'd still be a General come the morning. The Yodelling Bastards had pulled the wool over his eyes, and S.T.E.A.M. before them. In fact, he'd been played for a sucker since the days of his liasons with the Fourth Earth Batallion. And before them... what? Who had Jack Scorpio been before he studied under Channon? What had Reed been up to before he joined Yankee Bravo Seven?

What did S.T.E.A.M. look like when all the masks were off?

"Quite often, the goals of S.T.E.A.M. and the goals of the country were the same. Take Hawthorne, for instance. He was one of ours – a triple agent – and it was his job to persuade the Nazis to build his time platform, thus wasting incredible quantities of rare cavorite on something that would have benefited us rather than them, if it benefited anyone at all. Enough cavorite for eight hundred wing-packs, squandered. Not to mention all those logic arrays – crushed under Marlene's new toy." He grinned. "You'll find over the next few months the Luftwaffe become rather easier to handle, and robot production in the Fatherland takes a significant dip. Just watch out for Fortress Berlin, that's all." He chuckled dryly. "You did know about that?"

Zitron leaned forward and picked up the speaking-tube in front of him. "If Hawthorne was one of ours... or rather yours..."

"Why did he decide to warn the Nazis about the 'rescue mission'? Well, he did resent our intrusion into his life; we were more than a little heavy-handed about recruiting him, but you have to understand what a prize he was for our side."

He smiled enigmatically. Zitron sighed, wondering what *our side* meant this time.

Reed continued, frowning. "I have to assume, based on the evidence, that he wanted to claim the Stone for himself, and we showed up ahead of his schedule. He must have found out what it really was..."

The General sighed again. "What was the Stone, Doctor Reed?" Reed considered the question for a moment, as if he wasn't quite certain himself.

"I won't go into the science. I'll just say that if I'm right – and I am – the Stone is a potentially limitless energy source for mankind. If the Devil's Eye Incident is even half true, we're looking at an infinite supply of cavorite at the very least. The very *least.*" He took a breath. He was getting excited. "We'd better hope we can find someone else as clever as Hawthorne someday. I mean, that was a man who made me look like... well, like *you.* Too bad we broke him." He grinned again, and there was something deeply unpleasant in it.

The President sighed, rubbing his temple. "Let me see if I understand this. The Yodelling Bastards were sent in to Castle Abendsen to foil a plot that S.T.E.A.M. had generated and fed to the Nazis in the first place?"

Reed smiled sadly. "They had the technology, we didn't. The plan – in terms you morons can understand – was to let them do all the heavy work, then extract Hawthorne and the Stone. Except Hawthorne had other plans, and in the end so did the Keeper of the Stone. So there we have it." He smiled. "Look on the bright side, though – our little plot managed to cripple the German war effort – not to mention stealing the legendary King Tiger and piloting it back to Italy, thanks to the lovely Marlene. In a saner world, I'd be getting some kind of medal." He shrugged. "Instead, I'm in prison for life. There's gratitude."

General Zitron leaned forward. "One more question." It was a lie. He had so many questions – *who the hell was Jack Scorpio anyway? Did I ever really know him at all? Did anyone?* He restricted himself to the relevant one. "If the Stone was as important as you say, why didn't Jack Scorpio shoot?"

Reed shrugged. "Some problem with cold-blooded murder, I imagine. I wouldn't worry." He grinned that unpleasant little grin again. "We'll fix it on the next attempt."

"So what now?"

Marlene drank the remains of her white wine and looked over at El Sombra. "Now? We all go our separate ways. Reed's in custody for being too sly a spy, poor Jack's dead, Savate's vanished – I've a nasty feeling he's switched sides again – and you've quit the team. That doesn't leave me much to work with, even if I wanted to lead."

El Sombra shrugged. "You four guys did pretty good. America's got the King Tiger now, thanks to you. Makes for a lot of dead bastards."

"Well, we're breaking up the band anyway. Mike's a full time medic now, Lev's back in the Navy despite his little problem..." – she hesitated, and El Sombra detected the barest hint of a blush – "...and... Johnny and me are taking one of the new USSA Tigers for a bit of a working holiday, as soon as it's built. I hear deep behind enemy lines is lovely this time of year."

El Sombra raised an eyebrow. "You and Johnny, huh?"

Marlene smirked. "He is awfully good at pulling my triggers."

"I'm not touching that one." He smiled and shrugged, nursing his own *cerveza*. "You know... I always figured there was a chance..."

"Oh, I still haven't forgiven you for killing my car back in New York." She mock-pouted prettily as the barman brought another round. "But if I ever do, I know exactly where to find you, don't I?"

El Sombra nodded grimly. "Six more months. Then I'll have my hands at his throat. I've wasted enough time."

"Six months? As long as that?"

"Make it three. It's not like he'll be hard to find, right?"

He grinned.

"How long could it take?"

THE LAST ENEMY

Seven years.

Djego stared at himself in the mirror above the bar and listlessly sipped his schnapps, counting the lines around his eyes and the flecks of white in his black hair.

The back of his head still itched occasionally where the knot of his mask had rested, even after all this time, but it was barely noticeable – phantom pain from a severed limb. Sometimes, during the night, the memories would return and haunt him – bullets slamming into wedding-guests, tearing flesh and bone asunder, his brother's eyes accusing him before the light left them; but upon waking, he felt a vague sadness and nothing more. His muscle definition had softened and he was developing a slight but noticeable gut, although the days he spent gardening kept him in reasonable shape.

El Sombra had been gone for seven years now.

He took another sip of schnapps, and turned to look through the bar window. Over the tops of the houses, he could just about make out the polished glitter of the Berlin Wall.

Bastard City, part of him thought, but did not emerge into the light of his mind. He nodded. Yes, Bastard City.

Fortress Berlin.

He stared for a moment, trying to dredge up some emotion, but nothing came. A vague feeling of pity, perhaps, for the poor souls trapped there. No more than that.

After a moment, he shook his head and returned his gaze to the drink in his hand, and his thoughts lingered on his brother's sword.

He still had it, on top of his cabinet, wrapped in newspaper, and it was as sharp as it ever was. He remembered the weight of it in his grip, the feel of the sword-hilt in his hand, the little push of resistance as it cut through flesh and bone. The adrenaline rush of the kill. Those times he'd had it taken from him, it had felt like losing an arm, or an eye, or some part of his soul.

And now it rested on the battered oak cabinet in the room he paid for with gardening work on the outskirts of Brandenburg. Wrapped in newspaper.

He still had a scrap of the mask, for what it was worth. He kept it in his pocket, like an alcoholic's badge of sobriety.

Coincidentally, it had been seven years since the first time El Sombra drank.

HE REMEMBERED VIVIDLY that first and last drink with Marlene, although it was El Sombra who'd sat there, not him. She'd been talking about her plans for the USSA version of the King Tiger that was being built for her – the Sherman Wildcat, they were calling it, a little sleeker than the German design, with better treads, and the standard .88-calibre machine-guns at the side replaced with the American multi-ammo model; still, it was very much the same beast. It wouldn't automatically win against a Tiger, but it'd even the odds, especially with Marlene at the controls and Johnny Wolf manning the guns. He'd almost wished he could have gone with them, but experience had taught El Sombra that he worked best alone, and it wasn't that much of a walk to Berlin. As Marlene had pointed out, behind enemy lines was lovely that time of year.

Unless you walked into a full-scale battle between Wildcats and Tigers, of course.

It was two weeks after he'd set out. He'd been ambling, taking his time, killing as many of the bastards as he could. He'd returned to the Luftwaffe base he'd visited with the Yankee Bravo team, catching them in the act of rebuilding. He'd killed the replacement ground crew, then the new squadron as they landed; it was nice to know that he could pull something like that off on his own, and he celebrated by blowing up the newly-rebuilt officer's mess. Perhaps the Luftwaffe would decide that particular area was bad luck.

He'd swaggered five miles north, ducking through the forests, killing the occasional sentry, feeling pleased with himself – and then he'd heard the first explosions, and the roar of the great steam engines. Over the next hill, he'd seen it – three King Tigers together, an unimaginable force. Presumably the Führer had decided, in the face of the new competition from the Americans, to group them together instead of spreading them out, and sent them south to take on the Wildcats as they were sent out from the Italian and French borders. Right now the three Tigers were chasing two of the Wildcats straight towards him, and all five of the tanks were exchanging fire – massive explosions of gunpowder, dynamite and peroxide, and great sprays of .88-calibre fire and dum-dum rounds. El Sombra turned to run back down the hill for the relative safety of the forest –and then one of the Tigers had missed its target and the shell had exploded close enough to send him flying through the air in a shower of mud and his own blood. He'd had just enough time to register that his mask had somehow come off in the blast, and then he'd passed out.

He didn't wake again for eight months.

By that time, the war was all but over.

THE SURVIVING WILDCAT crew had recognised him from the newspapers, and, as a veteran of Yankee Bravo Seven, Djego was afforded the best of medical care at the hospital in Venice.

El Sombra was nowhere to be found.

His mask had been torn off in the explosion, along with

some of the meat of his leg and arm. He walked stiffly, now, with a pronounced limp, and his left arm was all but useless, hanging limply at his side. The Wildcat crew had salvaged his sword, but Djego had little interest in using it. For him, it was a memento of times long past, not a weapon to be used.

Gradually, he regained his mobility, though his arm had lost most of its strength and the limp would never leave him. The back of his head itched constantly, and he suffered from horrendous mood swings, when he would rage against the Führer and the bastards, or weep helplessly, like a child. But gradually, he found his personality stabilising in the gentle, antiseptic atmosphere of the hospital. He found that Djego – so long despised as a weakling, a coward and a fool – was capable of a kind of gentle, melancholic wit that made him popular, although the self-depreciation still occasionally curdled into self-loathing. He found himself falling into a casual relationship with one of the nurses, a sunny brunette named Savina, who relieved him at last, after a decent interval, of the burden of his virginity; when finally she decided it was best to break it off, he took the blow with a grace and good humour the old Djego would have been incapable of.

Djego healed and grew, and the itch in the back of his skull began to subside, as El Sombra relinquished his grip.

MEANWHILE, THE WAR was ending. Castle Abendsen had been the death-blow for the Nazi forces; Reed had been correct in that the Ultimate Reich had sent their most precious resources to be destroyed on a fool's errand. The old-fashioned Rocketeers were being phased out in favour of squadrons of Hawk-Men to battle the winged Luftwaffe on an even footing, just as the King Tigers were being outfought and outmanoeuvred on the ground by the new Wildcat Mark IIs, 'compact tanks' that sacrificed some of the indestructibility of the earlier design for added mobility; it was no good having the largest gun in the world if your opponent could move faster than it could track. From his prison cell, Richard Reed designed new Locomotive

Men based on his ancestor's designs, and they were cautiously tested against the few Zinnsoldats that remained. Very quickly, the allies began taking the cities, then the towns. There were patches of guerrilla warfare here and there, but for the most part the general populace surrendered without too much trouble.

The Nazi High Command had their own plan, in the event of total failure. They were already in the middle of building it.

Fortress Berlin.

A gigantic bunker, thirty miles across, stretching from Potsdam to Werneuchen - a great metallic dome, with walls two hundred feet high and ten feet thick, made of concrete and steel and the hardest known alloys. There were doors into it, that never opened and could not be broken down, but there were no windows. There was no sunlight.

One year after the incident at Castle Abendsen, having managed, through an inhuman effort, to hold off the attacking forces, the remaining Nazis simply closed the door and shut themselves away.

The European leaders debated the strategy. Were they building up forces? At some point in the future, would the Ultimate Reich stream like an army of ants out of its great mental anthill and swarm over them all? But then, what would they re-arm themselves with? Perhaps, some scientists considered, they were building a bomb, some great annihilation device to take everything they had lost with them. But from his cell, where he was provided every luxury as long as he continued to be useful, Richard Reed pooh-poohed the suggestion; it simply couldn't be done with what they'd left themselves. In his opinion, they were waiting it out – waiting for Europe to grow complacent, or waiting for history to forget them. Or maybe they'd just turned the board over and built a place to sulk in.

The rest of Germany was split neatly in two, with half going to France and half to Italy, and their combined forces guarding the bunker against the day it opened. What the Russians though of this remains unrecorded, but Magna Britannia seemed happy enough with the outcome; easier to deal with the French and the Italians than with the Ultimate Reich.

A year and a half after he'd woken up in the hospital, Djego finally felt strong enough to travel from Venice up to the remains of Potsdam, and the edge of the dome. The Franco-Italian armed forces, who knew of his reputation as a war hero, let him pass, and he'd placed his hand on the metal, warm in the sun, and felt the itch in the back of his skull return, stronger than ever. There was a strong part of him, buried deep down inside, that wanted to smash his way in somehow, even though the most powerful shell could not; that wanted to kill every bastard in there, to storm the bunker like an avenging ghost until it was ankle-deep in blood. But his sword was back at his hotel room, and his mask was lost, and he was a man in his mid-thirties with a pronounced limp, and the door was solid steel and four feet thick, and behind it there was likely another door the same. So he turned around and left.

Oddly, he did not feel like a coward. After all, even El Sombra in his prime could not have broken in, and he was only Djego.

There was little to return to in Venice, so he headed west, eventually finding himself in Brandenberg – a French city now – where, while engaged in some cash-in-hand work to pay for his meagre lodgings, he discovered within himself a talent for gardening. It was good, physical work, and it kept him in shape and allowed him to think of nothing but the task at hand for hours at a stretch, and at the end of it, he was rewarded by beauty. The walls of the dome could be seen in the distance, above the houses, like some vast, forbidding mountain, but increasingly, that did not trouble him. He could not forgive the bastards – never that – but he found that he could forget them for a while, as he toiled and tilled the earth, and grew the flowers.

Djego healed. Djego grew. He became a fixture of the city, laughing and talking with the other residents. His gardening business grew. After a couple of years had passed and he had put down roots, he became romantically involved with a woman called Helga Vogt, whose husband had died in the war. Djego did not ask the circumstances, and she did not ask anything of him. The past was the past, and they had a good enough life in the present to let it rest.

Occasionally, Djego would still feel the urges from that other part of his mind, but they were feeble things, buried deep and easy to shrug off. If El Sombra was still some small part of him, he surely knew the situation was what it was, and there was nothing to be done.

Surely.

On these occasions, Djego quieted the old ghosts by visiting the local bierkeller and sipping schnapps alone, counting the years and reminding himself of how much time had passed. It had always worked before.

He was thus engaged when the thin man approached him.

"Djego the poet?"

Djego blinked, turning to study the newcomer. He was tall, thin and bald, with sharp green eyes, deeply tanned skin and a curious blond-and-black stubble that seemed to cover most of his face. He seemed uncomfortable in his crisp black suit, though it fitted him excellently.

"No, that's not me," Djego said, warily. "I haven't written poetry since I was a teenager. I am Djego Rossi" – they had given him the surname at the hospital, for records purposes; it was a traditional placeholder – "or, if you prefer to address a man by his job description, Djego the Gardener." He half-smiled and fumbled in the pocket of his shirt for a business card. "My schedule is fairly full at the moment, but if you have any weeding that needs to be done..."

"Weeding. Very good." The thin man grinned, and Djego noticed that several of his teeth were missing, notably the canines. The effect was unnerving. "Yes, I suppose that's as apt a metaphor as any." He tittered, softly.

Djego sipped his schnapps, wondering if he should make an excuse and leave. "And your name is?"

"Leonard," the thin man said, and grinned again, as if at a private joke. "Leonard De Lareine." He tittered again. It was deeply unnerving.

"You're French?" Djego's eyes narrowed. The man's accent

was very difficult to place, but it did not seem native to any part of Europe he knew of.

"Are you Italian, Mister Rossi?" De Lareine's grin did not leave his face. "Or is it Mister Sombra?"

"El Sombra," Djego sighed, feeling a renewed burst of itching at the back of his skull. It happened sometimes. El Sombra had been a famous figure during the war, and occasionally people made the connection, or discovered Djego's whereabouts through some means, and asked him to tell stories, or sign newspapers, or fight them, and he would courteously explain to them that he was not El Sombra and never had been. Then he would walk away, letting them believe it or not as they wished.

"I am not El Sombra, my friend," he heard himself say, "and in truth, I have never been El Sombra. Believe it or don't, as you wish. For myself, I would prefer to finish my drink alone."

"Yes, of course," De Lareine smiled, and there was a long pause, during which the strange, thin man did not leave Djego in peace, or do anything but stare at him, body twitching strangely. After a moment, he began talking in a low, purring voice. "How could you be El Sombra? You can just about walk, with a limp – not quite run. You leave the sword that was sacred to El Sombra in a dusty apartment room, wrapped in old paper, and spend your time poking at worms and soil when blood is crying out to be avenged. You are a coward –"

"Go away!" Djego snapped, incensed. "Leave me alone!"

"You are a coward in the way that all comfortable men are cowards, Djego who was once a poet. You allow injustices to continue, do you not? And for what reason? Simply that it would make you uncomfortable to end them by your own hand."

Djego cursed, hand reaching to scratch furiously at the back of his head. "Damn you! What do *you* know?" He slammed his glass down on the counter, then reached into his pocket for thirty francs to pay his tab for the evening and slammed them down next to it.

De Lareine tittered, and tossed a long piece of red cloth onto the money.

Djego felt his heart seize in his chest.

The cloth was missing a scrap at the end, and there was mud ground into the fabric along with the old bloodstains; but it had two evenly-spaced holes in it, and was unmistakably a mask.

It seemed to be looking at him.

Djego shook his head and tried to step back from it, but his legs wouldn't move.

"No," he whispered. "No. Please."

De Lareine only smiled, like some great cat.

"I was happy," pleaded Djego. "Doesn't that matter to you?" He picked up the cloth in trembling fingers, looking into the empty eyeholes. "Doesn't that mean anything?"

There was no answer. The barman looked up for a moment from polishing the steins, and shrugged. The other patrons of the bierkeller did not even notice anything was happening.

"I was happy," Djego choked, and then, in one spasmodic motion, he pulled the mask onto his face, and secured it tightly, so that the knot once again rested at the back of his head, where it belonged; so tightly that it might never come off again.

El Sombra looked at his hands.

He prodded his belly, amused at the rounded shape of it, and took a couple of steps back from the bar. The limp was gone.

He laughed, very softly, so as not to disturb the patrons. Then he turned to De Lareine.

"How did you find me, amigo?"

De Lareine tapped the tip of his nose. "I followed my nose." He sniffed the air twice, then tittered. "Come. You have something waiting for you in Djego's apartment, I think. Wrapped in newspaper."

The two of them walked out of the bar, smiling like old friends.

The barman watched them go, then picked up the thirty francs.

THE DOOR TO Berlin swung open with a low creak, and El Sombra stepped inside, De Lareine padding behind him.

Outside the metal dome, it was a late summer afternoon, passing into early evening. Inside, it was a black, moonless night. What little light there was came from an oil lamp De Lareine held, although El Sombra could make out the occasional pinprick of light ahead of them.

"How did we get in?" El Sombra muttered. "The Franco-Italian forces have been banging on this door with explosive shells every day for years, and you just knock a few times and it opens for you." He frowned, hefting his brother's sword.

De Lareine tittered and smiled his gap-toothed smile. "The doors are controlled by clockwork arrays, wound every day by the human robots of Berlin. You know of them?"

El Sombra shuddered. "People conditioned to be robots, because they couldn't afford to mass-produce the advanced droids Magna Britannia has. They tried to turn my hometown into a human robot factory." He glanced at the thin man. "You already knew about that, didn't you, amigo?"

"I did. Look, there's one now." He pointed at a figure in the distance, walking stiffly along the road ahead – a woman of thirty, beautiful once, but now sallow-skinned and hollow-cheeked, her head shaved and a tattooed number gracing one temple. On the other was a lobotomy scar. She had not eaten in some days, and her teeth were black, as if before that she had eaten nothing but rotting meat for some considerable time. She passed them without comment, eyes staring dully ahead, as she walked her circuit of Fortress Berlin, moving from task to task.

El Sombra felt suddenly nauseous. It was as if De Lareine had conjured her from the air by speaking of her. De Lareine's smile widened, as if to confirm the notion. *"Now go not backward. No, be resolute,"* he said, and El Sombra knew he was quoting something, but what it was he had no idea.

After a pause, the stranger spoke again. "The knock is a password. It is heard by the machines and the signal is given for the door to open. It's supposed to be used from inside, but the signal works both ways."

"People can't open the door from the inside without the

code?" El Sombra said, surprised, then he shook his head. "No, of course not. Nobody gets to escape."

He looked around as they walked, at the deserted countryside, the empty buildings, the endless night. Occasionally, on the road, the two of them would see one of the Nazis, cold and dead, riddled with bullets or stab wounds, occasionally beaten to death with bare hands.

De Lareine tittered softly.

"How do you know the knock?" El Sombra asked, suddenly.

De Lareine looked at him for a moment. "Suspicious of me? Going to turn on me?" He tittered. "Will we fight?"

El Sombra scowled. "Yes; maybe; and it depends on whether you answer the question. Speak."

The tall, strange man licked his lips. "It's my job to know things. I'm an agent."

El Sombra's eyes narrowed. "Of S.T.E.A.M.?"

"S.T.E.A.M. no longer exists, but yes. Once you take S.T.E.A.M.'s mask off, we are what you find underneath. Agents of the Queen."

"Victoria?" El Sombra blinked, dumbfounded. Surely *she* couldn't be... no, not after what had happened.

"No. The other Queen." De Lareine smirked. "The more important one. She has decided it would be best for the world to come if the Führer, too, no longer existed."

El Sombra raised an eyebrow. "So why involve me, amigo? I mean, I wouldn't miss it for the world, but..." He stepped over the rotting corpse of an *Oberstgruppenführer*. Something had been eating it.

In the distance, one of the human robots slowly trudged across the road, between buildings.

"The Queen knows you." De Lareine grinned. "Eleven years ago, in New York. You made quite an impression. She remembered this was an ambition of yours." He grinned. "Aren't we generous?"

El Sombra frowned. "I don't need S.T.E.A.M. in my life, or whatever you call yourself now." He muttered petulantly, almost under his breath. "I was doing fine on my own."

"You *were* doing fine on your own, weren't you?" De Lareine smirked. "You had a good job, working with your hands. You were trying to fall in love. You were content. But you weren't walking through a city of death in an endless night to kill the man who murdered your soul, were you? No. For that, you did need us." He let out another noxious giggle. "You made your bargain, El Sombra. Too late now."

El Sombra decided not to reply to that.

"WHAT HAPPENED HERE?"

The corpses were piled in the streets, and the stench of putrefaction was so bad that El Sombra and De Lareine had been forced to hold their hands over their faces from a mile distant; eventually, the thin man had produced a pair of breathing-masks to fit over the mouth and nose and block the very worst of it, for which El Sombra was grateful. Here and there, the Nazis were pushed into great, obscene piles of flyblown flesh, as if some attempt had been made to clear them from the streets, and every so often one of the city's remaining human robots would stagger mechanically through the stink and the flies, retching despite itself. One, an old man, collapsed in front of them, and when El Sombra checked his pulse he had already died; another they saw in the distance, engaged in pulling rotting meat from the bones of the dead and chewing mindlessly at it.

"They were sealed in." De Lareine smiled. "The Ultimate Reich had a history of thinking big; Fortress Berlin was to be a gigantic bunker to control the war and the world from. Then... Castle Abendsen. And suddenly the war was lost, thrown away, and the bulk of the high command were locked inside their bunker waiting for an opportunity that would never come. There was talk of remaining in the bunker for a thousand years, like a Phoenix in its egg. The kind of grand plan the Führer was known for coming up with. And in a thousand years, he would still be here to see it." Another titter. El Sombra was finding himself as unnerved as Djego was by it.

"So they were all sealed in. Outside, there were jews, and blacks, and other races, and travellers, and homosexuals, and everyone else they wanted to eradicate; inside, only themselves. Aryans. Their dream of a pure Aryan world, on a tiny scale."

El Sombra sighed. "But some were more Aryan than others, amigo?"

"Exactly!" De Lareine laughed, mockingly, as he swept his arms wide to take in all the corpses littered around them. "It helped that food was becoming scarce. No sunlight, you see. A diet composed principally of mushrooms. It's shocking nobody thought of it earlier." He sniggered. "But people were growing discontent. And in the face of discontent..."

"...they found someone to blame."

"The redheads were first. Oh, they defended themselves tooth and nail, but eventually the city was made pure once again. You will find the bulk of their bodies in great storage-houses, the remainder in the form of ash. After that, brunettes, and once the problem of hair had been sorted out, those whose eye colour differed from the correct shade of blue. Then those with freckles or blemishes on the skin. And of course, anyone with a physical or mental deformity had to go, which was increasingly everyone." He smiled, as if savouring the thought. "Mushrooms are no diet."

El Sombra shuddered. "I can guess the rest."

"Eventually, it was just the immortal Führer and his closest and most Aryan underlings. When they finally turned on each other, it was just a fight over whether or not they'd be allowed out. And that was that. The end of the Ultimate Reich."

"How do you know all this, amigo?"

"Many spies have many eyes, my friend. We know because we watched." De Lareine smiled his maddening, unsettling smile, as if trying to keep a giggle from spilling out. "We have certain technologies available to us that you would describe as magic, but are quite common in our homeland."

El Sombra nodded. "You're from Zor-Ek-Narr. The Forbidden Kingdom."

"I wondered when you'd guess."

The eyes behind the mask narrowed, as El Sombra took in the all-over stubble, and the catlike twitch of De Lareine's walk, and the canine teeth that had been surgically removed to better allow him to blend in with *Homo Sapiens*. "You're a Leopard Man."

De Lareine grinned.

"So Doc Thunder's ex-girlfriend is the Secret Queen of the World." El Sombra shrugged. "Why doesn't that surprise me?"

"The Queen was the first to exist in this world, along with the original Keeper of the Stone, the Shaper of us All and the Weeper of Stars, whose domain was sorrow. And the Sacrificial Lamb, of course, but there are always sacrifices, aren't there?" The cat-man sniggered. El Sombra could hear the capital letters – which struck him as unbearably pretentious – and he didn't much like the talk of *sacrifices* either. His hand gripped the hilt of the sword.

"We" – De Lareine continued, warming to his theme – "by which I mean Us, the Hunting People, all descend from the Shaper's first machinations, which precipitated a great Battle of Gods, at the end of which the Shaper and the Weeper were destroyed by the Titans and the Keeper set free from –"

"Who else was in this mythology of yours?" El Sombra interrupted. "The Peeper? The Leaper? The Creeper? Not that I'm saying Maya made all this up to keep you lot in line, amigo, but she could have picked better names."

"Not a fan of mythology?" De Lareine giggled. "But here we are, in the realm of Dis, among the rotting corpses of the damned, going to kill a Dragon. Mythology's everywhere we look. This is a world of mythology, my human friend."

Something in that jogged El Sombra's memory. "There is another world," he murmured. "There is a better world..."

De Lareine smiled again. "Different, certainly. They're rioting in London, you know."

El Sombra looked at him, mildly curious at the seeming change of subject. "Really? I'll admit, I've been expecting it since Victoria –"

"Oh, not *that* London," De Lareine said, and giggled. The giggle, El Sombra decided, was worse than the titter.

They walked towards the Reichstag in silence.

*   *   *

INSIDE, EL SOMBRA could hear the soft chug of steam machinery filling the air, the puffing of great engines, the slow ticking of clockwork.

He could hear the Führer waiting for him.

He breathed in, ignoring the stench of the rotting dead, and tried to still his mind. But it had been a long time since he'd had to do that, and he found stray thoughts still bubbling up from the recesses of his mind. He had been waiting for more than twenty years for this moment, and now it was here, and his sword was in his hand. His body had become older and fatter in his absence, but that didn't matter. His leg – the one he forced to walk without a limp – was stiff and in constant pain, but that didn't matter.

Nothing mattered now.

When the time came – in the next few minutes – he knew he would be able to move fast enough. He breathed in and out, slowly, imagining the battle, running the different scenarios through his head. The Mecha-Führer, huge in its chamber of smoke and steam, would perhaps rear from its throne, bellowing in fury, and smash one great metal fist down to smash the marble floor underneath, but El Sombra would already have leapt away...

...or perhaps Hitler would unleash a barrage of machine-gun fire from hidden weapons in its arms, the heavy .88-calibre bullets chewing up the walls and floor and even the ceiling as El Sombra dodged like a dervish, his blade coming close and closer to the hydraulics that were the Führer's lifeblood...

...or perhaps there would be time for conversation first, a few deathless words exchanged between the most evil man in the world and the avenging ghost who had walked across a planet to destroy him utterly...

...or El Sombra would fight to a standstill, and then one great fist would reach out and crush him, ending his life and the hopes of the millions of unavenged dead the monster had left in his wake...

...or Adolf Hitler would fall to his metal knees and weep, and beg forgiveness...

...or this, or that, or any other thing.

El Sombra smiled, and he was standing at the door to the great central chamber, the office of the Führer. At the door of history.

He announced himself with a laugh.

It was rich, and full, and it carried over the dead and rotting corpses strewn through the corridors of the Reichstag. It touched the human robots milling endlessly through the streets on their meaningless tasks, making them look up in the endless darkness and remember, if only for a moment. Even De Lareine lost his maddening smile for a brief instant in the face of it.

It was such a laugh...

Then, El Sombra opened the door to the Office of the Führer, and stepped through.

The Führer was waiting for him.

The massive metal body, more than three stories in height, sat upon a vast iron throne, motionless. The immense bronze head, frozen forever into an expression of pure hate, gazed down at El Sombra with black, empty eyes. The weapons bristling from every part of its body could, he knew, destroy him in an instant.

All around them, there were the sounds of machinery, endlessly grinding and turning and clicking in the walls and floor, but the Mecha-Führer was completely silent, utterly motionless.

In the centre of its chest rested a tank of toxic green fluid, and on the surface of the fluid, a human brain floated, like the corpse of a goldfish.

It was quite dead.

El Sombra stared at the Führer for a long moment. Eventually, he spoke, and his voice was cracked and raw, and choked with rage.

"Is... is this a *joke*?"

His hands shook like an old man's.

De Lareine smiled his terrible smile. "The Führer's body needed a great deal of maintenance and repair, you know. After two years, one of the processes delivering oxygen to his brain failed... and there was nobody left to repair it. He died, slowly." Another smile. "There would have been some pain, at the end."

El Sombra slammed his fist into the great iron throne on which the massive body sat, shattering his knuckles and tearing the skin from them. He didn't seem to notice. *"Some pain,"* he choked, through gritted teeth.

"They were going to upgrade him." De Lareine shrugged. "There was another body waiting for his brain to be transferred to in the laboratory, but the final trouble started before anything could be done. There was some speculation on whether one of the higher-ranking Nazis would implant themselves in that second body and stage a coup. What a coup it would have been, eh?" Another infuriating giggle. "Two giant robots smashing each other through the ruins of the Reichstag, and to the victor goes the Ultimate Reich. That would have been an ending, wouldn't it? But I suppose nobody wanted to give their humanity up." He grinned, wider. "If only you'd arrived sooner, eh?"

El Sombra was still staring into the empty, dead eyes of the Führer.

"This isn't right," he said, eventually, in a strangled voice. "How... how can it end like *this*?"

"Why shouldn't it?" De Lareine shrugged. "Here's a thought. Maybe, despite his twenty-year tantrum and all his dressing up, spoilt little Djego is not the centre of the universe –"

El Sombra turned, face red, tears streaming from his eyes, and charged at De Lareine, slashing his sword in an arc aimed at tearing the guts from the Leopard Man. But El Sombra was forty years old, and a little fat, and his leg hurt, and De Lareine was faster even than his father, who had won the Last Great Games in the golden temple of Ig-Nur-Hoth, against a mechanical minotaur built for the purpose.

El Sombra crashed down onto the floor, into the soot

scattered about, as De Lareine walked around him, speaking in his nonchalant purr. "Did you really believe Adolf Hitler would wait around for your sword? Did you not imagine that it might be *better* for him to seal himself off in a hole to die, instead of murdering and enslaving continents until you finally got around to him? Did you think you were the hero of your own little story, El Sombra, with your mask and your laugh and your –"

"Shut up!" El Sombra cried out, scrambling to his feet, the sword shaking in his hand, tears and snot running down his face. *"He was mine! He was mine to kill!"* He lifted the sword, the tip trembling. *"Bring him back,"* he screamed, *"do you hear me? Bring him back to life!"*

De Lareine had to laugh at that.

El Sombra lunged haphazardly forward, slashing blindly. De Lareine languidly ducked the wild stroke, then stepped aside, allowing the masked man to lumber past him like a bull past a matador. Then, before El Sombra could lose his footing again, De Lareine turned and struck, aiming the heel of his hand at the middle of El Sombra's back.

There was a sickening *crack,* like the branch of a rotten tree, and El Sombra crashed once more onto the filthy marble floor, and this time he did not get up again.

After a moment, he spoke in a small, weak voice, like a little boy's. "I can't... I can't move my..." He swallowed, staring into the distance. "What happened?"

"Life," De Lareine replied. He sniffed the air, twice, then left the room.

"Don't go –" El Sombra called after him, but he was already gone. The minutes passed, and though El Sombra felt no pain, he could feel himself growing weaker, and his vision was starting to blur. He wanted to look up at the lifeless robot towering over him – to make his last sight the dead brain floating in its tank, as if that would bring him closure – but he found he could not turn his head.

"How could it end this way?" De Lareine's voice echoed from the corridor, along with the rattle of metal on metal. "Because it was *always* going to end this way. You were always part of the Queen's history, little Djego, passed from Queen to Queen... a Chinese whisper in an empty room... a joke in reverse... first the laughter, then the sick, twisted *punchline.*" He squatted in El Sombra's line of vision, the tray of surgical instruments in his hands, letting him see the scalpel, the chisel, the saw, the tank of nutrients waiting for the brain. "You'll understand in the end, don't worry. You'll look back and laugh."

"No," said Djego, in a small, frightened voice, as the tears dampened the red cloth over his eyes. De Lareine only smiled.

"Your chariot awaits," the Leopard Man said, and began to cut.

THE DOOR TO the dome opened again at sunrise.

From inside, there was the ugly sound of metal on concrete, of something impossibly large and heavy being dragged by something even larger.

Then the metal man emerged from his hole, dragging the corpse of the Führer behind him.

They were both around three stories tall, although the metal man was slightly taller, and from a distance they might have looked the same; but on closer inspection there was little resemblance. One – the dead Führer – was a fearsome construction of sharp edges and jagged metal, exposed pistons and gears scraping against the earth. Its ugly bronze head was contorted into an expression of endless rage and hate, and in the glass tank at the centre of its chest, a lump of dead flesh still floated obscenely, visible to the world.

The metal man was of more modern design – a thing of sleek muscle and sinew sculpted in steel and copper, whose inner workings gently whirred and purred where the Führer's had screamed and ground. His body had never been customised to suit its original purpose, so he wore no swastika, and he was thankful for that. The bronze head that sat atop his great shoulders was similarly unsculpted – a placeholder, bald, and possessed of the serene expression of a shop window dummy, or perhaps a Buddhist monk.

Like the Führer, the metal man's chest contained a tank of life-giving fluid, though this one was opaque rather than transparent. To the undiscerning eye, the metal man would appear a simple robot, although a very large one. Nevertheless, the tank contained a human brain, and unlike the Führer's, it would need little in the way of support. The brain in the metal man's chest would, perhaps, live for thousands of years.

He wondered how he would spend the time.

He remembered little of his former life; he had been a man named El Sombra, or perhaps Djego. He had been stupid – he realised that now – but that was something he would never be again.

Apart from that, there was only a succession of faces, the memory of laughter and of a final, awful betrayal that had destroyed him. But there was also the sense that a great and terrible mission had ended at last, and it was time for a new life to begin. Perhaps, as time went by, he might recall more of his past; for now, there was only the wonder of being alive, and new, and filled with purpose.

He knew he would have to explain himself, to convince the humans who would come for him that he was not their enemy, but he was confident that he could do that. The calculating arrays inside him were whirring efficiently, supplied by the data from his living brain, and he knew he was much more now than he had been. Yes, he could explain.

He could explain everything to everyone.

The metal man took a last look back at the great dome of Fortress Berlin. Somewhere in there, the Leopard Man was hunting, freed from his own mission. And in the Führer's old office, the empty, lifeless clay of El Sombra – or was it Djego? – lay, discarded, like a butterfly's cocoon.

The metal man thought on this, as the Führer rusted at his feet and the tanks began to approach from over the hills ahead.

He would need a new name.

PLUTO

"Even if someone walked through that one, I'd still believe it," Carina Contreras-Ortega said. She was looking through a window into a minimally decorated room, where two people, a man and a woman, had been playing the Japanese game Go for some considerable time, each of them lost in thought. Occasionally, Carina thought she heard a frustrated sigh, or saw one of them make a tiny movement, but for the most part they simply stared at the pieces on the board, which were all a uniform grey. There was no way to tell which piece was on which side, or whose move it was.

Except there was no room, no players, no board, no window. It was all painted canvas. The breathing of the players, their irritable sighs, the tiny movements of their bodies – all were illusions created by the sheer realism of the image. Despite herself, Carina found herself completely drawn into the world it presented; the posture of the two motionless grandmasters suggested detailed histories, a relationship stretching back years. The pieces were grey, Carina realised, because the true game was not found on the board, but in the players.

It really was a breathtaking illusion, and quite the most realistic she'd ever seen.

But then, illusion and reality changed places so often in France. Carina smiled, turning to the man standing by her side.

He turned towards her, and the clockwork in his head ticked absently, reminding her that he was not a man, in the strictest sense of the word; rather, the illusion of one.

His name was Anatole-744, and he was twelve years old, which meant that his skin was pale pink, but still obviously painted metal, and his green eyes did not move. His voice was deep and a little grating, never changing pitch or timbre or volume; it was the same harsh monotone whether he was talking of the tourist hot-spots of Marseilles or of Nazi war atrocities. The black hair on his head, brushed into a conservative style, was the most realistic thing about him; horsehair, perhaps. The hotel had been very sorry that they could not provide a newer model, but they had assured her that Anatole-744 was fully programmed as a guide.

After another click, the robot cocked his head. His face was set in a vague half-smile that could pass for a number of different emotions at once, but Carina was getting better at reading his body language, and when he spoke, she read mild confusion into the metallic drone of his voice.

Or the illusion of it, at least.

"I'm sorry, Madame Ambassador, I do not understand," he said, then straightened, awaiting new input.

She smiled, searching for the correct terms to explain it. "I was referring to an experience unique to myself," she said.

Anatole-744 nodded. "I see. Human experiences are fascinating to me," he said. "I would like to hear more about this one."

She almost laughed out loud. It was the third time he'd said that in response to some statement she'd made. The first time, she'd taken it at face value, as an honest expression of curiosity, but now the illusion of humanity was slipping and she found herself amused by the naked programming beneath; people liked talking about themselves, so the guide would invite them to do just that.

She considered telling Anatole-744 that she had once been

a turtle swimming in a giant bowl of rice, just to watch him accept it without a qualm and relate the anecdote to some piece of tourist ephemera. Instead, she told him the truth.

"Once I saw a painting so realistic that for years I thought it was the view from the window." She smiled, then continued, without knowing why. The memories still disturbed her. "It was painted over my window, to make me think things hadn't changed after the Nazis..." – she shuddered – "...after the Nazis invaded my hometown. My father was trying to protect me; I never quite forgave him for it."

She turned her head to Anatole-744, expecting him to break in with a comment about some tourist exhibit in Marseilles that related to the Ultimate Reich, or windows, or fathers, some destination she hadn't seen yet. Instead, he kept a respectful silence, and she found herself warming to him, almost forgetting that all his responses were built into the clockwork in his head and chest.

"I was imprisoned behind those paintings for nine years, until our village was liberated," she continued. "Actually, the man who freed us went on to be quite a big name in the war. I heard rumours he'd retired and was living in Germany, but by the time I went looking for him he was long gone." She shrugged. "But at one point he was quite the minor celebrity... have you ever heard of El Sombra?"

There was a clatter of gears and tiny wheels inside Anatole-744's robot brain, and he seemed to shudder. Eventually he responded, haltingly. "No, Madame Ambassador. That story was fascinating to me. May I make a recommendation?"

Carina smiled wanly. *Ah, here it comes.* "Please," she said, politely.

There was another long clicking and whirring of gears, then a great grinding whine from inside Anatole-744's head, and Carina stepped forward suddenly, to touch the robot's sleeve. "Are you all right?"

"That story was f-f-fascinating to me," Anatole-744 said, his hands shaking. "May I make a recommendation?"

"We should get you to a –" Carina started, and stopped. She

was going to say *doctor,* but that wasn't the right word. The illusion again. "A – a mechanic. You sound in pain."

"May I recommend – mend – mend –" Anatole-744 stuttered, "that you visit Pluto?"

Carina blinked. "The planet?"

"Yes. No. Yes." Anatole-744 stumbled backwards, crashing to the floor. "May I recommend Pluto. Pluto."

Carina knelt at his side, tearing open his shirt to reveal the pink-painted metal underneath. She looked for a hatchway, some means of entry into his inner workings, but there was none, and she did not know what she would have done even if she'd found one. "Can you tell me what I can do?" She asked, desperately. "How can I help? Is... is there a button? A switch?"

"Pluto." Anatole-744 said, at a lowered volume. "Pluto lives in Paris."

Then he shuddered again, and ceased to move.

His green eyes stared ahead, lifelessly, but then they always had.

THE DEAD ROBOT was shipped back to the hotel, and Carina remained at the museum until a new one could be sent to her. For a moment, she had been astonished at the seeming callousness of the crowd, who had simply watched; but then she shook her head at her own foolishness. What was lying on the floor was nothing but mechanical parts, a machine that had gone wrong and broken down, that was all. Any personality she had chosen to imbue it with was all in her mind – *the illusion,* she thought. Her word of the day, it seemed.

She had to smile. She had always been willing to believe a beautiful illusion over reality.

While waiting for the hotel to send the replacement guide, she continued viewing the exhibit, a collection of Japanese art recently loaned to the Musee Cantini. The artist Kichida was responsible for the canvas depicting the game of Go, and also a tryptich of scenes inspired by Warhol; these were scenes of empty cities, overflowing with trash and vegation. In the rightmost painting were two children fighting over the corpse of a dog. The scene was covered with lights of every shape and size, the glass bulbs Warhol had popularised, but they were dark and dead. The only light came from the glow of the moon. Many had said the work was a commentary on society's addiction to coal; Kichida's only comment was that the work had come to him in a dream, as it had to Warhol, but most took that sort of talk with a pinch of salt these days, as more and more artists and writers tried to jump onto the dreampunk bandwagon, with varying success.

Carina shuddered inwardly at the grim spectacle, and moved on, examining a work by the line artist Urasawa; the corpse of a dead robot, captured in ink on paper. The work was called *Pluto*. The coincidence made her uneasy.

Anatole-744 must have been directing me to this, she thought, examining it carefully. *Why did he think it was in Paris?*

Her reverie was interrupted by a polite cough behind her, and she turned to see another android, more advanced than Anatole-744. This one had a thin rubber coating, making him look like a dummy in a high-priced shop window. His eyes moved, and he could smile, after a fashion. Somehow, it seemed more artificial than Anatole-744's motionless metal features. *There's a term for that,* she thought. *The uncanny valley. Try too hard to create the illusion, and the illusion vanishes completely.*

"A pleasure, Madame Ambassador," he said in a musical voice which rose and fell harmoniously, but seemingly at random, like a child's singing. "My name is Jean-Claude-56621, and I'm here to be your guide for today."

"Hello, Jean-Claude-56621," Carina smiled, offering her hand. The robot pantomimed kissing it, his rubber lips brushing the back of her hand in a way that made her wince slightly. They were cold and clammy, and the effect was not nearly so charming as when Anatole had simply shaken her hand on their first meeting.

"I can converse on many topics," he said, as if that was the most appropriate comment to make. Then he nodded, quite unnaturally, at the Urasawa piece. "*Pluto!* One of several pieces by Urasawa that homages one of his idols, the artist Tezuka. Would you like to know more?"

Carina shook her head absently, wishing the robot would go away. "Anatole-744 said Pluto was in Paris."

"I'm sorry, I do not understand." Jean-Claude-56621 smiled, and his eyes moved back and forth, like a doll's. Carina scowled.

"Wait here," she said, in a faintly disgusted tone. Then she made her way back to the hotel on her own, and told the concierge that she was almost sixty years old, an Ambassador for The South American Union, and more than clever enough to use a map and a guidebook.

FOUR DAYS LATER, she met Rousseau as she came off the train.

"Madame Ambassador," he said, in a warm, deep, rich tone, and offered her his hand as she stepped onto the platform. "My name is Rousseau. Welcome to Paris." His hand was warm, and his blue eyes sparkled, and she found herself thinking for a moment that Jorge would surely not find out, though he had the last time, and the time before.

Then she smiled, breathing in the Paris air for a moment. "No number?"

He raised an eyebrow. "No. How did you know?"

"I didn't, until now. You're extremely advanced." Now that she was looking for it, she could perhaps detect a slight regularity about the skin, an infinitesimally plastic quality. And his movements were a little too efficient, his teeth too even. But then, he looked no more artificial than some of the older kinema-stars in Hollywood or Odessa. "May I ask how old you are?"

Rousseau smiled warmly. "You may, but the answer is complex. When you change the head or the handle of a broom, how old is the broom?" He paused, then lifted her bag from the train, holding it easily with one hand. "My body is very new – three months. The latest model. Most of my clockwork is about two years old, and parts of my memory array are almost fifteen. Ancient, in robot terms. Obviously, back then, my thinking wasn't nearly so good as it is now..."

Carina nodded absently as he carried her luggage to a sleek black towncar. "I was going to say that your syntax was excellent. You sound... well, human."

"Thank you."

"It must be strange," she said, musing, "to have some parts of you so much older than others."

"Oh, it's no different from your situation. Most of your cells renew themselves many times over the course of your life – for example, the fat cells in your body are completely replaced every ten years. Other cells, like the neurons in your brain, never replenish themselves, in the same way that the core of my memory array is still as it was fifteen years ago, when it was first built." He held the door for her, smiling. "We're not so different, you and I."

As Carina settled back into the plush leather seating of the towncar, there was a clashing metallic noise in the street behind her, and she turned to see an old, horse-drawn wagon loaded down with scrap metal as it rattled past; an incongruous sight on the streets of Paris. As the wagon clattered away from her, she noticed that some of the metal in the back was painted pink, old severed arms and legs, occasionally a head, mixed in with the other rusting scrap iron. Then the wagon turned a corner and was gone.

"Not so different at all," Rousseau murmured, and slipped into the driver's seat. The automobile started smoothly, the hydraulic engine propelling it forward at a steady pace. Once upon a time, such a car would have been prohibitively expensive, reserved for royalty; now, with the recent technological advancements, every citizen of France could have one, and most did. Rousseau parked in front of the hotel and helped her once again with her bag, then returned to the towncar while she rang the bell at reception.

"Madame Ambassador," said the manager of the hotel, "it is a great pleasure. Please, accept our apologies; your decision to visit our fair city was very surprising and we were not able to have all the facilities in place..."

"Facilities?" Carina frowned. "Is there something wrong with the suite?"

"Ah, *non*, Madame, the room is in perfect condition for your stay," the manager smiled reassuringly. "But I can only apologise that we were not able to send one of our androids to meet you at the station."

Carina raised an eyebrow. "You weren't?" She turned, looking back to the entrance, but Rousseau was gone, and the towncar with him.

TWO DAYS LATER, she met him again.

She was enjoying a cup of excellent coffee in a Parisian café – sampling the fruits of her labour, she supposed – and watching the beautiful people go by. There seemed to be so many of them; the men well-turned out in sharp suits with t-shirts underneath, the only signifier of age a dash of salt and pepper in their hair, the women ageless and uniformly beautiful in chic summer-dresses and kitten heels. Everyone seemed to follow the fashion, and yet no two of them were dressed alike. It wasn't quite Milan – Paris followed the trend rather than set it – but it felt close.

Even the robots were beautiful; very few were flesh-toned, instead painted with smooth pastel colour schemes, or with polished metal surfaces exposed to the world. Her waitress looked quite dazzling – an android in female shape with a high, pointed head, styled like the Chrysler building. Carina left her a large tip, to the stares of those at the next table: a portly old man and his over-tanned wife. They were dressed impeccably, but there was something ugly about their eyes and the set of their mouths, and their conversation was loud and boorish. They smoked incessantly, building a mountain of dead cigarettes in their ashtray.

Occasionally, as she watched the crowds and sipped her coffee, she would try and spot another of the very latest model androids, like Rousseau, who looked so completely human. Despite this, she did not notice him approach until he sat down at her table.

"Why did you tip the waitress?" he said, in his easy baritone. "It usually isn't done to tip a robot. Gives them ideas above their station." He smiled. "Or so I've heard."

Carina blinked. "Don't sneak up on me like that, Monsieur Rousseau. You'll give me a heart attack." He grinned at that, showing off those perfect, artificial teeth, and she found herself smiling back. "If you must know, I thought her service was excellent. And she was herself a work of art."

Rousseau shrugged. "The fashions are changing. Once, people preferred androids to be humanlike – now, they find that distasteful. New robots produced in France are beautiful sculptures, like your waitress, rather than crude shop window dummies like poor Anatole-744, or Jean-Claude-56621. Some of the newer ones aren't even humanoid – I believe there is a bar along the Seine where you can be served drinks by a mechanical octopus." He smiled, absently. "Not so popular, that one."

Carina nodded. "Which raises a question about you."

Rousseau raised an eyebrow for a moment – the exact same gesture she had seen him make before, when they'd first met. "Oh?"

"You are – if I may be indelicate – the epitome of the humanlike android, and your body is only three months old. Unless all of the robots I've seen today are even newer than you are…"

"Then I'm not a French robot. Very good, Madame Ambassador." He smiled. "Actually, I was assembled in Britannia. My name really is Rousseau, though – no number, or Number One if you absolutely must. I am unique."

Carina sipped her coffee. "I was under the impression British android technology had slipped far behind the European models, particularly the French. You put the most advanced robot I've seen here to shame." She winced. "I'm sorry. We have very few robots in the Union – is it a *faux pas* to discuss your manufacture?"

Rousseau grinned again, that easy, perfect smile. "Your French is excellent. No, British robots are still rather clumsy things, slightly behind the Jean-Claude series. My blueprints came from... elsewhere."

"You're stringing me along, Monsieur Rousseau." Carina frowned. "Why did you meet me at the station yesterday?"

"Why did you come to Paris? Your business was in Marseilles – a trade meeting, I believe? Coffee exports."

She fixed him with a cold glare. "You know a little too much about me, Monsieur. I'm not so sure that I like it."

Rousseau shrugged again, leaning back in his chair. "I know what I read in the papers, and what I hear on the diplomatic grapevine. Why *did* you come here, Madame Ambassador?"

Carina looked at him for a moment, frowning. "I've never been, and I can just as easily get the dirigible to Mexico City from here. I'm enjoying seeing the sights." Rousseau did not respond. She sighed, and told the truth. "Pluto lives in Paris."

"Ah." Rousseau smiled. "You want to meet Pluto."

Carina smiled. "Well, I'd like to know who he is first."

Rousseau nodded. "Pluto is, allegedly, the world's largest and most intelligent robot."

"I never heard of him."

"You won't have, unless you spend your time reading freesheets devoted to arcane conspiracy theories. Doubtless you've heard rumours that the current wave of technological breakthroughs pushing the French so far ahead of Britannia is down to assistance from cybernetic intelligences..."

"Like MARX," Carina said, referring to the vast 'distributed analytical array' that had been so useful to pre-war Italy.

Rousseau snorted, as if Carina had mentioned a drunken uncle or backward cousin; the family joke. "The Italians still talk MARX up as the future of artificial intelligence, but it's the French who are leading the field these days – especially here in Paris. And it's all thanks to assistance from Pluto."

Carina nodded for a moment, before she remembered that she was talking to an artificial intelligence herself. "I think it's you that leads the field, Monsieur. And you're not French."

"You're too kind." His smile was almost flirtatious. "I think of myself as the exception that proves the rule."

She nodded. "And Pluto? Did the French create him?"

"No, no," Rousseau shook his head. "Pluto has the distinction of being the final and most powerful creation of Hitler's Ultimate Reich."

Carina spilled her coffee.

"I'm all right," she muttered, as Rousseau helped mop up the spill with a napkin, "I'm all right, I'm all right..." She took a deep breath and tried to keep her hands from shaking. The people at the next table were staring at her again, but they soon returned to their meal. "I'm sorry," she whispered, after a pause. "I just... I had assumed everything the Nazis had built had been destroyed after the war." She took a deep breath, held it, then let it out slowly. "I thought it was all over."

There was a crashing sound from the street; metal on metal.

Carina turned to see a small boy – no older than twelve – running after a blue android in a pale cream suit. The suit was torn, and the robot was limping, and Carina quickly saw why; the boy had a metal pole, and was hitting the robot as hard as he could, aiming for the joints, the weak points in the design. After every strike, the robot murmured, "Well done," in a faint voice, and the boy would laugh. None of the other passers-by seemed to notice or care. A plump matriarch in a fur coat followed the boy, calling after him, "Not too loud, Marcel! Not too loud!"

They turned the corner, and were gone.

Rousseau shrugged. "It's a fad that took off," he said. "Some psychiatrist a few years ago decided that a child's destructive urges should be given free rein on some piece of furniture that doesn't matter. Most households have an extra robot now – an old model, essentially bought to be beaten until it no longer functions. For what it's worth, the children do seem slightly more polite, so there may be something in it." He smiled again, though now there was a humourless quality to it; Carina found herself thinking that whoever sculpted his face had done well for him to be able to convey such subtleties. "There are places in most towns where grown men can go to exorcise their demons, release their inner frustrations. Every gym now has an android hanging alongside the heavy bag, and most offices dress a flesh-coloured robot in a CEO's old suit, with an iron bar or a baseball bat handy. You've mostly been enjoying the galleries and restaurants, I take it, so you won't have encountered this trend." He frowned. "Are you all right?"

Carina shook her head, feeling sick.

"It's not such a phenomenon in Britain – and, of course, robots never did become popular in America or Russia. Western Europe is still at the forefront of technology, so perhaps there's some correlation there..." He tailed off. "But you were saying you thought it was all over."

Carina looked over to the next table. The beautiful waitress was leaning over, gathering the cups and plates, her mechanical movements somehow infused with an impossible, balletic grace. The portly man took a drag on his cigarette, then stubbed it out on her derriere; his companion laughed, a high, shrieking, discordant note.

"Monsieur Rousseau," she murmured, "would you take me back to my hotel?"

FOR A MOMENT, in the bedroom, the illusion fell away, and she felt the hand in her hair as a claw of steel and brass, and his movements inside her as a program, a set of commands to be executed logically, emotionlessly.

But only for a moment.

AFTERWARDS, SHE BRUSHED his dry skin with her fingertips, marvelling at the lack of sweat. *Poor Jorge,* she thought, feeling a momentary pang of regret – but then, surely he didn't have anything to be concerned about this time? After all, he wasn't jealous of the wind-up toy in the bedroom drawer that she sometimes used. It was the same principle.

Wasn't it?

Rousseau had been rough with her, as she'd directed, and now she felt sore, almost bruised. *And yet,* she thought, *he feels nothing. He felt nothing during it, and despite his exhausted pose, he feels nothing now. No sensations at all. A machine.* She couldn't decide how she felt about that. She supposed Jorge wouldn't be able to either, if he ever found out.

She traced the outline of his abdominal muscle with her fingernail, marvelling at it; so perfectly sculpted, so perfectly artificial. No, she decided, there'd be no difference; Jorge would be just as miserable and angry as he had been when he'd discovered her last indiscretion. It wouldn't matter that she hadn't slept with another man.

The illusion of a man would be enough.

The robot made a show of waking, though he had never slept, and smiled lazily, as whatever programming directed him in these situations told him he must. "Mmm," he said, in a voice modulated by an internal array of muted, impossibly miniaturised clockwork, "what are you thinking about?"

It was, Carina presumed, one of a large database of comments relevant to the situation. The illusion had slipped again, and that frustrated her. "I was wondering why you were made... anatomically correct, I suppose." She ran her hand over him; he still felt like skin, warm to the touch. "What were you built *for*, Monsieur Rousseau? If you don't mind me asking?"

"Well, what were *you* built for?" he said, and grinned in that same infuriating, enigmatic way. "I'm... an ambassador, if you like. A diplomat of sorts."

"Who for? Britain? Or your manufacturers?" She looked at him warily. He turned to look into her eyes, reaching with his fingers to play with her earlobe, and the gesture was enough to catch her off guard. "All right," she said. "Tell me more about Pluto."

Rousseau shrugged, lying back again. "Hitler's attempt at immortality," he murmured. "You're aware that since his crippling injuries in 1945 his brain operated from a robot body?" Carina nodded. "It wasn't built to be used for long periods. Pluto was the solution – a new, advanced body designed to last for centuries. Three stories tall, with a great head of brass and an internal brain far in advance of the old model." Rousseau chuckled dryly. "Of course, it wasn't calling itself Pluto then. It was just the second body of the glorious, undying Führer."

Carina frowned. "Calling *itself*?"

"The internal brain, you see. A body that big needs one in addition to the, ah, human pilot – otherwise the human brain would go mad trying to lift one finger. The internal brain acts as an interpreter, like a nervous system... this one was designed to do more than that." He glanced over at her, noting that he had her full attention. "Pluto's internals were designed to augment the pilot's intelligence – boost the IQ, allow the pilot to perform complex calculations instantly. I imagine Hitler hoped it would allow him to become some super-strategist, to turn the tide of the war... but, by the time it was built, he was already locked away in Fortress Berlin, with all of the civil wars, and the purges, and the coups. And so Pluto sat, unwanted and unused, with no programming and nobody to transplant the Führer's brain into it. Eventually, that monstrous brain died a lonely death" – he shrugged again, as if dismissing something of no consequence – "floating upside down in its glass tank. An interesting little epilogue to *Mein Kampf*, there. In the end, his great struggle was to keep a few more neurons firing."

"He deserved worse," Carina said coldly. "So sometime after that, Pluto... turned himself on?"

"Accounts vary," Rousseau said, "but essentially, yes. He dragged the Führer's giant mechanical corpse out into the daylight and handed it over to the Franco-Italian alliance, and himself with it." He smiled. "Emphasis on the *Franco*. The French forces knew what they had, and didn't bother telling the Italians about it, although they suspected. That's why relations have been so tense for the past couple of decades."

"And Pluto is France's technological secret weapon."

"His fingerprints are all around you – the high-speed train you arrived on, the lightweight dirigible you'll leave us in, the shiny new automobiles purring on every street... and most of all, the robots. Every technological improvement to come out of France in the last thirty or so years came from the electronic mind of Pluto. Everyone else is playing catch-up." He paused, staring into the distance for a moment. "For the most part."

Carina smiled. "Your manufacturers."

"Yes. But France will build someone like me soon enough. They're nearly there already, with the Charles series. A little work on the outer casing, that's all..." He looked at her, studying her face for a moment, his expression suddenly serious. "You're wondering if it's Pluto I'm working for."

She shrugged. "Don't worry, I don't expect you to tell the truth. I didn't invite you here for your honesty."

Rousseau shrugged, swinging his legs off the bed and sitting up. "Why did you?"

"Oh, I don't know. Maybe I just wanted something to talk about." Carina smiled, humourlessly. "That's the difference between humans and robots, isn't it? You're informed by a program directing your every action. We flesh-and-blood people don't always know exactly why we do things."

"Don't you?"

She didn't answer him. Eventually, he began pulling his clothes back on. Carina watched him for a moment, still fascinated by his apparent humanity. Eventually, she spoke. "Why did you accept the invitation, Monsieur Rousseau?"

He smiled, shrugging on his jacket. "To give you something to talk about," he said, and left.

SHE WOKE, LATER, to the ringing of the telephone.

"Madame Ambassador? You have visitors."

There were two of them, and they stank of bureaucracy and academia in equal measure. Apologetically, they explained that a person of great power in France wished to talk to her on certain matters; indeed, he was unusually insistent. She could, of course, decline; they stressed that emphatically, over and over, so much so that Carina assumed they were trying, none too subtly, to put her off.

"I'd be delighted," she murmured, and watched them slump, defeated.

An hour later, she was face to face with Pluto.

"LEAVE US," HE said.

"Pluto, I can't possibly –" the chief scientist said, looking pale and drawn.

"Leave us." The great voice thundered again, and the scientist shot a pleading look at Carina, as if she could change the massive robot's mind. Then he and his team left the great metal chamber Pluto was stored in, shaking their heads as they went.

As they left, she looked up at the great brass head; for some reason, she'd expected to be staring into Hitler's face, but Pluto's head looked nothing like the Führer's; it was quite bald, and serene as a monk's. Perhaps Hitler had wanted a change of image.

Pluto was sat on a huge metal throne, festooned with hydraulic pipes leading to vast networks of arrays on either side; for her part, she was sat on a smaller, more comfortable chair, in front of a small coffee table the scientists had provided for her, complete with a full pot of freshly-brewed coffee. Pluto waited for the door to close, then spoke again. **"They've realised that they need me more that I need them."**

"Won't they be listening?" Carina said, pouring herself a cup to steady her nerves.

Pluto leaned forward slightly, and the effect was terrifying; Carina nearly dropped the pot. Seeing the effect on her, he leaned back again, and now his voice was softer, though still loud enough to echo off the burnished metal walls. **"The room is soundproofed, and I'd know if they found other ways to listen in. We can talk as we please."** He paused. **"They're wondering why I want to talk to you at all."**

Something in his cadence was oddly familiar, but Carina couldn't place it. "I'm wondering the same."

He looked at her for a long moment, or seemed to, through

those great brass eyes. "Do you know me, Carina? Do you remember me?"

She looked at him for a long moment, but did not understand. She only shook her head. His own head bowed, and the shadows cast by the lights overhead seemed to give the great bronze face an expression of infinite sadness.

There was a long silence, and Carina wondered if she should go to the great iron door and bang to be let out; the whole situation was strange and she felt increasingly anxious about the true intentions of the metal behemoth. Eventually, he raised his head. "No, I don't want you to remember. Not you. But then, how should I put this..." Another pause. Carina fidgeted. "I'll start at the beginning.

"Most of the robots now in Western Europe are of my design. All of them have an internal radio system, so they can, if necessary, communicate with each other via morse code, and with me. I know what they know. However, I've found that with some of the older models, this form of communication can be a great strain... it's a matter of processing power."

Carina nodded. "So the Anatole unit who died..."

"Was signalling me across the robot network. I tried to speak to you through him. His arrays were old and near to failing, and the effort was too much for him."

Carina noticed hands were trembling. "Do your handlers know about this... wireless network?"

"They do. I do not know if they are aware of all the potential uses yet."

"And why did Anatole-744 signal you?"

"Because you had indicated to him that you were someone I could trust."

She took a long drink of the coffee. "Trust?"

"I have a question. I know that I can trust your answer."

She placed the cup down, and waited for the question. The room was silent for a long moment, as if Pluto was weighing it up. Eventually, he spoke.

"Is there a difference between a human and a robot?"

Carina blinked.

"Isn't that obvious?" she asked. "One's made of metal, for a start."

Pluto did not respond.

Carina sipped the coffee again. "...You know, I was talking about this earlier today. I suppose you were told about that. Rousseau probably sent a coded message."

"Who is Rousseau?"

She sighed. "Someone I... never mind. I said to him that the difference between a human and a robot was that a robot was programmed. It's programmed to follow a particular path, and human beings aren't." The words sounded bitter in her ears. "That's the difference. A robot can't be a person. All a robot can ever be is the illusion of a human being." She stared into her cup, waiting for Pluto to say something in response.

There was silence. The great brass head simply looked at her. She finished her coffee, thinking to herself. "Except..."

She put the cup down on the table and looked at her hands.

"My husband is a good man, and a kind man. I've been married to him more than thirty years." She spoke slowly, evenly. "I was running a town, trying to pull it out of the hell the Nazis had left it in, becoming more and more involved in the larger Mexican political arena. I had no particular desire to get married..." She laughed to herself. "As a matter of fact, I have a slight phobia about big weddings. I liked Jorge, I thought I loved him, but I didn't especially want to get tied down. But... his mother was constantly asking when he'd make an honest woman of me. And there were people who wouldn't take me seriously as a political candidate without a husband. And my father hadn't liked Jorge, and I still hadn't quite forgiven my father. And I didn't see any reason not to get married." She scowled. "It's like I had a special checklist of all the worst reasons you can walk down the aisle, and I checked every single one of them off before I did."

She looked up at Pluto. The massive robot did not move.

"Jorge is a wonderful man, you understand. We're happy together. I certainly don't want a divorce. But..." She shook her head, looking away. "I don't know why I'm telling you this."

Pluto did not respond.

Eventually, Carina spoke again. "Since I became an Ambassador-at-Large, I've done a lot of travelling. More often than not, while I'm on these trips, I find a good-looking young man who I don't give a damn about and who doesn't give a damn about me and I fuck him. And it fills a need Jorge can't." She shrugged. "I don't cover my tracks particularly well. He's always hurt when he finds out. I always promise I won't again. I always do."

She stared up at the motionless brass face. "You didn't know that, did you?"

There was a long silence. Eventually, Pluto spoke. **"No."**

"So when you wanted to talk to me, you wanted to talk to an illusion of me. When I tell Jorge I won't cheat on him again, and he believes me, he's talking to the illusion, too. And when I look in the mirror and promise myself, across my heart, that I won't ever be so cruel to him again..." Her eyes stung, and she realised that she was crying. "Maybe we're all illusions of people. Maybe we're all just programmed."

Pluto looked at her for a long moment. When he spoke, it was quiet.

"Is there a difference between a human and a robot?"

Carina shook her head. "I don't know." She took a handkerchief from her purse, and wiped her eyes. "Is that the answer you wanted?"

"It's the answer you gave me. And I trust you. More than myself." There was a great grinding of metal as Pluto lifted his arms to his chest. **"I was hoping all the bastards had died. But it seems there will always be bastards, Carina. And those who need to be saved from them."** A metal fist slammed into a metal palm with a sound like two massive tanks colliding. Like an angry god pronouncing judgement.

Carina stared up at him, suddenly feeling a terrible sense of vertigo, as if the floor was dropping away. "What are you saying? Who... who *are* you?"

But she already knew.

"You should leave Paris tomorrow." Pluto paused, then settled back onto his throne. **"Goodbye, Carina."**

Eventually, the doors opened again and the scientists shuffled back in, pale and concerned. It was clear they'd rather what happened didn't go any further. "There are people who want to shut this whole facility down," the chief scientist said as he led her out of the building, sweat trickling down his brow. "We'd really rather this didn't happen again, you understand."

"I don't think it will," Carina said, feeling numb. The chief scientist nodded gratefully.

"Madame Ambassador... what did you talk to him *about?*"

"People," she replied. "We talked about people."

THE NEXT DAY, as she was taking her seat on the airship, she saw Rousseau for the final time. He was dressed in a dark suit and smoked glasses, sitting in the midst of a phalanx of similarly-dressed men surrounding a tall, elegant black woman, who Carina vaguely recognised as having recently married into the British royal family; Maya something.

Rousseau lowered his glasses and smiled. Carina asked the stewardess if she could have a seat in a different section.

The only seat they had was in Economy, and they said they'd have to charge her, but Carina smiled patiently and said that it was just until the stopover in London, and after that she'd return to First Class. It was just that there was someone she was hoping to avoid. The stewardess seemed puzzled, but promised to bring Carina a complimentary wine during the journey.

Carina made herself as comfortable as possible. It was a window seat, at least.

As the airship reached five thousand feet, swinging over Argentuil, she spotted the first explosions.

UNDER THE
RED SUN

THE SUPERMAN STARED at himself in the mirror.

He ran his fingers slowly over his chin, then the bald dome of his head, touching the scalp gently. No hair would ever grow there again, but over time he'd become used to that. Likewise, his eyes would never be the same shade of piercing blue they had once been, but occasionally he felt their new colour suited him better; near white, and icy cold.

It had been almost two hundred and eighty years since Doc Thunder had received the touch of death.

The first fifty had been the worst – unable to stay awake more than five minutes at a time, barely able to breathe on his own, an unmoving lump of poisoned flesh, rotting in a medical chamber in the palaces of Zor-Ek-Narr. Occasionally, during his brief spells of lucidity, he would see Maya looking in on him – at first with love and sorrow, then with pity, and finally, towards the end, with something approaching indifference, as if he was a houseplant she was taking care of for a neighbour. When he'd finally left – when he was finally able to leave – he'd felt a great weight fall from his shoulders. There was nothing even approaching love between them any more.

Monk had apparently visited him as well, though he hadn't

been awake for that. He wished he had been, just once; Monk had died twenty years into his long sleep. A heart attack, brought on by encroaching age and the strain of his own monstrous physiognomy. The Doctor had felt a great, crushing wave of grief when he'd first heard; he still wished he'd had the chance to say goodbye.

But there was a small, selfish part of him that was glad his friend and lover hadn't lived to see what he'd become.

On a whim, the Doctor intensified his gaze, watching in the mirror as the flesh of his face seemed to melt away, then the layers of muscle, until he was looking at the smooth whiteness of bone, the grinning skull beneath the skin. It was a nice trick – with a little concentration, he could have seen right through himself. Or, if he focused his eyes a little differently, right through the mirror and into the next room. From his brownstone in New York, he could read the President's personal mail, if he wanted to, or search for microscopic life in the sands of Mars. There were only two things in the entire solar system that his gaze could not penetrate: the wall of mist shrouding Zor-Ek-Narr from the eyes of mortal men, or the other wall of mist Maya had set up an ocean away, around Britannia. She needed her secrets, he supposed.

Perhaps he should have worried about that – or about the network of operatives she had evidently maintained since the eighteenth century, if not thousands of years earlier – but increasingly, he found it difficult to care.

He had become aware, soon after regaining full consciousness, that his brush with mortality had not weakened his system at all. If anything, it had strengthened it beyond measure. The moment he'd received the touch of death, his superhuman body had gone into overdrive in an effort to save his life, and had remained that way ever since. Wounds healed almost instantly. He couldn't remember the last time he'd been sick.

He no longer aged.

Every so often, he performed this little ritual; he stared into the mirror, focused the strange new powers of vision he was acquiring, and peered through himself, through flesh and bone, into his smallest cells, examining the loops of his DNA for some clue as to how long he might live. He did this even though he knew the answer already.

Forever.

Forever and forever. He was immortal now; that which could not kill him had made him stronger, whether he wanted it or not. He'd never grow any older. Never get any less powerful.

Only less human.

He concentrated, and the eyes in the skull glowed a fierce red.

The mirror melted, dripping onto the floor in a pool of red-hot slag, threatening to set light to the floorboards. It pooled around the Doctor's shoes, setting them alight, and his trousers in turn; soon all of his clothes were ablaze. And he felt nothing.

Not quite true. He felt like screaming.

"Good morning, Doctor. Is that your new party piece?"

The Doctor turned to see Lars enter with the morning coffee. He feigned surprise, although his senses told him exactly where his housemate was at all times. If he thought about it, he knew where everyone in the world was at all times.

Except for Maya, of course.

He quickly blew out the flames – using a tiny fraction of the air super-compressed within his lungs – and turned his attention to Lars, resisting the urge to look inside him. Lars Lomax was another one like himself. Another immortal.

He had suffered a debilitating setback of his own around the same time that the Doctor had received the death touch; he had been stabbed through his invulnerable heart, then decapitated by shaped explosive charges, and his immense head, horned like Satan's own, stored in a jar at Langley for the CIA to poke at. Like the Doctor, Lars had Thunder Serum flowing through his veins – although this was a mutated variety created from a stolen sample of Thunder's own blood – and, like the Doctor, his death had been a temporary measure, an inoculation against mortality. He, too, would live forever.

In the jar, he had begun growing a new body from the stump of his neck. It had taken about thirty years; the mass needed to come from somewhere, so as his body had grown, his head had shrunk, until it was of normal human size – a man's head resting atop a child's body. The Doctor hadn't seen that stage, and the thought of it made him feel nauseous. He wondered, sometimes, how Lars had stood it.

They'd tried killing him again – and again, and again – but it had never quite worked, and eventually those scientists who remembered his atrocities died off and were replaced. The new crop remembered only that Lars was charming, funny in a deadpan sort of way, and that he enjoyed debating current affairs from inside his glass prison. He especially enjoyed taking the position of Devil's Advocate. His little joke; although he looked almost human, his skin was still a bold shade of red, and a pair of satanic horns still grew from his temples. Occasionally, to complete the picture, he would grow a beard. The new scientists thought he was quite the joker.

The Doctor did not think so.

The Doctor had seen inside him.

They were already enemies before immortality took them. Lars Lomax – who'd once called himself the most dangerous man in the world – was a genius on the level of a Richard Feynman, a Galileo Galilei or a Franklin Reed, who'd used his terrifying intellect for evil, even as the Doctor had used his own powers to uphold the forces of good. It seemed like a minor philosophical difference in the face of immortality, but it had been enough to make them eternal foes, just as having immortality thrust on them and their humanity stripped from them at the same time had made them unlikely friends; they understood each other, and there was nobody else in the same hemisphere who did.

There was a word, the Doctor thought, that had seemingly been invented to sum up their relationship, and that word was *stalemate*.

Roughly ninety years ago, the Doctor had had Lars Lomax released into his care, so he could keep an eye on him; and vice versa, because the Doctor did not entirely trust himself, and he felt a friend and enemy like Lars would ask the difficult questions. Like whether trying to immolate yourself with your eyes and a molten mirror is a new party piece.

Implicit in that question were a dozen other questions, a hundred, a thousand, and all of them about his mental state. The Doctor didn't feel like answering any of them.

Instead, he reached for the coffee. "Is this the French blend?"

Lars shook his head, a little sadly, as if the Doctor had disappointed him somehow. "Hydroponically grown, from Kew. Much as I enjoy watching *Homo Mechanicus* recreate Western Europe in their own image, robot coffee isn't really up to par." He handed the Doctor one of the mugs. After a pause, he indicated the melted mirror with the other. "I haven't seen you do that before." His voice had an edge to it.

The Doctor shrugged his massive shoulders. "To tell you the truth, I'm not entirely sure how I do it yet – telekinetic acceleration of molecules, perhaps. It raises some questions."

Lars nodded. "A few."

The Doctor suppressed a sigh. He'd discovered the ability two months ago, and had practised occasionally since then, finding a childlike joy in melting great rocks out in the desert. While nobody else had known about it, the feeling of projecting heat from his eyes had been oddly relaxing; now that Lars had seen it, the whole thing felt grubby, like he'd been caught masturbating.

Lars nodded, sipping his coffee slowly. "I'd be interested to see how well you perform the ability over distances." Again, a hundred thousand words unspoken in one sentence. All their conversations seemed unspoken nowadays. The Doctor found himself wishing Lars would attack him with a flamethrower or a killer zeppelin or a robotic lion; anything but this endless barrage of unasked questions.

There was an awkward pause, then Lars spoke again, "In the meantime, you've got a call waiting. From an old friend."

The Doctor instinctively moved towards the telephone extension, and Lars shook his head. "It's in the study." He grinned. "The crystal ball."

The Doctor nodded, perking up slightly, and walked to the study. He hated the telephone. The crystal ball was different.

In the past two hundred and eighty years, he'd gone from

being the hero of the American people to being a virtual recluse, only coming out to handle the occasional natural disaster, talking to his government as a voice on a phone, an emergency service to be contacted only when necessary. Occasionally he wondered if it was losing his hair that had caused the withdrawal – seeing that stark, angular face reflected in the mirror instead of the warm blond beard. But no, the disquiet ran deeper than appearances; it was in every cell of his body. Before the touch of death, before he'd evolved into what he was now, he'd enjoyed talking to people.

Not now.

Any human friends – and now that qualification, *human*, slipped regularly into his thoughts, *human*, because he was not human, not any more – any human friends had long since died, and now there were only two other people in his life who really appreciated what it was to be immortal. Two people in the whole world he could talk to.

One of them was Lars.

The other was Maya Britannia.

AS HE STRODE towards the study, the Doctor found himself musing on the double anniversary.

It was the year of the Quincentennial – five hundred years since America was freed from British rule – and, by coincidence, roughly a hundred years since Magna Britannia had quietly and almost imperceptibly fallen under the rule of Zor-Ek-Narr, and the two most advanced civilisations in the world had become one. The Magna Britannia of 2276 was a bizarre mix of cultures where Leopard Men and their high priests walked the streets, rubbing shoulders with the mechanical men of Europe and Japan – some so lifelike that there was no way of telling them apart from human beings – and the twilight entities of the Night Kingdoms of Russia. These days, London was so exciting and diverse it made New York look like a picket-fenced suburb of old. The Doctor had to admire Maya's achievement, and it had all been done without a single shot fired, or a single life lost before its time.

As far as he knew, anyway.

A military invasion of Britannia by the Forbidden Kingdom would have doubtless been effective, but it would also have resulted in a global apocalypse; first France and Italy would have had to become involved with a war on their very doorstep, and then, while their attention was distracted, the Night Kingdoms would have doubtless attacked them from the East; Russia had always resented France and Italy slicing Germany up between them without inviting Hitler's most implacable foes to the party, and they'd have relished the chance to take a piece of it for themselves – if not the whole pie. The Doctor was sure such a war wasn't in Maya's plans, whatever they were. He found himself wondering how she'd have gone about stopping it.

Sometimes, he wondered what he'd do in her place, if he were the one guiding the great powers from behind the scenes, shaping history for his own benefit. Probably not bother doing it from behind the scenes – no, use his strength instead, his ever-growing power. Stare down the massed armies until they ran together like wax, bodies shrieking in furnaces of liquid metal. Shake the earth and topple cities with a single punch. Bathe in blood and fire. Rule over the fragile insects, the mayflies, the human species. Until he got bored and snuffed out the Earth like a candle.

During these nightmarish reveries, he found himself wondering just how serious he was, and something very much like terror would creep slowly up from the base of his spine.

Sometimes, he wondered what would happen if that feeling of terror ever left him. If the nightmares didn't seem so nightmarish any more.

What he might do.

At any rate, Maya had chosen a different route.

Instead of starting a useless war, in the years between the Third Great European War and the Fourth – the Robot War – Maya had simply married into what was left of the Royal line. She was a Princess, after all.

She'd used the cultural and social status this gained her to slowly influence politics, parlaying the role of consort into a position of visible power and legitimacy within the British government. It hadn't hurt that the strained Franco-Italian alliance had collapsed when France's territory had been forcibly taken over and transformed into the Mecha-Principalities; she, or rather the late Rousseau-1, had been the one to broker a peace between Britannia and the robot kingdom, which had earned her the plaudits of a grateful nation.

Eventually, her ascension to the throne had seemed like the most natural thing in the world. It had taken over a century to accomplish this slow sleight of hand, but Maya was one of the immortals, and as such she had all the time there was.

The Doctor had no real feelings for Maya any more. Before the death touch, this would have saddened him, but not worried him; now it was a source of dread. He found himself wondering if his ability to feel things, simple emotions like *love* or *hate,* was atrophying slowly, shrivelling like some vestigial gland no longer required. During those nights when he lay in his bed and stared up at the ceiling, knowing that if sweat could come it would be icy cold, he always found himself giving thanks to whoever might be up there for the primal terror he was feeling. As long as he could feel that horror of becoming inhuman, it meant he still had some humanity left in him.

Maya – and Lars, come to think of it – didn't seem to have the same problem. Maya's love for him had cooled, yes – to someone who'd lived as long as she had, he supposed he'd been nothing more than a one-night stand, if that – and Lars had certainly mellowed with the years, seemingly content to potter around the brownstone, making vague plans for future schemes.

They both seemed more emotionally active, *alive* in a way he no longer felt. It was possible, he supposed, that they, too, were feeling that terrifying disconnect – but then, Maya had been immortal as long as he'd known her, and a thousand times longer than that, and royalty to boot; Lars, meanwhile, had never seen himself as being any part of the common herd. Maybe the problem was that the Doctor, alone out of the three of them, had always preferred to see himself as an ordinary human being.

And now he was the least human out of all of them.

"Maya?" he said, entering the study. The large spherical crystal in the corner was alive with a blueish light, and in it he could see Maya looking through a sheaf of papers, signing each in turn; she looked up at the sound of his voice, and he smiled.

"I prefer 'your Majesty,' Hugo," she said, unsmiling but without reproach.

He winced at the 'Hugo.' He'd always hated that name, and she knew it. "Well, I prefer 'Doc.'"

"It doesn't fit you any more."

He sighed. "Doctor, then."

"How's Lars?"

The Doctor shook his head. "Still... Lars. Always some scheme or other. He's talking about colonising Venus – creating a slave race from his own cell tissue. I think it's just idle talk at the moment, unless he's worked out a way to terraform the planet somehow, or build dwelling-places that compensate for the temperature and atmosphere... maybe coat them with reflective surfaces to mitigate the sunlight..." He realised he was trying to solve Lars' terraforming issues himself, and tailed off. Maya shrugged.

"I wouldn't put it past him. Do you think he wants to be on his own for a millennium or two?"

The Doctor rubbed his temple. "I think he just wants to go to war with us again. He misses it."

"Do you?"

"No." The Doctor thought about leaping over buildings, smashing his way into crashing zeppelins on fire over mountain ranges, fighting hand to hand with golden robots and abominable snowmen for the fate of the world. He missed it all terribly.

Once he'd thrown off the worst of the sickness, he'd tried to get back to that, but while he'd been away it had become a different world. People were nervous around him. The President, depending on which of the many new parties he was affiliated with, would routinely invite the Doctor to the Oval Office the day after inauguration; most often, during these meetings, the President would nervously make it clear that, while he or she thanked the Doctor for the sterling work he'd done in the past to safeguard the nation – and while he or she would certainly appreciate any help the Doctor could provide when it came to Acts of God, plagues, meteors, earthquakes or what-have-you – he or she would prefer that the Doctor not take too active a role. "We humans prefer to do things our own way," one President had said, smiling, not understanding why the Doctor had winced.

The Doctor would invariably shake hands, congratulate the President on his ascension to office, and then return to his brownstone to enjoy another four-to-eight years as a useless hermit. And those were the good meetings.

At the bad meetings, the President would smile a little too wide, shake the Doctor's hand a little too hard, and talk about all the things America would be able to do with the superman on their side. How *nobody would push America around now,* as if they'd been pushed around before. After those meetings, the Doctor would again return to his brownstone to be a hermit for four years. Occasionally there would be calls and requests for another audience, but he ignored them, and the bad Presidents weren't bad enough to try to force the issue, or bad enough for him to take a stand, the way he had against McCarthy. They were just ugly, unpleasant little people.

Little *humans.*

The Doctor shuddered. "Sometimes I do miss it, I suppose," he muttered, without specifying what *it* was.

Maya smiled sadly. "Maybe you should go and rule Venus. Or go conquer Mars. Or Lars could have Mars – there's a certain poetry there. Lars of Mars... But you should find something that fits you. You're obviously not happy where you are."

"I'm happy enough," he lied.

"You're stagnating. I can tell. I've seen it happen before. You need something to do..." Maya looked at him for a moment. "Do you still play chess?"

The Doctor shook his head. "Not really."

Maya smiled. "Lars and I still play, for old times' sake, but... it's too small a game, when you think about it." She cocked her head, looking at him strangely, and her eyes seemed to be sizing him up, as though she was weighing something in her mind. She spoke the next words slowly, very carefully, as if worried she might break them. "I think you need to get out of the house."

The Doctor shook his head. "I'm not sure..."

"Get out of America. Or at least out of your own head, which seems to be where you spend most of your time these days. Go somewhere different." She leant back, studying him enigmatically, and the Doctor was reminded of when they'd first met, when she'd seemed so evil to him. He'd been thinking in human terms then; Maya was just old, that was all. So old as to be beyond simple definitions. "You're clearly not well, Doctor. You haven't been for some time. You've been under stress ever since... well, you know." She smiled. "You need to relax a little."

"Maya, I can't –" He thought about the molten mirror, and what might happen if an idle thought struck him in a populated area. About the immense care he had to take, every second of every day, over everything he touched, in case he flexed his fingers carelessly and destroyed what he was holding. His words tailed off.

"I think you have to. What's the alternative? You stay cooped up in that brownstone of yours until you go mad? Is that your plan? No wonder Lars wanted to escape." Her voice softened. "Trust me. You need a holiday."

Something in her manner put the Doctor on edge. Maya was hiding something, and for a moment he had visions of superhuman beings in white coats bursting into the room, restraining him with a butterfly net made of woven titanium. He almost laughed, but he was worried he might not be able to stop.

Maya was right. He did need a break.

"All right," he said, in a shaky voice. "Where do you suggest?"

*   *   *

Paris had changed a lot in two hundred years.

The Doctor wandered, directionless, through the thick smog that made the city seem like some alien planet, and for a moment he imagined himself walking the streets of Venus. He nodded absently to those androids who passed by in all their varied shapes and colours, some humanoid, walking briskly, others clattering on a multitude of metal legs, strange monsters leering out of the yellow mist. The alien feel of the city extended to the architecture; where the old brickwork had crumbled, or been eroded by acid rain, it was replaced by strange metallic structures, designed for mechanoid rather than human use. The Doctor felt like an explorer in an unknown galaxy.

Maya had been right. This was just the place to take his mind off things.

The great robot revolution of the mid-twenty-first century had led to most of the human population being driven out – first from the big cities, and then even from the surrounding towns and villages of France. Even the most organised guerrilla unit couldn't compete with beings who could, to all intents and purposes – by virtue of wireless radio frequencies – communicate telepathically. And while humans were extremely adaptable, new robots could be built for any situation; as the Doctor walked along the Seine, he noted that the streets were being cleaned by a large mechanical beetle, about the size of a dog, spraying water from jets poking from its sides. Once, it had sprayed napalm, to burn guerrilla fighters out of the forests; the humanoid robots passing by tipped their hats to it.

There was little sound. Most of the robots around him communicated telepathically, though the more polite ones wished him a pleasant afternoon as they passed.

The French purges had led to war between robot-held France and Italy, with the other nations undecided about whether or not to step in; however, before the war had entered its second year, Maya had stepped in, using her man Rousseau and the almost-defunct intelligence system TURING to broker an uneasy peace between the various factions, focussing on reparations to the dispossessed French, and then a trade deal that would give everyone something approaching what they wanted. Italy renewed their old alliance with France, which immediately raised tensions with Russia, and suddenly the Mecha-Principalities were supplying them with advanced weaponry, in return for coal and oil.

Especially coal.

He passed a robot slumped in a doorway; twenty years old by the look of him, perhaps a little more. Looking inside him confirmed the worst; his internal boiler had run down from a lack of coal. The Doctor considered using his vision to heat the water inside him to steam, giving the machine enough power to perhaps get home to its loved ones, but he decided against it. His control wasn't the best; he could just as easily melt the robot into a puddle of slag. It was true that if he did cause some damage to these people an overzealous handshake, say, or an idle thought while looking at a limb – they could be repaired, unlike flesh and blood. But that didn't mean he should take chances needlessly. Besides, where would it end? Heat one, you'd have to heat them all. There just wasn't enough coal to go around.

The lack of coal was becoming a serious problem in the developed world; some of the poorer European countries were already at each other's throats over it, and China had – quietly and without fuss – gained the status of an economic superpower by judicious export of its coal reserves. Their own economy was more agrarian, which the Doctor had always thought was a wise move; occasionally, on the rare occasions when he slept – a luxury rather than a necessity – he had dreams of Manhattan as a place of empty, forgotten spires, coated with vegetation, with a feudal society growing crops in the ruins and the cracks in the pavement. These dreams were filled with dead, lightless bulbs – the signifiers of the dreampunk movement, after the death of Warhol. Presumably, they signified what was waiting if the world continued on its present course. Agrarianism was the future, assuming a new power source didn't appear out of nowhere any time soon.

America, Italy and Japan were all deeply indebted to the

Chinese regime, having used up their own supply of coal more than a century ago, but nobody was deeper in the hole than the Mecha-Principalities. Coal wasn't a matter of power to them, or technology, or even civilisation; it was their food and drink, it was life itself, and they got through it at an appalling rate.

The Doctor sniffed the air, wincing as tendrils of yellow smoke entered his lungs; the pollution index was higher in Paris than in any other part of the world, including Magna Britannia, which accounted for the sharp drop-off in tourism. Paris had been a popular destination in the decades immediately after the Robot War, as humans plucked up their courage to explore the astonishing sights and sounds of the City of Machines; it had been a glittering paradise of strangeness and charm, populated by some of the most famous androids of the era. There was the red-suited robot gladiator, Magnus, who could punch through steel... the novelist Zane Gort, whose mathematically-precise tales had been translated into dozens of languages, including binary... Deckard, the robot detective who, through a quirk of his internal arrays, believed himself a human being... the great robot rights lawyer Andrew Martin, who won the 2069 Nobel Peace Prize for his work with Rousseau-1 on the Universal Declaration of Sentient Rights, and lived for almost two hundred years... and towering over them all, the gigantic King of the Robots, Pluto. Tourism, more than anything else, had cemented the fragile peace between man and robot into something lasting.

And now the smog had separated man from robot once again. The robots didn't need to breathe, of course – and neither did the Doctor – but, outside the toxic cloud of yellow mist that was drifting ever further across the borders of Italy, Spain and Switzerland, that had swallowed Luxembourg and half of Belgium, the humans muttered darkly that the machines would poison the whole world if they were allowed to.

The Doctor sighed. He couldn't help but wonder when the Fifth European War would begin, and what his part in it might be.

Thinking of Pluto, he remembered a report he'd read a year or two ago on the titanic robot leader, about how he was working to find a new power source and end the dependency on coal that was slowly killing the world. He'd made some strides forward with geothermal energy, but little of practical value. Still, it might be interesting to talk to Pluto again – they'd exchanged a few words in the early twenty-second century, and the Doctor had always meant to speak to him further, but they'd never had the chance. Idly, the Doctor focussed his vision, looking through the smog, through the crowds, through buildings, flicking through the city like a book of maps...

...there he was, tending to a vast array of clockwork; presumably another iteration of the MARX system, or something based on it. On a whim, he looked closely at the King of the Robots, looking through his mechanisms, studying his inner workings. Most of them had been replaced over the centuries, but the central core of his personality was still as it was; right at the centre of the great brass and steel body there was a small core of parts over two hundred years old, and in the middle of that, there was a small metal tank...

The Doctor blinked, and looked again. He stared at the lump of pulsing grey matter, staring inside it, reading the DNA spirals, translating them in his mind. It couldn't be. It simply couldn't be.

And yet, it was.

"El Sombra?"

"EL SOMBRA?"

Pluto froze at the words.

He was standing inside the massive iron structure that had replaced the French Parliament – a gigantic cube of burnished metal that squatted in between the older, acid-damaged buildings. The interior of the structure was no less strange; in the centre of the metal floor was a vast, steel-lined pit, leading down hundreds of miles, through the planet's crust and into the magma below. Around the outside of the pit, various pipes carried superheated lava from below, using it instead of precious coal to heat vast tanks of water, funnelling steam through a vast network of valves and hydraulics. These in turn powered an immense thinking machine, twice as tall as Pluto himself and several times as broad, a massive network of analytical arrays hundreds of thousands of times more complex than anything ever attempted before. The machine, with the somewhat prosaic name of the Variable Integer Calculator, was in its twentieth iteration now; the VIC-1 could have out-thought all of the old-style distributed arrays, like MARX or OSMAN or TURING, put together. The VIC-20 made it look like a child's toy; however, like all the VIC series, it could not think on its own. It merely augmented what was already there.

The computer was built in the shape of an immense throne.

Slowly, the great brass head turned to look on the intruder. The Doctor had not bothered with the cube's doors - though he could have easily opened them, despite their massive weight. Instead, he had simply torn a hole for himself in one wall, bending the steel like cardboard.

"El Sombra?" he repeated.

Pluto gazed at him for a moment, then responded. **"Once."**

"All this time..." The Doctor shook his head incredulously. "I haven't seen you since – well, since you came bursting into the warehouse..." *And ruined my life,* he thought, but that wasn't fair. It was Jason Satan who'd cursed him with immortality. He couldn't start blaming El Sombra for it just because the man – or whatever he was now – happened to be standing in front of him.

Still, he felt a wave of resentment and anger wash through him. "What happened? All this time, we thought there was no brain inside there –"

"The French forces who discovered me thought there might be, at first. There were plans to take me apart and find out." The voice was deep and loud, and the Doctor realised with the chill that there was nothing human left in it. **"It was relatively easy to persuade them that I was worth more to them in working order. Since then... if something is presented as common knowledge, it will be believed."** He returned to his tinkering.

"What happened to you? Good God, man, how did you end up in there?"

"I remember little. Memories of my old life are hazy at best." His speech patterns were different – more refined, more considered. The Doctor kept waiting for an 'amigo,' but none came. "I remember being taken into Hell. I have a vague recollection of my mind... fracturing. And then... I remember waking up. And for the first time, being able to think – to *really* think, on a level I was not capable of before."

He paused, as if working out how to say it without causing offence. "I was very, very stupid in my old life, Doctor. Most humans are."

"Excuse me?" the Doctor said. That feeling of resentment was growing stronger.

"Oh, I don't include you in that group." The Doctor's fists clenched involuntarily. "If your intelligence is limited, it's because you restrict your thinking. You want to be human, so you think in human terms. You should try to be more like the others of your kind – Lomax and Maya Britannia. Use the full potential of the superhuman mind."

"And what if I'd rather be human?" The Doctor's voice was an angry whisper.

"You never were in the first place."

The Doctor said nothing, but the knuckles of his fists were white.

"You should accept what you are, Doctor. I've learned to enjoy this existence, despite its imperfections – and there are many. I miss being able to feel things. I remember I used to laugh..."

"You were more full of life than any man I'd ever met," the Doctor said, quietly. "And now you're... this."

"Exactly. I am 'this,' as you say. I won't give it up." He paused, marshalling his thoughts. "From inside this body... this mind... I can make things better, Doctor. I can change the world."

The Doctor scowled. He hadn't really liked Pluto before, and knowing what he knew now, he liked the King of the Robots even less. "How? By driving people from their homes and putting machines in their place?"

"Those 'machines' you're talking about *are* people. I'm not ashamed of forcing you to see them as equals. But I have bigger plans now. You're watching them take shape, as a matter of fact." He picked up a huge bank of arrays – easily weighing a ton or more – and slotted it into its place. The machine he was constructing chattered briefly as the clockwork sprang to life.

"The VIC-20?"

"Imagine expanding your consciousness – your intelligence – to hundreds of thousands of times its normal capacity. What wouldn't you be able to do? I've been using the VIC series to build more and more powerful iterations of itself for the past half a century, and I've yet to reach a limit. I've been able to solve problems that have puzzled the human species for centuries."

The Doctor narrowed his eyes. "Isn't there a weak link in the system?"

"Ah, yes. My organic component –"

"Your brain." The Doctor gritted his teeth. "Your *humanity*."

Pluto continued as if he hadn't spoken.

"– my organic component isn't designed for this kind of use. Not to mention that the Ultimate Reich technology keeping it alive is pitifully out of date – it's not going to continue functioning for that much longer. In as little as a decade, that part of me will start to fail, and I'll have to remove it." He paused again, and his hands moved slightly, in a dismissive gesture – the three-story robot equivalent of a shrug, the Doctor assumed. "My personality will change slightly, of course. I won't be able to retain my current degree of creativity or initiative. Still, most of the essential information of myself will remain, and evolve. I will continue to exist."

A vague chill was creeping up the Doctor's spine; a sense of unimaginable, indefinable horror. "So you'll just remove your... your self? Your *soul*? Like changing the tyre on an auto?"

There was a long pause, and then Pluto made a series of short, staccato noises. The Doctor took a moment to realise it for what it was; a mechanical chuckle. "Oh, Doctor," he said, his voice tinged with something approaching amusement. "I wouldn't have thought a man in your position would worry much about the condition of his soul."

The Doctor looked down at his clenched fist, then up at the brass head. The serene expression that the gigantic head permanently wore seemed somehow smug now, taunting him from above. *I should leave,* he thought. *That isn't the man I knew; nobody's how I remember them, they're either dead or changed and I can't connect with them any more, or anyone else. I should take Maya's advice – go to Venus, or Mars... or just shoot myself out into space and be alone...*

Another thought struck him; it was Maya's idea that he come here in the first place. Had she known? And if she had, why would she want him to find out like *this*?

Maybe she'd sent him to confirm her own suspicions. The Doctor felt a terrible weariness settle over him; he wanted to be free of all of it, of the endless schemes of the immortals and the petty needs of humanity. He wanted it to all be over, he wanted to just go to sleep and forget everything, he wanted to – *go ahead and admit it, to yourself if nobody else –*

– to die.

Once and for all, he wanted to die.

But he couldn't.

Well, maybe in the blackness of endless space, he'd find some equivalent of that; some kind of peace. The more he thought about it, the more he liked the idea. He wouldn't even need a spaceship – he could just drift, naked, through the solar system and out into the emptiness beyond. Why not? He didn't need to eat, didn't need to breathe, didn't really feel cold or heat as such – though he did notice it, in the same way a normal man might notice a particularly loud or garish colour.

He couldn't help but notice it, in fact. The interior of the cube was like a furnace.

He gestured towards the large, open pit. "What *is* this?"

"You're aware of our issues with coal – not to mention the pollution aspect. It's not the reason I built the VIC-20 array, but the problem of limited resources is the one that I'm trying to solve at the moment – hopefully, if I can find a solution to our coal addiction, the pollution will ease in time..." He made a slight gesture towards the open pit. "To generate the amount of steam necessary to ensure proper running of the VIC-20, we'd need to burn enough coal per day to power every robot in the Mecha-Principalities for a month. Instead, I decided to create a prototype geothermal pump – the first of its kind. By funnelling lava up through the boiler instead of shovelling coal, we can run a hundred VICs if we have to, and once my organics wear out, I may need to do just that. It's an elegant solution, you must admit, if a little dangerous..." He turned his head in the Doctor's direction. "Well, for me. You'd probably survive a fall down there."

"Only probably?" The Doctor raised his head for a moment, then returned to contemplation of the pit. "It doesn't seem overly practical..."

"No, it doesn't, does it? It's a possible solution for large, stationary, power-hungry machines like this one, but ideally, we need something to replace coal, oil, all the other limited resources in one fell stroke – and something clean, to boot." A hissing burst of steam cascaded from the valves on his shoulders; a mechanical sigh. "I'm on the edge of something, I know, but no matter how intelligent I make myself... well, I'm still bound by the laws of physics. The frustrating thing is that I can't help feeling that we're missing something, something crucial – like we're trying to reach the moon without cavorite, if you'll pardon the metaphor. Everything becomes a thousand times harder." He continued fiddling with the computer, his gigantic hands capable of surprisingly delicate work. "Didn't you experiment with an alternate form of energy at once point? Sigma energy? Something like that?"

"Omega energy." The Doctor nodded. "Similar to being struck by lightning. Maya hated it." He shrugged. "I'd almost forgotten it. I used to use it to supercharge my brain, but it took a toll – I suppose it was my equivalent of your VIC machines." He shuddered. "I built this horrible chair, all straps and wiring, to flood my system with bursts of Omega energy and bring on visions – 'the Omega effect,' we called it." He laughed mirthlessly, shaking his head. "There was probably an easier way to bring that on, come to think of it. I used to have a thing – a kink, I suppose – about getting strapped into strange contraptions. That was probably part of it..." *Part of the thrill,* he thought, *back when life was all about thrills and adventure. When did that go? Was it when Monk died?* He looked down at his hands. *Or when I stopped loving Maya?*

Jason Satan killed me. That's the problem. He killed everything happy in me and left an immortal, undying husk, a zombie walking around with a tiny piece of Doc Thunder trapped inside it looking out. Just like Pluto has a tiny piece of El Sombra inside him – the thing he's planning to scrape out and replace when it finally dies. There's no difference between us.

No, I'm lying. There's one difference.

Eventually, he's going to die.

He found himself saying it out loud. "When *are* you going to die?"

Pluto turned to look down at him again. **"What?"**

"You said that when El Sombra's brain dies, you'll carry on regardless. Well, when are you planning to die, Pluto? Are you planning to just go on forever?" The Doctor's voice was trembling, and he realised he was gritting his teeth.

Pluto looked at him for a long moment. His face, as ever, was unreadable. Eventually, he spoke. **"Why not?"**

The Doctor stared at him for a moment, then sighed. "One more for the club, then. Lars and Maya will be pleased. Goodbye, Pluto. We won't see each other again." He turned to leave the way he'd come.

Pluto continued talking.

"Earlier, you talked about the soul. It's a uniquely human notion – the idea of something that survives after death. Think of it from a robot's perspective." He turned away from the machine, giving the Doctor his full attention. **"As the arrays that make up our minds and personalities wear out and grow obsolete, we have them replaced, upgraded. To me, this organic component – the brain – is just one more array; a unique and irreplaceable one, true, but nothing I can't do without. My information is recorded elsewhere within me; I will not die. I have no need to."**

"Maybe you're already dead," the Doctor muttered.

"Maybe there is no death; no freeing of the soul. Maybe only a change of function. Humans biodegrade to become food for the local environment; my kind, at the end of their functioning existence, might expect to be melted down to build new robots. Usefulness continues. Still, it seems a poor reward for the loss of self."

"The soul." The Doctor almost whispered it. Pluto's speech hammered against his ears like the tolling of some graveyard bell, the words harrowing in their terrifying practicality; a robot's gospel, bare and without warmth. He began to walk away.

"The *awareness*. There is no part of me that is the seat of it, just as there is no particular cell in your body that is the seat of yours; but it has more value than any other use our bodies may be put to. We should protect that awareness, that most fragile part of what we are. Extend it as long as possible; indefinitely."

The Doctor stopped in his tracks, Slowly, he turned to face the gigantic android again.

"What are you saying?"

"Remember when I said I'd answered questions that have plagued mankind for centuries? I've solved the oldest problem of all, Doctor. The problem of death."

The Doctor stared, and what little colour he had drained from his face. "No."

"Yes. Immortality, Doctor. I'm going to share your gift with the world."

HE'D ATTACKED PLUTO, of course.

He'd stood and listened, in a kind of numb horror, as Pluto had described his nightmarish plans for humanity: "There's no real difference between my people and yours, Doctor. I propose our species take advantage of this, and merge. I've lived centuries, and will live for millennia more, but the next generation won't even have to make the changes I'll have to in order to survive. Their fragile organics – their 'souls,' if you wish – will be protected and nurtured by mechanical systems that will keep them alive indefinitely. If they'd prefer, they can look and feel completely human, just as the most advanced robots did before the war..." He'd tailed off, and his serene and motionless brass visage had seemed to the Doctor in that moment like the face of some mocking demon.

"Doctor?"

The Doctor had leapt up, and punched the brass head hard enough to tear it from Pluto's body. A rain of tiny cogs and gears fell, shimmering, from the severed neck; but the head was mostly brass, and the arrays in it were mostly connective, created to link with other systems. Pluto was far from damaged beyond repair.

"Doct%r?" He said, the voice emanating from somewhere inside his neck, as the Doctor reached in to grab great handfuls of the clockwork, tearing it free and scattering it. "Doctor, you're £mpairing my worki%gs. We can t&lk about this... *Doctor...*" One of Pluto's great hands reached up suddenly, grabbing hold of the Doctor in a crushing grip, actually hard enough to hurt; the novelty of pain shocked the Doctor into letting go, and the great King of the Robots took the opportunity to hurl him across the chamber and into one of the great steel walls. He impacted hard enough to deform the metal, and the whole building shook with a terrifying sound like some huge gong breaking in two.

"The arr&ys –" Pluto cried out, turning his headless body slightly as he perceived the tiny gears and switches being jarred and thrown out of their alignments; something that would take hours, perhaps days of painstaking work to restore. The Doctor, pulling himself free of the metal wall, saw the opportunity; a way to hurt his foe, perhaps a way to stop this insanity once and for all.

His eyes glowed a fierce red. After a moment, so did the VIC-20 – red hot, then white.

Then it began to melt.

"N%!" screamed Pluto, the crackling distortion caused by the damage to his body adding a note of pain and horror that an artificial voice could never have achieved; helplessly, he watched as his life's work, the great clockwork he had been working so long and so hard on, collapsed into a flowing pool of molten metal and flowed across the floor, taking its secrets with it. Great gouts of steam hissed from it, filling the room.

Pluto turned towards the Doctor and charged.

One great iron foot, treaded with rubber, smashed into the Doctor's face, lifting him up through the air like a rag doll; when he hit the wall, the entire building shook again, with an ominous creak and the sound of some hidden rivet springing loose. From outside came the crash of one of the decorative fixtures toppling from its corner, and the Doctor could hear the sound of ringing bells, a long honk of compressed air forced through a horn – robot screams.

Teeth gritted, he turned his killing eyes on Pluto's chest, aiming to boil the living brain inside the robot in its tank. The outer shell of the machine glowed a deep, dull red, but no more than that – whatever alloy it had been created from was as resistant to extremes of heat as the Doctor himself.

The Doctor grinned savagely. The fire of his own eyes might not be enough, but he knew where he could find better fire than that.

Behind Pluto, the great pit yawned. The shuddering pipes rising up from it were beginning to crack under the strain of the battle, spewing lava as the constant background noise of the pumps built itself up into a manic crescendo. Soon enough, the Doctor realised, they would erupt, drowning the city of Paris in boiling magma. Perhaps that would be enough to wipe Pluto's insane machinations from the face of the Earth. He hoped so.

He didn't plan to be around to see it.

Coiling the muscles of his legs into one final spring, he hurled himself at the gigantic robot, smashing into his centre mass like a bullet; the momentum sent him stumbling back to the edge of the pit – and then a step beyond.

The machine screamed, a single terrible howl of rage and pain, as it and the Doctor toppled over the edge, falling down into the endless shaft, lit from below by bubbling pools of searing liquid stone; the gateway to the core of the Earth. Desperately, Pluto lashed out, attempting to claw a handhold in the metal of the walls; but his flailing claw struck one of the larger pipes, and all he managed to do was shower them both in lava as they fell, until it flowed into his severed neck and silenced the howl of his mechanical voice forever.

The Doctor's rage drained out of him, and he had a few moments of freefall to wonder, fleetingly, if he'd been right to deny mankind eternal life; but what kind of life was that? Life as blobs of flesh inside machines? Wasn't that worse than death? *Then again,* he thought, *I do have a bias. Perhaps I just didn't want to see humanity throwing away something as precious as an ending.*

Still, he thought to himself, *did I have the right?*

There was no-one left to answer him. Seconds later, he splashed down into the magma, and the three-story robot melted and fused around him, encasing him in a core of molten metal. He breathed in, filling his lungs with it, trying to drown himself in the corpse of his enemy, but the pain was fleeting. Even as the Doctor began the long journey down, sinking to the core of the planet, he knew he would live through this. He would live through everything now, until the very end of the universe. And maybe a little beyond.

How powerful would he be by then? Perhaps this was the best place for him; far away from everyone he could hurt. Already, he was enjoying the solitude. The core of the earth waited to enfold him, like a nurturing red sun.

Inside a cocoon of strange alloys, the being that had once been Doc Thunder curled up, closed his eyes, and began his long wait.

JACOB STEELE IN THE
HOUR OF CHAOS

JACOB STEELE DRIFTS *in a haze of blue light, outside time, between one breath and the next. Sometimes, he thinks he's drifted there for a few minutes. Sometimes, it feels like centuries.*

Occasionally, the blue light lifts, and men flitting like hummingbirds are pointing guns at him, or preparing ways to trap him; but he is faster than they are, and he has plenty of bullets left for his gun. Jacob Steele has a sacred duty.

Jacob Steele is the Keeper of the Stone.

Occasionally, the Stone pulses in his grip, and shows him the true, binary structure of the universe; what should be, and what should not be.

A secluded glade in prehistory, where no star ever fell. Leopards who never walked on their hind legs. Great men of science once dead before their time, now living on to pull down lightning from the sky. Light in glass bulbs, spreading across the world in ever more arcane configurations, until the power runs out and it all collapses like a house of cards. Survivors fighting in the ruins, succumbing to diseases long thought banished, from cholera to fascism, but finally growing strong enough to fight the infection off. Green shoots, poking through the ruins.

Or crashing spaceships, evolution run amok, swashbuckling madmen, womanising superspies, superhuman beings brawling with demonic arch-criminals and giant robots. Monsters of history preserved long past any normal lifespan, watching the strange new beings springing up in a stagnated world, as the smog drifts slowly over it all. And behind them all, the puppeteer, the great red-handed Queen in her secret city, pulling the strings to keep things as they are.

Keep me, the Stone says to him. The world is locked into an unnatural configuration, a state of being that was never meant to be; but you can end it. You can bring things back to how they should be, if you can only hold on. You are the Keeper now; keep me. Hold on to me.

Don't let go.

"JACOB, I LOVE you! But we only have sixty minutes to save the world!"

"What?" said Jacob Steele, the time-lost gunfighter yanked from the Wild West into the strange, exciting world of the twenty-fifth century by forces unknown! On the leather seat next to his own, Maya, Queen of the Future Earth, writhed in helpless terror – and through the viewing screen was the reason why!

A vast star-destroyer, piloted by the insidious clone-forces of Lomax – the Space Satan! Diabolical ruler of the planet Venus, whose only desire was to enslave the planet he had once called home!

"That interstellar fiend!" growled Arcturus, noble knight of the Leopard People, from his position at the starboard cannon.

"Affirmative, sir!" agreed the hyper-intelligent android, Rousseau-5, as he plugged himself into the navigating table in a desperate attempt to plot an evasive manoeuvre that might rescue them from the very jaws of destruction. On the table, magnetic models of the ships whirred and pivoted – but there was no solution that could rescue them from their deadly fate!

"Ha! Ha! Ha!" A vicious cackle echoed over the ship's radio as the immense bulk of Lomax's flagship drew closer and closer to the *Jonah II.* "You've thwarted my insidious schemes for the last time, Steele! Now you will face your final doom! My missiles will seek you out, however you twist and turn – and blast you and your lovely Queen into atoms! The Solar System will be mine – *all mine!*"

"What?" Steele shook his head, wincing. "Who the hell is that?" He looked around the interior of the *Jonah II,* as if he'd never seen it before in his life. "Where am I?"

"The amnesia ray!" Arcturus gasped, the hackles on his neck rising. "It must have had a delayed effect! He's forgotten who we are!"

Steele looked at the huge half-man, half-cat as if he'd fallen prey to some terrifying space madness – and, at that very moment, a pair of sleek rockets roared out of the flagship, streaking across the vacuum of space towards Steele and his crew!

Instinctively, he jerked the wheel, and the great peroxide rockets blasted the *Jonah II* out of the missiles' path, but only for a moment! Then, the missiles turned, as if magnetised, and blasted towards the ship on their relentless mission of death!

"Sir!" Rousseau-5 cried out in his mechanical tones. "The rockets are homing in on something on board the ship! But what could possibly –"

"The Stone!" Maya screamed, pointing to Steele's left hand, and the mysterious artefact Steele had brought with him from the far past. The Stone, it had been revealed, was in truth a remnant of one of the lost star-lenses used by a corps of space sheriffs to bring law to a wild universe in times long forgotten, and, now polished down to a flawless gem, it served Steele as a ring capable of channelling strange and mysterious energies. Many times, Steele had used the ring to save his friends from all manner of deadly danger, but even its bizarre powers were no match for the vacuum of space! And now, a pair of merciless missiles streaked ever closer, drawn to the unique stellar mineral!

"There's only one way out," Arcturus snarled, his tail swishing. "Tear it off his hand and throw it out of the airlock! Better yet – fire it at the flagship! We'll see how Lomax likes playing cat and mouse with his own weapons!"

"It's the only logical solution," Rousseau-5 confirmed. "You must remove the ring, sir! Give up the Stone!"

"Wait a second –" Jacob scowled, looking down at his left hand.

It was bunched slightly, as if clutching something, and for a moment there seemed to be no flesh there, just a skeletal hand.

"Jacob!" Maya screamed, and he looked up – to see the missiles roaring straight towards him, a payload of death for him and everyone he loved! *"Take off the ring!"* she screamed, and despite all his instincts, he found himself reaching to –

Don't let go.

– he jerked the wheel to the side, and the missiles missed them by inches. "Now!" he shouted, and Arcturus opened up with the mass driver, spitting great balls of lead into the void as the rockets blazed past his position. A moment later, the massive bullets did their work, and the missiles exploded, buffeting the *Jonah II* in a torrent of fire and flame!

"Sir!" Rousseau-5 cried, "We've got a rupture in the main boiler! We're going down!"

The *Jonah II,* spewing smoke, began to spiral away from the welcoming stars, towards the green planet below. As Steele fought to level out the ship, he imagined he could hear Lomax cursing under his breath – but the radio was dead.

"THE WEDDING WILL be held in one hour, my dear Jacob." Lomax sneered, fingers toying with his elegant moustache. "It promises to be the event of the season at the Royal Palaces. And you will be the guest of honour – or should I say – *your severed head!"* The Space Satan threw back his head and cackled, a diabolical laugh that echoed around the arena and drew cheers from the crowd of red-skinned, reptilian clones who'd been assembled to watch this cruel gladiatorial combat.

Beside him – on her own golden throne – Maya struggled in her bonds, her dark skin glistening in the Venusian sun as she gazed helplessly at the terrifying spectacle.

Steele rubbed his temples with his right hand, frowning. Hadn't he been on board some kind of spacecraft a moment ago? How had he ended up here? Some sort of crash...

...no, of course not. He'd been here for years.

He felt a familiar weight in his left hand, and looked down to see the blue blade, Souldrinker, forged by the dwarves of Venus from the Stone he had brought with him on his trip through time... which had, of course, been revealed as a fragment of the mysterious Sword of Ancients, as wielded by the Gods of Venus in the time before time. Legend had it that the great Sword could drain the life from a world, and the dagger the dwarves had forged from a single chunk of it had the uncanny power to drink the life-force of any enemy and imprison it forever. A formidable weapon indeed, and Jacob's skill with it, through the long years of his exile here, had earned him the title of Warlord of Venus, and the undying love of the Queen of Southern Venus, Maya Br'tana.

Northern Venus, however, had long been ruled by the clone-hordes of Lomax, the enigmatic Space Satan, who would never rest until the entire planet squirmed in his iron grip. Steele gritted his teeth, readying himself for the combat to come.

"You should have stayed in your own forgotten age, my prehistoric friend!" Lomax sneered, running a serpentine tongue over his fangs. "Your soul-sucking blade will prove of little worth against – the *Derleth!*"

"No!" Maya cried out, squirming helplessly as the iron gate of the arena lifted slowly, revealing a squamous horror, a shambling mass of half-fused tentacles dripping with foul, black ichor. In the centre of the obscenely waving flesh was a single vast, unblinking eye, that looked upon Steele with an infinite hunger. Slowly, the Derleth slithered forwards, leaving a trail of noxious slime.

"Yes!" Lomax smirked, as the crowd bayed for blood. "I have woken the Derleth – the great Soulless One – from his aeon-long slumber beneath the deepest trenches of the Venusian sea. He shall be my weapon against all who dare to defy my rule! In particular, your so-called 'Warlord' – for how can the blue blade drink the soul of a creature that has none – that eats souls itself? No, my dear, your consort is doomed, quite doomed. And soon you shall have a new husband, and all of Venus shall have a new King!"

"Oh, you fiend!" she sobbed, "You unspeakable fiend!"

The deadly Derleth slithered closer, slowly feeling its way across the arena floor. Suddenly, one of the tentacles shot out with the speed of a moray eel, a plethora of fanged mouths at the tip opening wide to drink Steele's blood and absorb his very spirit. He dodged to the side just in time, then lashed out with the glowing dagger, slicing away the beast's tentacle before it could close about him. The severed chunk of slime-coated flesh dropped to the arena floor – then melted, leaving a puddle of bubbling goo behind.

With any other foe, the first blood drawn by Souldrinker would mean the end of the combat; but the Derleth had no soul to steal, and it pressed the attack harder than ever.

"It's after the dagger, my love!" Maya screamed, and at that Lomax showed the first sign of anger.

"Shut up, you little fool –"

"Don't you see? It's an eater of souls – it wants the souls captured inside the blade! Hurl it away from you!"

"No!" Lomax roared, shrinking back. "If he throws that blade at me, the Derleth will devour my soul with the rest! You can't! You mustn't! Oh, demons of the afterworld, have pity upon me –"

Jacob Steele grinned mercilessly, dodging another flurry of tentacles as he drew his arm back to –

Don't let go.

– he leapt forward, driving the point of the blade deep into the grotesque creature's single eye, bursting it like a balloon. Unmentionable jelly squirted out of the ruptured mass, stinking of ancient rot, corruption unknown since the first days of the universe. Still, Steele drove the blade deeper, working it into the creature's brain as the tentacles thrashed madly for a moment, before going limp at last.

Perhaps the Derleth had no soul for the blue blade to absorb. But a dagger was still a dagger, and a monster from beyond the dawn of time still had a weak point.

Lomax stood to his full height, pointed one trembling red finger at the Warlord of Venus, and screamed –

*   *   *

"– OKAY, THIS ISN'T working."

Maya raised an eyebrow. "Perhaps it's your scenario. The 'Venusian sun'? Why not just 'the sun'? And you really oversold it on the last run-through..."

"What, the stab-me-in-the-chest thing? That's called *incentive*." Lomax scowled, scratching the back of his head. "Anyway, look who's talking. '*Oh, you fiend, you unspeakable fiend!*' Really? And what's with all the helplessness? You're the least helpless person I know."

"Well, it's fun to pretend occasionally." She smiled, enjoying his irritation. "You lived with the Doctor for years, don't tell me you never did anything like that with him."

"I lived with a depressed bald man," Lomax sighed, "who was terrified of touching people or even talking to them. The whole experience was about as sexy as haemorrhoids. Poor bastard." His eyes narrowed suspiciously. "One of these days you'll have to let me in on how exactly you got him to destabilise France on your orders..."

"I just told him to take a vacation," Maya smiled, innocently. "Anyway, digressions aside, what do we do now?"

She looked over to the flickering column of blue light on the dais – interweaved copper, zinc and cavorite, supplied with crackling Omega energy and supervised by the mental power of a Commodore-class thinking robot.

It was fortunate that Pluto had arranged for his blueprints for the VIC series to be kept safe from any eventuality; her agent, Prometheus Quicksilver – bastard heir of the Quicksilver line – had retrieved them, along with notes from various other projects, during the chaos of the volcanic eruption. As a result – and with Lomax's help – the twin kingdoms of Britannia and Zor-Ek-Narr were once again at the forefront of modern technology, their incredible advancements making them the rulers of the world almost by default. From the philosopher-plutocrats of China to the warring isolationists of the American continent, there was no civilisation on Earth that dared to disobey an edict from the Immortal Queen.

Britannia was certainly, at this point, the only country

capable of reaching into the timestream for an audience with the Keeper of the Stone.

While computing power had increased in leaps and bounds over the centuries, thanks largely to Pluto and the new generation of machine consciousness, the basic method by which the Lonesome Rider was retrieved from his lonely vigil had changed little since its invention by the renegade S.T.E.A.M. agent, Philip Hawthorne, in the early twenty-first century; a gateway would be created, the Rider would appear from exile, and there would be a brief attempt, before the portal collapsed, to kill him and take the Stone from his corpse.

These attempts would, without exception, end with the deaths of anyone who tried. Even when the would-be assassin fired from inside a concrete bunker, or a tank, the result was the same. Jacob Steele would have been deadly enough, if you made the mistake of drawing down on him; the Keeper of the Stone was death personified.

After the Doctor's disappearance, Lars Lomax had flown to Britannia to join Maya as a scientific adviser; his already vast intelligence had only grown more subtle and devious over the years, and this seemed like the right strategic move. "I'm sure you'll betray me eventually," she'd smiled, shaking his hand on his arrival, "but you've got all the time in the world for that." He'd laughed at that, happy to be understood, and that night they'd played chess for the first time in years. The morning after, he started working on a means of bringing the Stone back inside current time, and keeping it there.

The solution was simple and elegant; force was never going to work against the Lonesome Rider, and – immortal or no – Lars Lomax had no desire to get shot through the head. So how to get the Stone out of his grip? "Simple," Lars smiled, in that way he had. "We ask."

Maya had leant back on her chair, studying him carefully. "Just ask him to hand it over?"

"Sure. Checkmate, by the way." Lars' smile widened as he theatrically knocked over her King. "The thing is – it's all about *how* we ask."

Maya had to admit, it was inspired. First, build your Omega platform; no change there. Her people could make one of those in their sleep. The hard part was building the Phantasmagorical Projection system over the top of it.

They'd been semi-popular attractions in Britannia towards the end of the twentieth century – bizarre brass coffins that promised to plunge the entertainment-hungry visitor into the virtual world of their choice; the default setting was *Alice in Wonderland*. Most found the notion of being submerged in a fictional reality oddly disquieting rather than enticing; had the punters known that the booths were fully capable of killing in the right circumstances, they would have been even less likely to volunteer themselves for the experience. Lomax's idea was to materialise the Lonesome Rider inside a Projector, and – while he was still reeling from the novel experience of not having anyone try to kill him – run him through various fictional sequences designed to make him reject the Stone.

It was difficult – obviously there could be no margin for error – but eventually they had a projector guaranteed to start working on Steele the moment he materialised in their timeframe.

After that, it was just a matter of writing the correct story...

LOMAX FROWNED. "ALL right. We have less than an hour before the cavorite reserves are drained, and we've used about forty minutes of it. Once our hour is up, Jacob Steele vanishes from the timestream, and if we ever want him back we're going to need to find our own weight in industrial cavorite from somewhere. Do we have that?"

Maya shook her head. "It was hard enough finding the latest batch. Cavorite's a lot scarcer than it used to be."

"Not to mention the fact that there's barely any coal or oil or even wood left, and the entire planet is a smog-filled ruin, thanks to our wonderful ancestors and their enlightened approach to the problems of pollution."

Maya chuckled. "Lars, we've both been around since at least the twentieth century. That was *us*."

"Well, remind me to think ahead in future. The point is, this may be our last shot." He sighed, scratching the base of one horn. "All right, all right... something in our scenarios isn't working. We're providing a world of adventure for him, so he's got something exciting to latch onto from the off. Then we're putting him, and those around him, in physical jeopardy – a jeopardy that he can only get out of by abandoning the Stone. If he won't abandon the stone, he'll..." – Lomax glanced towards the brass coffin on top of the dais, and lowered his voice – "...he'll die, and once again the Stone will be ours. Except we have a problem there, because he's not rejecting the Stone and he's not dying. He's *winning*."

"He's the Lonesome Rider, Lars," Maya said, frowning. "What did you expect?"

"Honestly? I expected he'd enjoy some thrilling action on beautiful, scenic Venus."

Maya shook her head, a half-smile playing on her lips. "You and your Venus. I know it was very disappointing that the terraforming experiments didn't work out, Lars, but it's time to let it go. Your little paradise can only exist over there now, in that brass box..."

Lars nodded, staring into space for a moment. "We've been fools," he said suddenly, and walked over to the mobile brain feeding the Projector, checking the hands of the clock built into the robot's chest. Fifteen minutes maximum before the cavorite exhausted itself. He'd have to work fast.

He smiled reassuringly at the brain, then flipped open its cranial hatch, fingers flicking over the gears and switches inside, conversing with it through mathematics. "You said it yourself; he's the Lonesome Rider. We've both read the histories – Jacob Steele was renowned for staying on the job until the end. He's not going to abandon his task because we threaten him." He snapped the hatch closed, and the robot nodded in silent understanding. Lars took a step back.

Maya cocked her head, watching closely. "What did you program in, Lars?"

"The end." He grinned. "Paradise in a box."

* * *

"STEELE?"

Jacob Steele blinked, dazzled by the setting sun.

Reed was in the middle of boiling water for coffee; he started at Steele's sudden arrival, then stared at him for a long moment, shaking his head. "Good God, man," he said, in a dry whisper, "I thought you were dead. Where did you go?"

Steele looked around. He was still on the mesa, but the floating orrery of rocks and stones had crashed to Earth, forming a ring of concentric circles around the twisted body of the madman Edison. Nearby, the Locomotive Man was a smoking heap of wreckage, steam still rising from the twisted metal.

"I wish to hell I knew," he breathed. He tried to remember the hallucinations; that strange spaceship, the arena, the blue void, the Stone whispering in his mind.

He looked down at his left hand. He was still carrying the damned thing.

Reed's look of astonishment cracked into a broad smile. "You vanished during the fight. Just... popped out of existence with that stone of Edison's. If I were you, I'd put the damn thing down now –"

Don't let go.

"Best to hang onto it, I reckon," Steele muttered, without thinking about it. With his right hand, he slipped his iron back in its holster, then fumbled in the pocket of his coat for a cigar. Lord knew he needed one.

Reed raised an eyebrow. "Well, if you insist... You know, I honestly through you'd been wiped out – disintegrated utterly. Stranger things, as they say, have happened." He laughed shakily. "Isn't that right, Mister Owl?"

Steele's eyes widened.

Grey Owl stepped out from behind the wagon, as hale and hearty as he'd ever been.

"By God," Steele laughed, shaking his head. "What the hell happened?"

Grey Owl shrugged. "One minute I was deciding not to shoot you, the next I was waking up in the back of that snake oil salesman's wagon."

Reed grinned. "Coffee," he said, pressing a mug into Steele's free hand. "As I understand it, prolonged use of that stone seems to disrupt time – you were transported an hour or so into the future, while Grey Owl's personal timeline was reversed into the past, to... well, to before he died." He shook his head. "I have to tell you, an event like this is completely unprecedented –"

Steele laughed, then sipped the coffee. It was the best thing he'd tasted in a hell of a long time, and he couldn't help but noting there was a mess of bacon sizzling over that fire as well, but that could wait a spell. He turned to Grey Owl, smiling broadly. "It's called a gift horse, Reed. Don't go looking it in the mouth. How are you feeling, Grey Owl?"

Grey Owl smiled back, a little cagily, as if sizing Steele up – then, on impulse, he stuck out his left hand. "That's up to you. Are we friends?"

Steele looked down at the stone in his hand.

Don't let go.

"Hang on a second, I got my hands full here," he joked, but he could see Grey Owl looked angry at that, the old fire of enmity flickering in his eyes. Steele looked around for a place to put his coffee, feeling like a damn fool while Grey Owl was standing there with his hand out –

Don't let –

– and he could see in the other man a kind of pained realisation developing, that all the talk back at Devil's Gulch had been just that, just talk, and there was to be no peace between these men unless it came out of the barrel of a gun –

Don't –

– and then Grey Owl's hand was slowly drawing back, and the hurt in his eyes was too much for Jacob to stand, and he put the damn stone down to shake hands like a man.

Except when he lifted his hand again, he was alone on the mesa, and when he looked down at his open hand it was a skeleton's, grey as ash and crumbling like wet sand...

THE BRASS COFFIN swung open, and the dust and ashes that had once been Jacob Steele tumbled out onto the dead platform.

"The stone was the only thing keeping him alive after so long," Lars sighed, shaking his head. "Too bad. I honestly think he'd have thanked us for freeing him of it."

Maya lifted an eyebrow. "Really?"

"No, not really." He nodded to the robots entering the chamber. "Make sure you pick it up with the tongs. I don't want anyone touching it – human or android. We don't want to have to go through all this again with someone else."

"There won't be much difference between humans and robots before long," Maya murmured, smiling. "All Pluto's blueprints were missing was a viable power source for his immortal hybrids. Now that we have a sample of xokronite –"

Lars grinned. "Xokronite! I like it. Catchy."

"– we'll have all the power we need, free and clean."

"We'll have to find out how to synthesise it," Lars murmured. "One sample won't be enough. And obviously, we have to work out how to actually get power out of it in the first place..."

"I'll tell you what I remember. You're smart enough to take it from there. We have enough time for that." Maya smiled, watching the stone glow with its blue inner fire as it was carried away. "We have eternal life, and infinite power. And soon all my citizens will have the same. We've taken a planet on the edge of total environmental collapse and created a world of gods."

Lars Lomax nodded. "Yes, we have," he murmured. Then he grinned savagely. "Now, what do we do with it?"

ONE MILLION
YEARS LATER...

THE RED QUEEN'S RACE AND THE RED KING'S DREAM

EPSILON TWO FOUR, thought Ull of the Silver Service. *I hate myself and I hate my life.*

The psychetecture of the great golden building responded to the agent's heartfelt depression, the outside of the great structure altering itself to best suit Ull's mood. Great sections of the palace detached themselves, reconfiguring to better promote a sense of well-being and harmony.

While the entrance of the palace was heavily protected – so much so that anyone entering who was not the Red King would have their atomic bonds instantly nullified – the psychetecture system was not; he'd reconfigured the talkeasy built into his frontal lobe to make it believe that he was a guest, and the system was now desperate to accommodate his emotional needs. Obviously, the punishment for breaking into one of the Royal Houses would be death – or worse, ejection from the timestream entirely. Should he be discovered, not only would his infinite life come to an agonising end, but all traces of him would subsequently be forgotten by history. It would be as if he had never existed.

Worse still, he would fail his Queen.

Best to get this part right, then.

Alpha zero five. I'm the best there is at what I do and this is the most fun I ever had.

The sections paused at the sudden change of psychological state, jerked in the air, and moved back slowly towards their original position, as if unsure of themselves. Ull moved quickly, the deep black of his skinsuit shimmering slightly as it propelled him hundreds of feet into the air, to land like a cat on one of the moving sections. Now came the difficult bit.

Beta seven seven. I wish I'd had a mother. The structure he was perched on stopped an instant before it would have slotted itself into place and veered left instead, compensating for the sudden oedipal urge. Ull leapt again, into the gap, changing his mood in mid-air to another suicidal burst of self-loathing. *Epsilon two six. I always let everyone down.* He had to be very careful here – the wrong emotion and he'd be crushed between the moving parts of the building's outer wall. *Delta nine nine. Cechenena is a genus of moths in the Sphingidae family,* he mused, the sheer dryness of the thought sending the sections juddering to a halt just long enough for him to snake between the gap. *Alpha three one. Isn't it great to be alive?* Another gap opened in front of him as the inner walls shifted themselves about to form the perfect complement to a sunny disposition.

A second later and he was through the wall entirely – and inside the palace of the Red King.

Delta four one. Good boy, he thought, and the psychetecture, relieved that its guest had seemingly made up his mind at last, settled into an ostentatious deco design with a soft mechanical sigh. Ull smiled, petting it with his mind.

Good house.

ONE OF YOUR pets just walked into my house through the cat flap.

'Cat flap.' You and your anachronisms.

Don't change the subject. He exploited the psychetecture – presumably he thinks I haven't noticed. I take it that means we're into the endgame?

There'll be other games.

Not with anything of importance at stake. After today, it'll just be for pride, or territory, or philosophy – but today, the game is for a universe.

It always was. Your move.

ULL STOOD, SNIFFING the air. He made a swift check of his selfsearch – under ordinary circumstances, he'd been trained to survive without it, but after the emotional rollercoaster he'd put himself through he needed a little grounding.

Alpha Four Seven, chattered the readout. *Wary confidence, slight fear. The superior man prepares for all eventualities.* How true. *Inner motivations (y/n)?* N. That was always a long one, and he didn't have the time.

The hallway was a strange mishmash of styles, all of them hundreds of thousands of years old. An elevation-field coiled up from the centre of the floor like a snake, glittering in reds and pinks; a visible field seemed oddly gauche to Ull, but it wasn't his place to question the décor choice of a King. Placed around the walls were a plethora of ancient art treasures: sculptures by Warhol, paintings by Kichida, poems by Tunos, all dating back to the pre-powered eras, before xokronite had solved the twin problems of energy generation and pollution once and for all. There were historical artefacts here as well, from the same long-forgotten past – an original copy of the Fourth Earth Battalion Field Manual, the diary of a suicidal slave-owner dated 1750, both more than a million years old. If they hadn't been protected by specially designed fields, they'd have crumbled away to nothing millennia ago.

Ull found himself checking his selfsearch again. *Gamma eight three. Curiosity, the edge of a great understanding. The superior man sees the hidden thread connecting all.* These disparate treasures had something in common, then. What?

There was a large, flat field distortion hanging on the back wall, a complicated interference pattern that seemed to make no sense until Ull realised that it was meant to be appreciated visually; the eddies and currents sparked colours that, on proper inspection, formed a green paradise filled with strange plants and populated by men and women walking hand in hand. It was oddly scandalous – the people in the image were missing the telltale markings that showed where their selfsearches and skinpatches had been implanted at birth, and what Ull had taken at first for flesh-coloured skinsuits was actually their naked skin, open to the elements. Most shockingly of all, the men and women in the image had hair cascading from their scalps, under their arms, between their legs; Ull felt vaguely disturbed by it. *Zeta seven three,* he thought, not needing to check. *Mild disgust, fear of the other. The superior man respects all difference and is secure in his own preferences.* He'd had that one several times.

He looked around the hallway, searching for exits aside from the central lifting field; that would certainly be monitored. He could rely on his augmented skinsuit to deflect surveillance to an extent, but this was the Red King's summer palace, and there could be no relying on –

– Ull felt something brush his shoulder. He looked, and there was the smallest rip in the fabric of his skinsuit, and a bead of blood peeking through. His blood ran suddenly cold. *Zeta zero six. Fear of death.* He tried to remember what the superior man did when faced with that particular emotion.

Something brushed against his hand.

When he lifted it to look, one of his fingers was missing.

Razorfields?

Remember when 'razors' were something that existed? Ask someone what a razor is now. Anyone younger than eight hundred millenia wouldn't have a clue.

Isn't that a little... primitive? Bloodthirsty, even?

He breaks into my house, pokes around my private collection and then sneers at my art – he'll get what he's given and like it. I'm particularly proud of that painting. I'm not having one of your drones turn his nose up at it.

'Painting.' Oh dear.

So I remember history. You know what they say – those who forget the past are condemned to repeat it...

And that's what this is all about, isn't it?

Your move.

IN THE ROYAL Hangars, the five-strong crew of the *Zor 714* stood stiffly to attention, arms at their sides, eyes forward. Behind them, the *Zor* hung in its gravimetric cradle, rotating slowly; a great spinning-top of shimmering silver metal. The crew had been waiting for several minutes, but they showed no sign of resentment, only a hungry anticipation; today, the *Zor* was no longer an ordinary mid-level scientific research vessel – one of thousands serving Habitat One.

Today, the *Zor* was under Royal command.

As a mid-level scientific research vessel, the *Zor* was usually commissioned for surveys on the various colony worlds; very occasionally, if there was a report of some asteroid or planetoid inward-bound from the intergalactic gulf, the *Zor* would be sent, along with several other vessels, to take its measure and make sure it was no threat to the various human-occupied worlds, the Habitats. It never was.

The crew had expected to comfortably drift through the countless millenia ahead of them, like all the other scientific research crews, mapping new planets and solar systems, surveying their flora and fauna, reporting to whichever of the two Royal Houses commanded their particular loyalty – or to both – on any discoveries thus gained. Perhaps when all the stars had been fully explored – when every scrap of life had been fully catalogued and categorised and exploited for whatever use it had – they would find something else to do. In the meantime, they were happy in their work, and the uneventful nature of the job was part of the charm. Captain Tura had never considered the possibility that the crew of the *Zor* would ever do anything too challenging or exciting. She'd certainly never thought her ship would carry out any vital missions for the Queen.

That was the thing about living forever. Given enough time, anything can happen.

A pair of floating silver drones swept into the hangar, their speakers serenading the crew and the ship with the deep musical trills of the Royal Anthem. The Queen's retinue followed, a group of six androids with silver and gold casings; they were occasionally referred to as the Rusos, or the Queen's Bishops, but the role had been purely ceremonial for hundreds of thousands of years. In this day and age, the Queen was best protected by an invisible field, raised around her at all times; it was enough to stop any anarchists or insurrectionists from making an attempt on her life, and the Red King would, it was agreed, never be so gauche as to attempt a direct attack.

Tura swallowed, avoiding the urge to check her selfsearch as she gazed on the glory of the Red Queen. She wore a skinsuit of shimmering royal purple, a hooded cloak of red, and a ceremonial helmet, which completely covered her head and included a mask of brass, fixed into an expression of serene and noble calm; nobody had seen the Red Queen's true face in countless millenia. However, there were rumours among the older residents of the Habitat that, in the ancient times of pre-powered society, she was known as Britannia.

"Your Majesty!" the crew chanted in unison, falling to one knee as custom dictated.

"My subjects," the Red Queen nodded, and Tura rose to her feet. "You are all, I take it, fully briefed on the specifics of your mission?"

"We are, your Majesty." Tura bowed her head.

"And there are no questions?"

Tura shook her head. Who would dare to question a direct command from the –

"Your Majesty?"

It was the voice of the new Security Officer. Tura turned pale, even as she noticed Unwen smirking out of the corner of her eye. She wanted to slap him, but in front of the Queen all she could do was keep her eyes forward and try not to scream.

The Queen turned her expressionless mask towards the speaker, waiting for her to continue.

"Your Majesty..." *Shut up,* Tura thought, desperately, *shut up, shut up...* "Your Majesty, I can't help but notice that these orders are extremely vague. You've told us to take the *Zor* to a very particular nav-point at a very particular time, but there's nothing out there that might warrant a survey – especially not from a biogeneticist like Unwen. Why are we actually needed for this?"

The Red Queen tilted her head. She seemed almost amused, but with the mask it was difficult to tell. "Because I commanded it. What's your name, Officer?" She asked the question as if she already knew the answer.

The Security Officer looked up at the monarch almost belligerently. "Maya."

Underneath the mask, the Red Queen smiled to herself.

"Of course it is."

THE PAWN BEGINS her journey up the board. Well played. Unfortunately, it's all for nothing if I can take your knight out of the game...

We'll see. Your move.

THE SKINSUIT WAS self-repairing. It would mend and strengthen itself as needed, taking care of any holes or gaps in its fabric; so would Ull's skin. His little finger, however, wasn't going to grow back. It would need to be repaired back in the Queen's Palace, if he ever made it that far. And the next razorfield might take his head off at the neck.

The razorfields were invisible to the naked eye, but it was possible for his skinsuit to put out a weak field of its own, distorting them enough for Ull to see their faint shapes flitting to and fro in the air. Their movements were almost random, but at the same time there were traces of a definite pattern in the way they circled the room, like a shoal of deadly transparent fish.

They were toying with him, he realised; evaluating what defences he had before moving in for the kill. Soon, the fields would close in, a storm of knives piercing and slashing at him from every side; and that would be that. His existence would end, and with it the misson. If his skinsuit were capable of distorting the razorfields more, he might stand a chance against them –

– *distortion.*

That was the key.

Gamma eight nine. Understanding in the face of adversity. The superior man thinks and acts in one moment. He reached out with the weak fields of his skinsuit – the same ones that allowed him to leap hundreds of feet in the air, or cling to any surface – and captured the decorative image on the wall. An image made up of billions of tiny distortions...

"No! Oh, you little hooligan –" The voice echoed from nowhere. Ull had never heard the voice of the Red King, but there was no mistaking who was speaking. Under other circumstances, he might have studied the voice, even configured the selfsearch to begin a full mental evaluation. Now, he was busy.

It told him he was being watched, at least.

He curled the image around himself, taking a certain pleasure as the deformation of it made the little people burst and run together, the colours of the green grass and the blue sky and the varied flesh tones melding and changing, flowing into each other in a riot of shifting hues.

The razorfields circled for a moment, as if deciding how to approach, then dove from all sides. As they swooped down on him, Ull stilled his mind and prepared for death.

But the decorative image acted as he had hoped; as the razor fields flew through the distortion field, they were themselves distorted – transmuted by the shifting field into harmless bursts of colour and light. Ull smiled to himself, then released his grip on the image; unable to bear the stresses he'd imposed, it trembled for a moment like a soap bubble before bursting apart into individual globules of every shade and tint. They floated lazily through the air for a few moments, before being absorbed into the walls or the lifting field in the centre of the room.

Ull waited to see if there would be any other traps, or if the mysterious voice would deign to provide further comment. But the Red King, it seemed, had nothing to say.

Well, the alarm had evidently been raised. Ull stepped into the lifting field, and ascended.

THAT POISONOUS LITTLE bastard. I can't believe he *did* that. He could have just let the razorfields chop him up, you know. He didn't have to destroy a priceless masterpiece.

Personally, I thought it had a certain symbolic value.

Really? I thought you said that piece was derivative.

It is. I meant the way he destroyed it.

Oh, ha ha. Well, we'll see who destroys what. That's only a picture – it's the reality I'm interested in. He won't be able to take that apart so easily.

Won't he?

...your move.

THE QUEEN WAS silent for a long time, as if contemplating what punishment to visit upon the Security Officer. Tura, pale and almost shaking with nerves, waited for the axe to fall – would it only be the insolent Maya who faced the penalty for incurring the Red Queen's wrath? Or all of them? Even Unwen seemed to have realised the severity of the situation, and poor Munn looked as if he might be sick.

Eventually, the Queen spoke. "...My move," she murmured, to nobody in particular. Then she addressed the crew as a whole. "The *Zor* will be ready to depart directly – as soon as the necessary changes are made to the fuel situation. A fresh isotope is needed."

"Fresh?" the Security Officer blinked. "One isotope of xokronite is as fresh as any other, surely? The word doesn't have meaning in the context of –"

"*Maya!*" Tura barked, almost shouting. "Be *silent!*"

The Queen's blank brass mask seemed to smile. "Thank you, Captain. I can speak for myself, you know."

"Yes, your Majesty." Tura blushed red at her outburst. "My most sincere apologies, your Majesty."

"As I said, the *Zor* will depart once preparations have been made. I suggest you all board the ship, find your domicells and get some rest – apart from your Security Officer." The Queen sounded distinctly amused. "Her I would speak with alone."

"Yes, your Majesty," Tura nodded, trying to hide her relief as she and the crew hurried away. A new Security Officer, then – for the best, considering. Maya had been a little too full of herself for the position, and now she'd dug her own grave. Mouthing off to the Red Queen like that; it was unthinkable.

Who on earth did Maya think she was?

Beneath her brass mask, the Queen smirked.

NOT MUCH OF a move. You're putting a lot of faith in your Knight...

I'm promoting my pawn. Anyway, he's a Silver. That bloodline's served the Queen since before you were born – when the Queen they served was just a mad old hag in a jar, ruling over her tiny little island. They can take care of themselves.

Still, quite a risk. I have Knights of my own, you know.

I know. And you should know how I play the game by now – I only put my faith in a sure thing, remember?

Oh, I'm well aware. Only that which has been tried and tested need apply. I seem to remember you were against stagnation once...

I'll take it over change for change's sake. You always did like rocking boats and rattling cages.

A little chaos in the morning gets the blood running. And you know I hate doing the same thing twice. My move, I believe.

Knight takes knight?

If I didn't know better... I'd say you were reading my mind.

*   *   *

AT THE TOP of the elevating field, Ull found himself in what looked like a maze of mirrored surfaces. Some of these, he knew, would be real-time displays presenting a doctored image – several would be light-reflecting fields set to move and shift when out of his line of sight. A very few would even be permeable; those would be the ones to watch out for.

Where the assassins would be hidden.

Apha Four Six. Calm readiness. The superior man stills his mind in preparation for action.

He stepped forward.

The first of them lunged out of the mirrored surface to his left – a similarly black-clad figure, wearing his face, or a very subtly distorted version. It was only to be expected, Ull thought, as he grabbed the attacker's wrists, twisting it to snap the fragile bones and then heaving him through the empty air to crash into the mirrored surface opposite, impaling him on the shattered glass. The Red King's Vengers were his elite forces – capable of adapting themselves to match their opponent exactly if need be, both physically and in skill. And who better to use in an environment like this, where a dozen different reflections of Ull gazed back at him with every step he took?

One of the reflections on his left caught his eye – he turned and struck in one quick, liquid movement, then stopped his palm a split-second before it hit home; it was one of the display screens, showing an image of a Venger rather than the real thing. Doubtless it was booby-trapped, and he had very nearly fallen for it. He was just chiding himself on so nearly falling for such an obvious snare – *Epsilon two eight, self-reproach* – when the real Vengers dropped from above.

Stupid! Why hadn't he looked up? One arm was around his throat, cutting off his air, one grinning parody of his own features leering in his peripheral vision as another landed in front of him. Both were armed with nano-sharp carbon-steel blades. He could smell the poison coating the metal.

Delta five six, he thought. *Acceptance of the inevitable. The superior man flows with all moments.*

Even the last.

*   *   *

THERE. KNIGHT TAKES knight.

We'll see if it does take. My move, I think.

"I DID THINK about killing you," the Queen smiled from behind her serene mask. "Snapping your neck with my own two hands. Not for the reasons you might be expecting, but... anyway, it would be a weight off my mind if I took your place. But I just can't risk it."

The Security Officer bristled. "With all due respect, your Majesty, you don't scare me."

"Really?" The Red Queen cocked her head. "Why do you suppose that is? Out of all of my subjects, why is it that you – and you alone – have no fear of the power I wield?" She paused for a moment. "Do you like this society, Maya of *Zor* under Tura? Do you think it worth preserving?"

"Yes, I do," the Security Officer responded fiercely. "With one caveat. I would see you gone from it."

The treason hung in the air.

"Either you're a very stupid and headstrong girl," the Queen murmured, "or you already know what I'm going to show you. I can't quite remember which it is, I'm afraid."

The Security Officer said nothing. The Queen shrugged, and – making sure nobody was there to see – she reached up to detach the mask and lift it away.

Maya looked into her own eyes.

After a long pause, the mask was replaced. "You understand now, at any rate," the Queen smiled.

The Security Officer swallowed hard and nodded. "How –"

"At the co-ordinates you are to investigate, there is a temporal wormhole that will take you to the prehistory of Habitat One – of Earth. The rest of your crew also has a role to play there – except the Captain, of course. But then, you'll learn for yourself that there are always sacrifices..."

"I don't understand."

"You will. You've studied your history – I made sure of

that. You have a clear understanding of the turning points that created our civilisation; you'll know when the time comes how to guide it into being, and you'll have thousands of millenia with nobody to stop you doing just that."

"But the Red King –" the Security Officer sputtered, fear showing on her face for the first time. "How can I possibly learn to fight him?"

"The Red King won't learn the game until you know it inside out, and by that time, you'll need the challenge like air in your lungs. And he won't know the secret until it's too late."

"The secret?"

"The wormhole; the one that's about to bring you to the beginning of everything – riding with the Shaper, the Weeper, the Sacrificial Lamb and the Keeper of the Stone. It doesn't take you *back* in time."

Maya blinked at the Queen's expressionless mask, uncomprehending.

"It takes you *forward*."

WHAT ARE YOU, the *Drama* Queen? People have postulated that time is a circle since time started. It's no big secret – it's a theory you happened to prove correct. And what's the difference between backwards and forwards anyway?

There is no backwards. First law of time – you can never go back. The illusion of going backwards in time is caused by going so far forwards that you loop around.

I'm more interested in sideways, myself. Right, my move –

Hardly. That was just chit-chat about strategy. My move is Knight takes Knight.

You're joking. Two of my most elite Vengers had the drop on – oh, damn, he's killed them.

What can I say? He's a Silver.

Damn it...

He's quick.

*   *   *

ULL WAS VERY quick.

He grabbed the hand holding the blade, twisting the fingers just so; the Venger gave a yelp of pain, his borrowed face shifting, and the poisoned dagger fell from his grip. Ull caught it by the blade, his skinsuit already analysing the poison chemical and dosing him with the antidote – then his arm flashed up, and the blade flew out from between his fingers, burying itself in the head of the man opposite. He toppled backwards with a low groan, his features blurring to blank, lifeless clay; but his own knife was already in the air.

Ull caught it in his shoulder – *Delta five eight, stoicism in the face of pain* – and felt a wave of dizziness wash over him for a second as the newly-created antidote went to war with the deadly poison; his skinpatch gave him a brief additional burst of *hosa* to help him focus, and he tugged down on the hand in his grip, slicing the Venger's thumb on the blade.

Evidently, the Red King hadn't thought to make his Vengers immune to their own poison; the man slumped to the floor, dead in seconds. Ull carefully pulled the knife out of him, checking that the flesh underneath the skinsuit was mending itself. His organobotics were functioning at peak efficiency; as a Silver, his immortal body was in far better shape than the common herd. A perk of the job, not that the job needed additional perks.

The honour of serving the Red Queen was enough.

He threaded his way through the maze, feeling the subtle pull of the tracker as it guided him to his quarry.

He was close.

WAIT, YOU DIDN'T *give them antidote? Really?*

They've never stabbed themselves before. Also, you've never sent one of your Silvers to kill them before – oh, the hell with it.

You're not resigning the game?

Never. It's my move, and I'm going to pull out the big gun. I'm going to stop this precocious little creep in his tracks.

Oh? How do you propose to do that?

I'm going to tell him the truth.

*   *   *

Exiting the maze, Ull found himself in a great, vaulted chamber of gold and rubies, the walls quietly reconfiguring themselves to best effect even as he looked at them. In the centre of the room was some sort of barrier of red cloth, hanging from rings attached to some kind of circular rail. Ull had never seen the like before.

Alpha four seven again, he thought. *Be prepared for anything.*

He took a slow step forwards, the poison knife in his grip. Suddenly, from beyond the ring of hanging cloth, there came a terrible, booming voice:

"I AM OZ – THE GREAT AND TERRIBLE!"

A great gout of coloured smoke shot upwards from the centre of the ring, and despite himself, Ull took a step back – then the cloth barrier parted.

Behind it, sitting on a golden throne, dressed in a black robe, was a well-toned, red-skinned man with a neatly-trimmed tuft of black hair on his chin – *Zeta seven three,* thought Ull – and a pair of horns growing from his temples. "I call that my Pluto voice," the Red King grinned, waggling his eyebrows. "The cute thing is, I'm actually a very bad man. But I'm a very good wizard."

Ull stared at the barrier of cloth as it parted further, revealing two shimmering containment fields on either side of the throne, each holding an identical glowing blue stone. The Red King noticed him staring, and rolled his eyes.

"They're called curtains. *Cur-tanz.* Philistine. Which reminds me, you owe me one priceless work of art, created by royalty, depicting a world only accessible in the dreams of madmen, artists and savants. I'll take a cheque." He leaned back on his throne, then turned to look at the identical chunks of xokronite, as if noticing them for the first time. "Oh, you're looking at *those!* Yeah, for this bit I ideally need two identical guards, one who only tells lies and one who only tells the truth, but, hey, I can play both those parts myself. Anyway, you get one question, and..." He frowned. "Oh, come *on,* kid, say *something.* This is good material I'm wasting on you."

"You..." Ull paused, drawing a deep breath. "You're the Red King."

"Funny story about that –" the King began, and then his hand moved, so suddenly it seemed to blur, and he snatched the thrown knife out of the air less than an inch from his throat. "Hey!" He scowled, tossing the poison blade to one side. "Not while I'm talking, okay? And by the way, we have rules about that. I'm being nice to you as it is."

Ull blinked, unable to believe what he'd seen. "You *are* the Red King..."

"Yes! God! Where was I?" He sighed, cracking his knuckles. "Yeah, the whole Red King and Red Queen business. Now, you're not going to get half of this, because you're a philistine who doesn't even know about Judy Garland, but that was originally a joke I made, way, way back when I first realised what was going on. This is about eighty millennia into the powered era, back when she was Britannia and I was just Lomax. We had a lot more accidents back then – colonising space is going to do that – and I hadn't invented *hosa* yet, so basically nobody remembers that far back. Except us." He smiled. "Anyway, the joke was that she was the Red Queen and I was the Red King, and it stuck."

"A... joke?" Ull was confused – *Zeta nine one, confusion*. Most of the words had little or no meaning for him. Where was Judygar Land?

"A gag, a bit. I make them sometimes, especially when I'm monologuing. Anyway, the joke fits because the Red Queen – Britannia – has spent her entire immortal existence working behind the scenes, pushing dominos, pulling strings and generally running her gorgeous hiney off... all to stay in the same place."

Ull just stared.

"The universe is the way it is because Maya Zor-Tura spent her whole life making it that way, because at this critical moment in history – when a temporal wormhole to so far into the future that it's all the way around past GO opens up, collect two hundred dollars – she sent her younger self through it to do just that."

He grinned again, leaning forward. "Except she can't do it on her own. She also needs to send a lump of xokronite – the magic mineral that steals power from the Big Bang and makes all this possible – through the hole as well. And not one of the ones we synthesised, either, because their atomic structures are ever-so-slightly different, so they might not behave exactly the same. It's got to be the original piece, the capital-S Stone, infinitely old and getting older with every circle around the timeline. Maybe that's what makes it the way it is..." He shrugged. "Anyway, I stole it. And you've been sent to steal it right back. Lucky for you... I've got it right here." He tapped one of the containment fields, then indicated the other. "Or is it over here? Want to take a guess? Could be lucky."

Ull gritted his teeth. *Epsilon one two. Anger. The superior man channels his anger towards his goals.* "Give it to me," he said slowly, taking a menacing step forward.

"Ah-ah-ah!" The Red King grinned, seemingly amused at the Silver's temerity in threatening him. "What did I say? You get a question."

Ull took another step forward, fists clenching, readying himself to spring forward. *The throat,* he thought. *The weak point.*

Then he stopped in his tracks.

The Red King was looking him right in the eyes, and his eyes were so, so old...

"Go ahead, kid," he said, unsmiling. "Make my day."

Ull took a faltering step back. "I..."

"Yellowbelly. Ask your damn question."

Ull swallowed hard. "Why... why are you the Red King?"

The Red King looking at him for a moment, then relaxed, cracking into a smile. "You're not quite as dumb as you look, are you, kid? Your great-great-ever-so-many-greats-grandpa would be proud of you. I remember he broke my jaw once – that was back when I could die." He stared at the ceiling for a moment, marshalling his thoughts. "The other half of the joke. I'm the Red King because I think Maya's wrong. I want us to wake up out of this. I want this whole universe to go out" – he snapped his fingers – "just like a candle."

"You'd kill the universe?" Ull said, horrified.

"I'd *change* it." The King looked irritated, as if Ull had missed the point completely. "Do you know what the world would be like without Maya Zor-Tura? Without the Stone? No, of course you don't. You're not a dreamer – I can tell by looking at you." He furrowed his brow for a moment. "You've never heard of Omega energy either, have you?"

Ull shook his head. "What is it?"

"A form of galvanic force. Only one person ever really got a handle on it, and he didn't know what he had – mostly because Maya – sorry, the Red Queen – was right there to keep him from asking the right questions. Just like she was there to murder anyone who was likely to get too close to it. She'd made sure her younger self knew all the history – or prehistory, I suppose, seeing as we count it from when we got the Stone off that poor bastard Steele." He grinned savagely, enjoying Ull's total incomprehension. "She'd worked it out. Steam technology drains resources, but Omega energy – *Electricity,* they call it in the dreamworld – would decimate them completely."

"I don't –"

"You don't understand. Okay. In simple terms, a world without Maya or the Stone is a world of Omega energy. Instead of the *Pax Britannia,* they have the *Pax Omega* – for as long as it lasts."

"As long as it lasts?" Ull was just about able to grasp the concept of things being finite, but he still needed a little help.

"Sure. Omega technology is a hungry little bastard – it runs rampant and eats every mineral resource on the planet inside a couple of centuries, maximum. We're talking everything from petrochemical deposits to good old-fashioned coal to rare elements like indium, helium – even gold. Humanity gets everything it ever wanted – or the rich few do at least – and the population explodes just in time for everybody to lose it again. Take a look at the dreampunk artists around the mid-to-late twenty-first century – you won't sleep for a week. Horrific stuff. Ninety-five per cent of the world just starves to death."

The King shivered, shaking his head. He looked genuinely disturbed. "Nobody gets out unscathed."

Ull sounded incredulous. "I don't know what's worse – that this might exist, or that you want it to."

The Red King sighed. "Okay – one, it's not a binary choice. There are a lot of variables to play with. What happens if Maya goes back with a different Stone, for instance? One that isn't quite so ancient and magical? That might change things slightly – maybe just enough to knock this endless merry-go-round off kilter. Maybe stop the universe stagnating in an endless, eternal loop, forever and ever. Who knows? I'm willing to roll the dice – she's not."

Ull opened his mouth to speak, and the King shushed him with a gesture. "Two – that's not the whole story. The human race doesn't die out. For centuries, things are terrible, but people rebuild. They pick themselves back up. Except this time they have to do things differently. Technology isn't an option – they ruined that, and it's a shame, because it could have been great – but that doesn't mean they can't still grow." He smiled. "That's the wonderful thing about humanity. Whatever happens to it, the human race can still evolve. By the twenty-fifth century, you're got agrarian societies beating hell out of each other between lynchings – still not good. By the five hundredth, they're enlightened Buddhists. By the thousandth, they're beating hell out of each other again – it's a rocky road. Peaks and troughs. They don't have immortality to keep them nice and unchanging through the millennia."

"It sounds hideous." Ull shuddered. "What makes that world worth destroying ours for?"

"It's got potential. Ours doesn't. We're just going to sit here and twiddle our thumbs until the final heat death of the universe – although, Maya being Maya, she's set up the solution to that too." He sighed. "Poor bastard..."

"What?"

"Never mind. Like I said, we're in a loop that never ends. But you know who's living on that other Earth now, the one only savants can see? In the year one million and change? A race of hyperintelligent zen monks who communicate telepathically. That's how we *learned* about mental linkage – watching the dreamworld.' And do you know what they're doing, these guys? They're immortal too, just like we are. And they're using those superminds of theirs to explore and map the nine billion countries of heaven. And the whole history of their Earth, and of the infinite possible Earths that aren't theirs. And bring it all together."

Ull blinked. "That's impossible –"

"Odds are fifty-fifty they'll do it. My favourite odds." The Red King smiled to himself, looking into Ull's eyes. "You know I'm not lying."

Ull shivered. He knew.

"So what do you think? Are they going to make it? Do we take the risk and maybe all end up in heaven at the end of the story, Maya and El Sombra and Pluto and Doc Thunder and two Ben Franklins and Johnny Wolf and even the bad guys all together in one last happy ending? Or do we play it safe?" He grinned, leaning back on his throne.

After a long silence, Ull spoke, not without compassion. "I'll take one of those Stones now."

The Red King's face fell for a moment, then he managed a half-smile. "Want me to tell you which is which? That's the game. Heads or tails. True or false." He pantomimed pointing to each of the twin blue stones in turn: "Eeny, meeny, miney, mo..."

"My tracker unit has the exact atomic structure of the Stone on file," Ull said, flatly. "I knew which one it was all along."

The King's face fell. "Oh." He shrugged. "Well, I guess you'd better take it."

He scowled angrily, curling up in his throne like a petulant child.

"And don't let the psychetecture hit your ass on the way out, you sneaky little cheat."

CHECK AND MATE.
More like stalemate. Forever.

*Oh, you don't need to map Heaven, Lars, you'd never get in.
And there's no need to be such a grouch just because you lost –*
Did I?
He knew which Stone was which, Lars.
Yes, he did. He knew which was which. And he made his choice.

MAYA WATCHED THE *Zor* leave, sailing out of the hangar bay on the first leg of its journey, laden down with the Shaper, the Weeper, the Princess and the Keeper – and the Stone that bound them all.

And a Sacrifice, of course. The first of many.

She remembered those early days – the brittle arguments with Munn and Unwen, desperately trying to rush into the role of Queen before she was ready – then the long millennia in the jungle, growing into herself, making her plans, founding the Kingdom of Zor-Ek-Narr.

Zor-Ek-Narr; in the language of the Habitats, *Long live the Zor*

She'd commanded battlecruisers the size of suns, and star yachts that had flowed through the cosmos like dreams, but the *Zor* was still her favourite ship, and it always would be. Oddly enough, it was named after the Forbidden Kingdom. Where did that name come from, then? Where was the Stone from, originally?

She supposed it didn't matter.

As the *Zor* reached sub-light speed and winked out of sight among the stars, a terrible thought struck Maya. It was a thought she'd never had before, not once in the billions of years she'd been alive, and it felt like the bottom dropping out of the world.

Maya Zor-Tura, the Red Queen, stood watching the stars, and she thought, *What happens now?*

...OMEGA

Eventually, Earth died.

The stars went out and the planet crumbled to dust as entropy claimed the universe; and from out of the centre of the dust that had once been a planet, there drifted the egg.

The Being within the egg had been dormant for countless aeons, patiently waiting until all life in the universe had died a natural death. He liked being alone.

Although He had never been short of company.

From within the egg, He had seen and heard them all; everything that had ever walked, crawled or flown, from the smallest amoeba to the great immortals, in their eternal Habitats, and more powerful beings even than they.

He had never considered coming out of the egg until now.

He hadn't wanted to hurt anyone.

He was no longer simply powerful; that was a threshold He'd crossed billennia ago. Now, He was power itself.

Once, He had been called Thunder.

In the universe to come, some would give Him other names.

Slowly, over centuries, the metal of the egg flaked away, and He emerged from His cocoon, no longer human, no longer even humanoid. He cast his awareness to the very edges of the dead universe, and found no life. This universe was dead; there was nothing left of it.

There was not.

Nothing existed, and there was nothing in which to exist.

Over a timeless interval, during which time had no meaning, He considered the situation.

He existed. He was the only thing to exist. That did not feel correct.

He focussed His being, and spoke.

And there was.

AL EWING

Al Ewing has written four previous novels, including *El Sombra* and *Gods Of Manhattan* for the *Pax Britannia* universe. He also writes comics, notably *Judge Dredd* and *Zombo* for the British science-fiction anthology *2000 AD*, as well as the crime comic *Jennifer Blood*. In the alternate world of steampunk technology, he is a carnival geek and part-time hunger artist. Despite these reduced circumstances, however, he is still able to afford a sturdy pair of goggles and a top hat with gears on it for no reason.

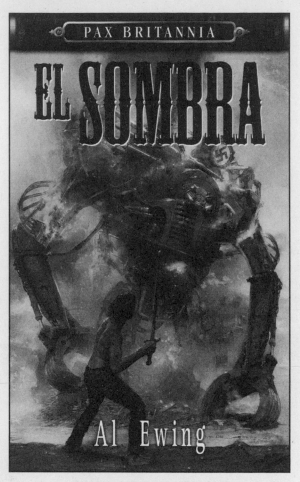

ISBN: 978 1 905437 34 4 • £6.99/$7.99

NO-ONE ESCAPES THE ULTIMATE REICH!

The terrifying Luftwaffe have come on their steam-driven wings and torn apart the sleepy town of Pasito, rebuilding it as a terrifying clockwork-town, where people become human robots. But they are unprepared for the return of a man the desert claimed nine long years ago, who has returned from the depths of madness to bring his terrible fury upon their world.

He defi es death! He defi es man!
No trap can hold the masked daredevil, the saint of ghosts men know as El Sombra!

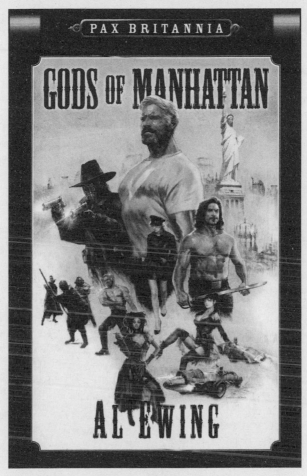

A RADICAL INNOVATION IN THE WORLD OF E-PUBLISHING!

Abaddon Books are proud to announce a fantastic new innovation in the world of electronic publishing! The eighth Ulysses Quicksilver book, *Pax Britannia: Time's Arrow,* is to be released exclusively in ebook format in three parts, starting with "Red-Handed" out now!

After the first two releases, the readers are invited to vote on the Abaddon website as to how they want the story to continue. It's like one of those *Fighting Fantasy* or *Choose-Your-Own-Adventure* books you loved as a kid, except you're choosing the outcome *as the book is being written!*

The votes from "Red-Handed" have already been counted, but it's not too late to be involved...

TAKING PART

Part One, "Red-Handed," is available through the iTunes and Kindle stores, through barnesandnoble.com, and through Rebellionstore.com *right now*, and Part Two, "Black Swan," will be available from March 2012. Voting on the next is through our website on Abaddonbooks.com, and will be open for two months from the book's release.

COMING UP!

Part Three will be produced in ebook format in summer 2012. Once all three parts have been published, the work will be collected and published once again – in both ebook and physical format – as a single volume, which *you* helped to create!

Embark upon an epic adventure with us – Quicksilver is depending on you!

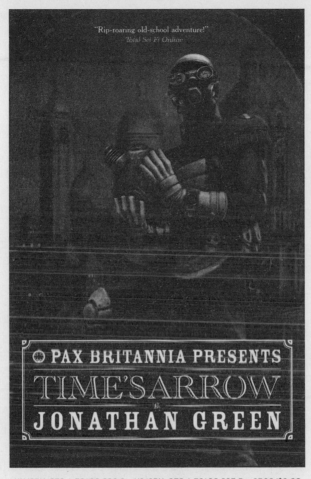

THE ULYSSES QUICKSILVER Omnibus

MASTERS OF ADVENTURE FICTION, **ABADDON BOOKS** PRESENT
THREE THRILLING TALES OF VALOUR TO DIVERT AND ENTHRALL

PAX BRITANNIA

UNNATURAL HISTORY • LEVIATHAN RISING • HUMAN NATURE

By

JONATHAN GREEN

UK ISBN: 978 1 907519 36 9 • US ISBN: 978 1 907519 56 7 • £9.99/$12.99

ULYSSES QUICKSILVER, AGENT OF THE CROWN, IN HIS FIRST THREE ADVENTURES!

Unnatural History – A professor of biology goes missing, while a catastrophic Overground train crash unleashes the dinosaurs of London Zoo. Is this the work of revolutionaries?

Leviathan Rising – A jolly ocean jaunt turns into a voyage of terror as a murder and an act of sabotage send Ulysses, and all aboard the *Neptune*, into the numbing depths

Human Nature – What does the theft of the Whitby Mermaid have to do with the mysterious House of Monkeys? And who is the enigmatic criminal known as the Magpie?